entangled

CAT CLARKE

entangled

Quercus

First published in Great Britain in 2011 by Quercus

21 Bloomsbury Square
London
WC1A 2NS

A CIP catalogue reference for this book is available
from the British Library

ISBN 978 1 84916 394 1

10 9 8

Typeset by Nigel Hazle
Printed and bound in Great Britain by Clays Ltd, St Ives plc

For Mum, for everything.

Elspeth Margaret Clarke
1947–2010

day 3

I met Ethan the night I was planning to kill myself. Pretty inconvenient, when you think about it.

The same questions whirl round and round in my head:

What does he want from me?

How could I have let this happen?

AM I GOING TO DIE? (That one's my particular favourite.)

This isn't quite how I planned it. And I *do* like things to go to plan.

First things first: let's just start writing and see where that takes me. I presume that's what all the paper is here for. And the pens. Seems to me there are enough pens to last a *long* time. This is very, very bad. Maybe I'll just lie down for a second.

1

Don't know how long I was out for. Don't have my watch. Or my clothes. The thought of him undressing me when I was unconscious is beyond embarrassing. And this gown thing is not exactly the height of fashion. I feel like I'm waiting to be operated on. God, I *really* hope that's not the case. I'm sort of attached to my internal organs. I must be losing it – cracking jokes at a time like this. But humour at inappropriate times always has been a speciality of mine.

I have to figure out a way to get out of here. Maybe I can reason with him. I just need to find out what he wants. But part of me doesn't want to know the answer.

Shit . . . I think he's coming.

⤳

Well, that was short and sweet. He just came in with my food on a tray, saw me sitting at the table, pen in hand, and nodded. He seemed pleased. I sat there like an idiot, gawping at him. He didn't try to read what I've written – just looked at me in that way that makes me sure he knows *exactly* what I'm thinking. And then he was gone. Door bolted behind him, of course.

The food was delicious. That's just one of the many, many weird things about this. The food is great. And how many kidnapping cases have you heard about where the victim has her own en-suite bathroom? And possibly the comfiest bed in the entire world. I just wish everything wasn't so *white*. It makes my head hurt. Sometimes I have to close my eyes to remind myself that there *are* other colours in the universe. At least these pens aren't white. That would have been pretty annoying, to say the least. Because writing is *definitely* helping. Just the mechanics of it: forming the letters which make up the words which magically join up to make sentences. It's sort of soothing. But what does he want me to write? And *why* does he want me to write? Weird weird weird. Still, maybe this is my big chance to be the writer I've always wanted to be. My last chance, probably.

Anyway, you're supposed to write about what you know, aren't you? So let's start with Ethan. Maybe someone will be able to find him one day (probably years after my skeleton is found at this bloody table with a biro still clutched in my bony fingers). I reckon he's about six feet tall. I'm basing this guesstimate on Nat, who maintains he's six foot but is clearly no taller than five foot ten. Liar, liar, pants on fire.

But back to Ethan. He is beautiful. I mean *properly* beautiful. He has black hair. It's somewhere between long and short, and there's this bit that's always falling

entangled

in front of his eyes. His eyes . . . well, they're grey.
Gunmetal grey? Slate grey? Sky-before-a-spectacular-
summer-thunderstorm grey? Maybe just plain old
grey grey. His face is perfect. Honestly, it's like he just
fell out of a painting or something. Cheekbones, eyebrows, nose, jaw. He's got them all and they're all just
right. And that mouth . . . he has the lushest lips I've
ever seen. I liked kissing them.

So what else, what else? He's pale, really pale. Like
never-seen-the-daylight-cos-I'm-actually-a-vampire
pale. For a brief moment of madness yesterday (after
an *entirely* sleepless night), I did entertain the thought
that maybe he *is* a vampire. Until I remembered that
my life *isn't* actually *Twilight*. Ethan's skin is amazing.
I would kill for skin that clear. I can't quite work out
how old he is. At first I thought he was maybe around
twenty, but it's really hard to tell. Sometimes he
looks older, and other times he looks like a lost little
boy.

He has a scar from the bottom of his nose to his
top lip. I remember tracing it with my fingertips. Some
scars are good.

It's no big surprise that his body is beautiful too.
Lean but strong. Smooth. And he wraps it up in pretty
decent clothes. That night he was wearing a white vest,
faded old jeans, and battered black Converse All Stars.

4

He's clearly not much of a colours person – greys, whites and blacks so far. Which is fair enough, but I *love love love* colours. Purple is good . . . and green. A green so bright it's like it's shouting. I miss green.

So, you might be thinking that Ethan sounds pretty hot. And it even sounds like I want him. I *did* want him, but the whole abduction thing seems to have put a bit of a damper on our relationship. And I think it's too early for me to have that syndrome . . . what's it called? Where a hostage starts to identify with her captor, falls in love with him, and then joins him on his evil kidnapping/killing/whatever spree. All I'm trying to say is that an impartial observer would think he's hot *as* – and I would have to agree.

I can't work out where he's from. I don't think he's a local boy – he certainly doesn't *look* like any of the boys round here (or rather, *there* – back home, I mean . . . where AM I?). On Monday night, I asked him where he was from and he said 'around', which *maybe* should have aroused my suspicions. At the time I probably thought he was just appealingly mysterious. Idiot.

Ethan. Perfect boyfriend material. Apart from the tendency to kidnap unstable girls who are too wasted to even realize what's happening. I can just imagine the lonely-hearts ad:

Tall, dark and handsome man WLTM green-eyed girl. Interests include films, long walks in the rain, Italian food and a just a teensy bit of kidnapping every so often.

Sane girls need not apply.

Things I know about Ethan (not including the whole looking-like-a-Greek-god thing)

1. He drives a newish-looking silver van.
   Man in van = obviously dodgy.
2. He doesn't seem to be your classic slasher-movie psychopath.
3. He's gone to an awful lot of trouble to make sure that I'm comfortable here. The bed, the bathroom, the delicious food . . . All unnerving in the extreme.
4. He didn't choose me. I chose him. I chose to go and sit next to him on the swings. Maybe he knew what he was going to do but hadn't got around to picking his victim yet. It's almost like he was the bait – all alone and shining like a beacon of hotness. He reeled me in good and proper.
5. He likes to listen. Not so much with the talking.
6. He hasn't tried to hurt me. Yet.
7. I don't actually have a seventh point, but seven is

6

my lucky number and I REALLY could do with some luck right now.

Night night. Sleep tight. Don't let the strangely alluring psychopath/vampire bite.

day 4

Well, wasn't I just the bizarrely upbeat little kidnappee yesterday? I reckon that's what someone who's been kidnapped should be called. Kidnapper, kidnappee. Makes sense to me. That rhymes.

Not feeling quite so upbeat today.

Why is this happening to me?

Stop thinking. Keep writing. Keep the pen on the paper and move your hand.

I needed a bit (OK, a lot) of Dutch courage before I went through with it. While I was getting ready, I swigged from the bottle of vodka that I keep under my bed. I chose my clothes with care. Just cos you're going to die, there's no need to look sloppy. I put on my new jeans, which make my legs look super-long and skinny. I went through practically every top I own, before settling on my trusty old green T-shirt (my *lucky* green T-shirt – ha!). Shoes were tricky, but I eventually went for comfort with my Adidas shell-toes. Not exactly glamorous, but they added a certain old-school chic. I put on more make-up than was strictly necessary, all the while looking in the mirror thinking, *No more eyeliner for me. Last lipgloss I'll ever wear. Last time I'll look in this mirror knowing I'll never be good enough,* and things to that effect.

Knife in bag, then good to go.

I tripped down the stairs like a girl without a care in the world. Shouted, 'I'm off to meet Sal. Don't wait up!' to Mum, who was watching telly in the living room. Maybe I should have just popped my head round the door for a second, instead of slamming the front door when I heard, 'Grace, wait a sec . . .' But I didn't. One more second in her presence would be too much to bear.

So I didn't say bye, and I didn't leave a note. I just didn't see the point. Suicide notes are lame *as*, anyway. And if I *had* left a note, then everyone would now be thinking I'm dead. Which I'm most definitely not (yet).

I caught the bus into town. Sat right at the back – unusual for me. My last ever bus journey, or so I thought. Come to think of it, that may well still be the case. As bus journeys go, it was pretty standard. A woman with loooong grey hair sat in front of me. The lank locks hung over the back of her seat, and the straggly ends brushed my jeans. It was revolting. Long hair after a certain age is just not an attractive feature. Thankfully Icky Hair Woman got off the bus before I started gagging.

I felt kind of peaceful after she'd gone. I closed my eyes and breathed deeply. I was going to do it – I was really actually truly going to do it. This was it. *Oh, they'll be sorry* ... The sing-song voice in my head made me smile.

I'm not sure how I feel about the yes-you-really-were-minutes-away-from-topping-yourself thing now. But I'm not ready to examine my feelings too closely. Not quite yet. It's like I have a bandage wrapped round me. I sort of know why it's there, but if I unravel it and actually *see* the festering wound underneath, all yellow and oozy, I may just lose my mind.

I got off the bus and skipped into an off-licence. I spent a good few minutes choosing my tipple. Went for gin, which is strange, cos I hate the stuff. It reminds me of Dad. So I headed towards the counter and the guy had the worst case of acne I have ever seen (apart from Scott Ames in Year 9, but at least that cleared up and now he's looking pretty fine). Then the most ridiculous thing happened: I got ID'd! Now you have to understand that this *never* happens to me. I've been buying alcohol since I was fourteen, for Christ's sake. Maybe it was a sign from God: 'Grace, you can kill yourself if you really must, but I'm not going to make things easy for you.' I gave Acne Boy my best you-have-*got*-to-be-kidding-me look and said, 'You have *got* to be kidding me. I'm twenty-two years old! Do I look like a kid?' He just pointed to the sign that said, 'If you look under 25 blah blah blah blah blah . . .' I wasted a couple of minutes spinning him a line about having left my ID in my jacket, and having left my jacket at home cos of the unseasonably warm weather we've been having. Still no sale. Irritating. But I suppose you've got to get your kicks somehow when you've got the most disgusting, pus-ridden excuse for a face, and no hope of getting sex (ever). I flounced out of the shop in an appropriately flouncy, indignant fashion, popped into the shop next door and bought exactly the same bottle two quid cheaper. So I guess God wasn't sending me a sign after all.

As I walked down the street with the bottle clutched under my arm, I passed a couple about my age. They were holding hands and laughing. *Go away go away go away!* The guy pushed the girl up against a shop window and kissed her. I missed being kissed like that.

I walked on, nearly bumping into a gang of townie boys with shiny shoes and questionable hair. One of them turned and shouted to me, 'Cheer up, love. It might never happen!' I grinned at him. *Oh, I think it will . . .*

I came to the park gates. My dad used to take me there when I was little. I'd feed the ducks, then run around like a crazy person. Dad would chase me and pretend to be a zombie. And then he'd push me on the swings – so hard that I was sure that I'd go right over the top of the crossbar, but I'd still shout for him to push harder. I never got bored of that.

After Dad was gone, the park started to mean other things to me. Things I'm glad he wasn't here to see. It meant smoking and drinking stupidly strong cider and doing things with inappropriate boys. And other stuff too.

A lot of memories in that park. Good and bad. (Mostly bad.) It seemed as good a place as any for my date with death. I'd decided on the den at the top of the climbing frame. I tried not to think about the possibility that some random kid might find my body. *Hopefully it'll be the park warden – the one that looks a bit like a paedophile. Urgh. He'd better not touch me. Even if I am too dead to care.*

I wandered past the duck pond. It had been drained years ago. It looked sort of sad at not being able to fulfil its one purpose in life. *Christ — already getting sentimental and I haven't even started the serious drinking yet. Next thing you know I'll be on about melancholy trees or despondent rubbish bins.*

I went straight to the den, climbed up into it and sat down. The floor wasn't too filthy, and I was glad. Not that it really mattered.

Took the knife out of my bag.

Stared at the blade and remembered.

Every detail of that night knifed my heart.

And every reason not to live twisted that knife — twisted it hard.

I opened the bottle and drank.

Drank some more.

Closed my eyes.

Took a deep breath.

I was ready.

Cut.

꒳

And then I heard something. A creaking, squeaking sound. *Too loud. Shit. Someone's out there.*

I peeked out of the den's window and saw him. On the swings. Back and forth, back and forth, going as high as he possibly could, just like I used to do.

Damn. Can't very well do it now, can I? Got to make him

go away. Leave me in peace. So I put the knife back in the bag, grabbed the bottle and clambered out of the den.

If only I'd just stayed put and waited till he went away.

He saw me coming and watched my somewhat unsteady progress towards him. As soon as I got close enough for a proper look . . . well, I don't need to go into that again. *Reckon there are worse ways to spend your last few minutes. Just talk to him for a bit. He'll go away eventually.* As I approached, he slowed the swing to a stop. He watched me and I watched him. I sat down on the swing next to him and said hello. There was something about the way he looked at me that I couldn't quite put my finger on. Now I think I know what it was – I think he *recognized* me.

And even more weirdly, I think I recognized him.

But that's not possible.

day 6

Day 6? How did *that* happen? Yesterday I stayed in bed, mostly alternating between crying and shouting (and sometimes both at the same time). It was awful. The first time Ethan came in I stayed under the duvet. I couldn't bear to look at ~~~~ And when he came to take away my food tra~~~~ pleading with him. It's just too e~~~~ I said, how I tried to bargain with ~~~~ *red* him. Most of all though, I just kept a~~~~ why. He stood with his back against the door, saying nothing for the longest time. I wanted to grab his stupid ears and smash his stupid head against the door until his stupid brains leaked out. Instead, I did nothing.

Oh, I've thought about attacking him. I've thought about it plenty. Even hatched some half-arsed schemes: the classic hiding-behind-the-door-with-a-vase trick being a particular favourite. Only one problem though:

I don't have a vase. And somehow I don't think a pillow would be quite so effective. Still, I could at least *try*. Kick him in the balls, gouge out an eye, bust some Bruce Lee-style moves (not that I know any Bruce Lee-style moves, but a girl could improvise). I can't quite work out why I've done nothing of the sort. Maybe he's put some kind of voodoo magic mind-spell on me. Yeah, that must be it.

Now where was I? Ah yes, the totally undignified pleading and snivelling and asking him why. He listened and watched me with those stormysexysmoky eyes. I seemed to be troubling him. He looked like he actually felt sorry for me. Like he *genuinely* cares. I don't get it. How can he look at me like that and yet STILL be putting me through this? If he wants me to be less pleady/snivelly he should FUCKING LET ME GO, SHOULDN'T HE?

Finally, when I was a crumpled, sobbing heap on the floor, he said softly, 'Grace, it's got to be this way. There's nothing you can do about it. I'm sorry.' He turned and opened the door, and with one last, particularly annoying 'I'm sorry' he was gone. I banged on the door with my fists until they were bruised and swollen, shouting, 'IT DOESN'T HAVE TO BE THIS WAY! IF YOU JUST LET ME GO, I WON'T TELL ANYONE! I PROMISE! ETHAN? ETHAN? COME

BACK . . . PLEASE, ETHAN, COME BACK!' Over and over and over again. Eventually I slid down the door and sat with my back against it – more hopeless than ever.

So yesterday sucked. Today's better, but not much. For one thing, my hands hurt like a bastard. Beating your fists to a pulp is not such a great idea when the only thing you have to occupy your time is WRITING. Stupid cow.

Before I get back to The Tragic Story of Grace Carlyle's Supposed Last Night on Earth, I thought it might be a good idea to describe my room/cell/whatever. It really is kind of nice.

My room/cell/whatever – a list in seven points
1. It's nearly double the size of my bedroom. The walls, ceiling and floorboards are all white as white can be. It smells newly painted too.
2. The bathroom. White again. Toilet, sink, shower. Two white towels (which Ethan takes away each day and brings back alpine fresh). There's even cleaning stuff under the sink, but he's got another think coming if he reckons I'm going to use it. Surely this is the one time a girl can skive off her chores without repercussions?
3. The window. Ah, the window – my least favourite

thing. Boarded up (with white boards, of course). Unfortunately Ethan's done a pretty good job of that. Even if I press my body up against the wall in a most attractive fashion, I can only see a tiny chink of light in the bottom left-hand corner. It's easy to lose track of night and day, but I'm doing the best I can.

4. The bed. White again (sensing a theme yet? Maybe Ethan's got some kind of complex or something? Purity. Innocence. Virginity? Sorry, you've got the wrong girl). Two white pillows, white duvet cover, white sheets.

5. The table and chair (white and whiter). In the middle of the room, facing the door. The paper and pens were on top of the table when I woke up that first day. There are forty-seven pens. They're Bics. I really would have preferred pencils, but I suppose beggars can't be choosers and all that. And if beggars could be choosers, this beggar would have chosen a slightly more comfortable chair to sit on. Numb bum. Anyway, there's also three massive wodges (reams?) of paper.

6. The light. There's a bare light bulb hanging from the ceiling, right above the table. It really lets down the rest of the decor, to be honest.

7. The door. Well, it's the way you come into or go out of the room, but I wouldn't know much about that. There's no keyhole. Sounds like there are a couple of deadbolts on the other side though. It seems a sturdy sort of a door.

✦

Nap time.

✦

Just woke up. Thought I was at home in my own bed. And then I crash-landed back to Earth with an almighty thump. Worst feeling ever.

It's the not knowing that's really getting to me. I'm not saying it would be better if Ethan had actually *done* something to me by now, but at least then I'd have some idea of what I'm up against. I could at least try and fight some perverted rapist. I can't fight Ethan . . .

✦

So I sat down on the swing next to this guy and said hello. And he looked at me in that weird way of his. I said hello again. He whispered a hoarse hello, then cleared his throat and said it again, louder. It reminded me of those mornings after a night on the piss. The ones when I lounge around watching kids' telly in a kind of hazy post-alcoholic stupor, and then the phone rings and I find that I can't speak properly cos I haven't said a word for twelve hours or something.

I introduced myself and reached out to shake his hand. He looked at my hand like he wasn't quite sure what to do, and then just as I was about to take it back, he reached out and shook it. His hand was soft and strong, and his grip was firm. Forgot to mention before, but Ethan has perfect hands too. Like he'd be awesome at playing the piano. God, he has beautiful *everything*. It's really quite sickening.

He told me his name and I was surprised. Mum once told me that if I'd been a boy, I'd have been called Ethan. I've never met an Ethan before.

I asked if he wanted a swig of my gin. He shook his head slowly and looked at me strangely, cocking his head to the side and looking kind of quizzical, as if to say, 'Are you sure you should be drinking that?' Since he hadn't actually said the question out loud, I thought I was perfectly within my rights to ignore it. I took a few gulps. It was starting to taste pretty good.

So far the conversation wasn't exactly flowing smoothly, but I wasn't going to let that put me off. I asked him where he was from, which is when he said 'around' (the suspicious-to-anyone-who's-actually-

paying-attention-and-cares-whether-they-live-or-die
'around'). Anyway, I started babbling about nothing:
the park, the irritating guy in the off-licence, the
weather (yeah, the *weather* – can you even believe it?).
Then I moved on to other stuff. *Proper* stuff. And somewhere along the line I forgot that I was supposed to be
getting him to leave. I drank more, and soon got that
oh-so-familiar feeling of the words that I wanted to say
being very slightly too big for my mouth, so that I had
to be careful to EN-UN-CI-ATE VE-RY CLEAR-LY.

Ethan didn't seem to mind my onslaught of chat.
Occasionally he'd smile at me, or ask a question about
something I'd said.

Come to think of it, he asked a lot of questions.
But whenever I asked *him* a question he evaded it
neatly, either by being Master of Vagueness, or by
chucking the same question right back at me. That's
cheating.

I didn't feel wary of him at all. In fact, I felt strangely
safe. I wasn't *happy* exactly. I mean after all, I was still
planning on topping myself. How happy can a girl be
in that situation? It's just that I felt that talking to Ethan
really was the *right* way to spend the time I had left.
And I felt like we had some kind of connection. Urgh.
That looks even lamer written down than it sounded
in my head.

So, moving on to the Main Event, which I re-member surprisingly well. The time passed, the gin dwindled, and my head became more than a little bit fuzzy. I realized that I wanted to kiss Ethan; I wasn't loving the idea of Nat being the last boy I ever got to kiss. I knew I would go for it eventually. It was just a matter of timing . . .

We'd been sitting in silence for a few minutes (a nice, friendly silence, I thought) when I scooted my swing nearer his. Ethan turned to me so our faces were really close. He looked at me through the bits of hair that fell in front of his eyes. I gently touched the scar above his lip, and asked him how he'd got it. He shrugged. And that's when I kissed him. It seemed to take him by surprise – not that I'd hidden my intentions *at all*. His lips were warm and soft and comforting. But he didn't exactly kiss me back.

I asked him what was wrong, and he shrugged. Again. 'I don't think it's such a good idea. Sorry.' *Ouch*.

I did what any self-respecting girl would do in the face of a knock-back like that: I started to cry. Pathetic. But how was *I* supposed to know that I was trying to pull a boy who was planning on kidnapping me?

Ethan put his arm around me and made comfort-ing 'shhh, don't cry' noises. I was confused as hell, and drunk, and probably starting to remember that there's-something-I-have-to-do-tonight-so-I'd-really-better-get-on-with-it-if-it's-OK-with-you.

And that's when I puked down his vest.

~

Well, there's not really much more to say about that night. Post-puke, it gets even more hazy. What I do remember is that Ethan didn't react like I would have done if some random had vommed on me. I was apologizing like crazy (still crying, I think) when he just whipped off his vest and chucked it in the bin behind the swings. He said something like, 'Time to go,' and held out his hand to me. I must have mumbled something about wanting to stay in the park, but I was feeling so dog-rough that I let him haul me up from the swing and lead me away. I remember seeing the van. I remember him leaning over me to buckle my seat belt. And then . . . not a lot. I *think* I remember that we were headed towards my house. Damn that gin – such a bad move. All I know after that is that I must have fallen asleep. And I woke up here.

day 7

No change. Nothing.

day 8

Today is dark.

day 9

Onetwothreefourfivesixseveneightnine.

day 10

Ready to write'n'roll. The last few days have been pretty crappy. Not much to tell; a lot of pacing back and forth. It's driving me insane, not being able to move around. I need some space. Or at least a treadmill. Ethan has washed the bed sheets, and he's replaced my surgical gown with some new clothes – I now have two pairs of bright white pyjamas to choose from. Might be progress.

He's hardly said a word to me for four days. Pretty much every time he's come in I've been lying in bed. He often glances over to the table hopefully, and he seems disappointed (deflated?) that I'm not there, scribbling away. If he comes in and sees me now, it'll probably make his day. Don't want that happening. Sometimes I glare at him, just daring him to say something. And sometimes he looks as if he's about to speak, but then thinks better of it. What is his deal?!

The longer this goes on without anything happening, the more confused I get. I don't exactly feel scared any more. Maybe there's only so long you can maintain that level of fear, before it gets too exhausting.

I've been here ten days now. I wonder how Mum is doing. Frantic, probably. Maybe engaging in a spot of retail therapy to distract from her trauma. Or sitting on the sofa next to a policewoman, like a character in a TV drama. Acting like a good mother – one who cares. I wonder if the police are still looking for me. Maybe they'll have given up by now. Maybe there's only so long you can maintain that level of hope too.

I keep thinking about Sal. Does she feel bad? Does she feel *anything*? Are her insides writhing and twisting in guilt and shame?

Sal. I don't even know where to start. The beginning seems like as good a place as any. She moved here from Edinburgh with her parentals and annoying little brother just over a year ago. Before Sal arrived, I was sort of good friends with Those Girls at school – the ones who think they're better than everyone else. I was always on the fringe though, never too close to anyone. I never thought I was missing anything by not having a real proper best friend.

The first time I saw her, I knew we'd end up being mates. I just knew it. She was sitting in the corner of the common room, frantically scrawling in a note-book. None of that self-conscious new-girl air about her. She had awesome hair and good clothes. Not that I'm superficial, but these things help when you're try-ing to decide whether or not to make an effort with someone. OK, so maybe I *am* superficial, but so is everyone else.

I slumped down on the seat next to her, asked her what she was writing. It was a story. Something we had in common – we both liked to write. So that was how we got talking. I'd never really talked to anyone about my writing before. English teachers don't count. From then on Sal and I gradually started hanging out together at lunchtimes, break times, free periods. It seemed like every day we spent a bit more time with each other, until I barely bothered talking to anyone else. I stopped hanging around with my usual crowd and they barely even noticed.

After we'd known each other about a month, I felt ready to take the Next Step. It's a big deal when you make the leap from seeing someone at school to hang-ing out with them *in your own time*. But I was ready. I invited Sal round to my house one Friday when Mum was in London visiting a friend.

We ordered pizza and vegged out on the sofa. I found out some more about her: pepperoni was her favourite; we both thought social-networking sites were for losers; she wanted to be a lawyer or a writer or a marine biologist or star in a West End musical; she was totally in love with Chris, a boy from her old school, but she'd never done anything about it and he didn't have a clue and now it was too late cos he lived 200 miles away. Which was sort of lame when I thought about it, but I let her off. Just cos.

All in all, I was more than a little bit excited (secretly, of course) to have a New Best Friend. Not that there was an *old* one for her to replace. Sal was good for me. She was always so *happy*, and not in an annoying way. Just the right level of shiny. She was so damn optimistic about everything. Always sure that tomorrow would be better than today. So sure that we'd both get exactly what we wanted. Should have known that wasn't possible.

Sal and I became pretty much inseparable. I practically lived at her house at weekends. Mum didn't seem bothered. I think it suited us both: she got to pretend she was childless and carefree and I got to pretend I had a mum who actually liked me. And a dad too, just for good measure.

One night just before Christmas, I was staying at Sal's house (Chinese takeaway, wine, *Skins* on DVD). We were getting ready for bed, brushing our teeth in front of the bathroom mirror. I reached across Sal to grab a hand towel. She caught me by the wrist and said, 'What's this?'

My stomach did that horrible flip-flop motion, like a washing machine at the start of its cycle. I made a big deal of spitting out a mouthful of toothpastey foam while I thought hard. I don't know why I was surprised; it's not like I thought the scars were invisible or anything. I tried to play it down – it's nothing, just some scratches I got when I was a kid . . . from my grandma's cat?

It was hard to look at her. And even harder to look at myself. She put her hand up to my face and moved my chin so that I had to face her. 'Grace, you know you can tell me *anything*. You're my best friend.' I'd never been anyone's best friend before. No option but to tell the truth, the whole truth and nothing but the bloody truth. I followed Sal into her room, sat down on the bed and talked.

I'd just turned fifteen the first time I cut. I was in my room, writing an essay. My music was blaring, as usual. It was a pretty normal night. No more depressed than any other day. That's the thing: I was never happy, not really. Kind of just existed from day to day, on a weird plateau of feeling nothingness. That's not to say I didn't feel happy at times – of course I did. But they were fleeting moments, gone before I could even begin to appreciate them.

I was looking around for something to distract me from my essay. I drew round my hand and coloured in the fingernails with a red biro. Opened up my desk drawer and rooted around a bit. I found Dad's old Swiss Army knife. I opened up all the blades, and found some tweezers that I hadn't realized were there. The last blade I opened was the knife. Sharp and shiny and strangely appealing in a way I couldn't quite understand.

I pressed the blade against my thumb, applying just a little pressure – not hard enough to draw blood. *Huh. Unsatisfactory.*

I drew the blade across my forearm – hard. For a millisecond it looked like I hadn't really done anything. There was just an indentation in the skin. But then the blood welled up so fast. It was so red. And there was so much of it. *Better. Much better.*

It was mesmerizing. I held up my arm and watched the blood drip drip drip down into the crease of my elbow. One or two drops splashed onto the desk. I felt slightly floaty and weird – but mostly good.

A little pain. But it was a good pain, a clean pain.

That first night, I only cut myself once. No one

noticed. I don't exactly go around holding my arms out for people to inspect.

After that night, I cut more. Amassed a pretty serious collection of scars.

I got better at choosing where to cut, finding ways to hide the angry red slashes from the world. And later, hiding the silvery scars. I hadn't really thought there would be scars. Hadn't really thought.

To me, the scars are obvious. They stand out like they're screaming, 'Look at her! Look at what this freak does to herself!'

It's more like a whisper though, to anyone who's listening.

Sal was listening.

She sat opposite me, her legs crossed like a seven-year-old's in school assembly. I *knew* she was looking at me with a mixture of worry, pity and maybe something else (horror?). I didn't look at her to check though. Just concentrated really really hard on the duvet. *Red stripe, white stripe, red stripe, white stripe. Red. White. Red.*

When I'd finished my inadequate explanation and answered Sal's questions (also inadequately), she took my arm in her hands and looked. *Really* looked. My forearm was exposed in the harsh overhead light. The scars seemed to stand out more than ever before. She touched them with her fingertips, murmuring, 'What have you done to yourself?'

I had no words. Not even a smart-arsed joke. Just tears.

I cried more than I had ever cried in front of a real live person. Sal hugged me and stroked my hair and told me everything was going to be OK. I cried myself beyond red blotchy puffy-facedness and into sleep.

When I woke up, the room was dark and Sal was lying next to me wide awake. I apologized for making such a scene, tried to make light of it. I was embarrassed, big time. I'm not used to losing control like that.

Sal propped herself up on one elbow and looked at me all serious. 'I think you need to get help, Grace,' she whispered. I was horrified by the idea. We went back and forth for a while, until she realized that she was getting nowhere.

She made me promise that a) I wouldn't do it again, and b) whenever I felt I *wanted* to do it, I would pick up the phone and call her. She said she would come to me any time, day or night.

I actually believed that a) and b) were entirely possible.

I was *sort of* glad I'd told her. It was good to share

the secret. But I felt stupid and ashamed and pathetic at the same time.

Sal and I were closer than ever after that night. Bound together by my dirty little secret. That was just over nine months ago.

~

Ethan's just left.

He found me sitting at the table, sobbing. He brought my tray over and gathered up all the paper and put it on the floor. He put his hand on my shoulder ever so gently, and it stayed there while I cried. When the tears ran out, I picked up the fork and began to eat. I could only stomach a couple of forkfuls. I had to swig down some Coke just so I didn't choke. Ethan sat on my bed and watched me.

'How do you feel?' he asked.

'Why are you doing this to me?'

'You should eat. You'll feel stronger.'

'Why are you doing this to me?'

'Grace . . .' He looked at me imploringly.

'I don't want you here. Please leave.'

He left.

day 11

Had a dream about Sal last night. Hardly surprising really.

She was here with me and we were sitting opposite each other at the table. Ethan was leaning against the wall, watching us. Sal and I were talking about something important and Ethan was repeating every single word I said. I got annoyed, and told him to leave us alone. And just like that, Ethan was gone, replaced by Nat. A smug Nat who smiled too much. Sal got annoyed and told him to leave us. I smiled at Sal and reached across the table to hold her hand, but she morphed into Ethan and said, 'Maybe we're getting somewhere, Grace.' Then I woke up, wishing that dream people would at least have the courtesy to stay as the *same* dream people and not be so bloody confusing.

I thought I'd pick up where I left off yesterday, chronicling the complete life cycle of a friendship. After I told Sal about the cutting, things were OK for a while. No one else would have noticed a change, but I noticed a difference in the way she looked at me. I felt like she was always trying to gauge my mood. Like if I was in a mard for no particular reason (not exactly a rare occurrence), she'd cock her head to one side and look at me thoughtfully. I could practically *hear* her wondering if I was going to cut. Sal probably thought she was being subtle, but I often clocked her looking out for fresh cuts (which she never saw). I didn't mind all that much. She was acting exactly like a best friend should. It was nice.

Occasionally she'd try to get me to talk about it – about why I did it. I would listen to her theories and then try to change the subject. Why does there have to be a reason for everything? Some things just *are*.

So our friendship might have seemed a bit unbalanced: me being all self-pitying, Sal looking after me most of the time. She certainly took care of me enough times when I was puking in the toilets of some cheesy club. And she had a nice line in rescuing me when I was about to do something I'd probably regret with someone I'd *definitely* regret.

I didn't exactly relish the role of Pathetic Needy

Friend, but Sal seemed to want to look after me. And maybe I needed looking after.

Everything changed a few months ago.

I'd been to Glasgow to visit my grandma over Easter. Had a fine old time: bit of shopping, lots of reading, nice long chats over a lovely cup of tea. (It was always a *lovely* cup of tea, *never* an average one.) I came back all cheery and bearing gifts from Sal's homeland: a cuddly Loch Ness Monster and a Scottish bagpiper doll with super-scary staring eyes.

The Sal I found was not the ever-optimistic-little-ray-of-sunshine Sal that I left. Oh, it wasn't obvious. She laughed at the presents I'd brought her and listened in an interested enough way to my enthralling holiday tales. But there was something wrong – I knew it. It was subtle, like when you mess with the brightness levels on your TV. She was duller somehow, faded. She didn't seem sad or depressed or worried or anything you could put your finger on. She just wasn't quite Sal.

I asked her what was up almost as soon as I saw her, but she was adamant that nothing was wrong. I knew she was lying, so I pushed it a little, but backed off when she started getting annoyed. I figured she'd tell me when she was ready. I didn't realize just how long I'd have to wait.

Things carried on more or less as normal for the next few weeks. Sal was clearly doing her best to act her usual upbeat self, but I wasn't buying it. No one else seemed to notice that anything was wrong. Her parents were too busy dealing with Cam, who was being bullied at school. And everyone at *our* school was too busy being wrapped up in themselves, as usual.

About a month passed and I watched Sal closely, looking for clues. She seemed to be getting worse. I noticed her pushing her food around on her plate at lunchtime – completely out of character. And she looked like she was losing weight. But still she maintained that nothing was wrong.

My daily 'Hiya, how's it going?' now had a hidden meaning, as in 'Hiya, how *are* you, *really*?' But Sal wouldn't take the bait. She seemed more and more distant. I felt like she was backing away from our friendship. It was upsetting.

One Thursday afternoon just before our exams, Sal and I meandered towards the park. We were headed to my house for a bit of English revision. Not that we needed to do any, but we had to at least *look* like we were making an effort.

It had been a gorgeous morning, a kind of birds-singing, break-into-song, 1950s-movie-type morning, but as soon as we left school, top-heavy dark clouds seemed to fast-forward through the sky, finally letting loose a torrent of stupidly heavy rain as we passed through the park gates.

We just stood there, looking at each other and giggling. Within a minute or so, we both looked as if we'd taken a shower in our clothes. I grabbed Sal's arm and ran towards a huge old oak tree near the swings. We sat with our backs against the trunk, laughing and shivering and watching mothers frantically trying to fasten up waterproof covers on pushchairs. Soon, we were the only ones left in the park. Still the rain drummed on.

We sat there for a while, hypnotized by the show the rain was putting on just for us. Sal turned and looked at me like she was trying to read my mind – or maybe trying to weigh something up in her *own* mind. *Uh oh, here it comes*. I felt a bit sick. Scared.

'There's something I need to tell you.' Did I know that what she was going to say would change everything? Maybe not. But I knew it was going to be big.

'I think I'm pregnant.' Four words, that's all it took. All I could manage to splutter out was 'Jesus!' *Nice. Good work. Very supportive.*

Sal began to cry and it just about broke my heart. I put my arms around her and held her tight. She kept saying the same thing over and over again: 'What am

I going to do?' I said that it would be OK and that we'd figure it out and was she really sure? But I wasn't getting through to her, so I held her face between my hands and made her look me in the eyes. 'Listen to me, Sal. Are you sure you're pregnant? Have you done a test?' Sal shook her head and sobbed, 'I know I am. I know it, I know it. How could this happen?'

We must have sat there for a good twenty minutes before I noticed that Sal was shivering really badly. She looked terrible. We headed to the bus stop, me with my arm around Sal's shoulders, her stumbling along in a kind of dazed stupor. I think she was all cried out.

We sat in silence all the way home. I could *not* have been more shocked. *How could this happen? I thought she was supposed to be a virgin . . . Surely she'd have told me if . . . When? Who with? And why hadn't she told me before?*

I led her into my house and straight up to my bedroom. We changed out of our wet clothes. I even let her wear my favourite jeans. She sat at the dressing table while I ran a comb through her matted, damp hair. She was looking in the mirror, but I could tell she wasn't really seeing much of anything.

I looked at Sal's reflection. Would I call her beautiful? Maybe. Definitely. Blonde hair that skims just above her shoulders. She often gathers it up in some

complicated arrangement that always looks completely effortless. Brown eyes and permanently honey-hued
skin. Lucky cow.

When I was done with Sal's hair and had quickly
run the comb through mine (boring brown beneath
MANY layers of red dye), I sat down on the edge of
the bed. Sal turned around on the stool to face me.
We were practically knee-to-knee, but somehow more
distant from each other than ever before. 'So, are you
going to tell me what happened?'

She shook her head. No eye contact.

'Okaaay, how late are you?' The words almost got
stuck in my throat. *I can't believe we're having this conversation.*

'Two weeks,' she said softly. Two weeks? Could she
be two weeks late just from stress or something? Or
did it definitely mean she was pregnant? *Aargh. I haven't
got a clue about this stuff.*

'OK, two weeks. You know, you can't be sure till
you've done a test. You could just be late cos you've
been stressing so much. Let's not jump to conclusions
here.' That sounded all right in my head, but pathetically inadequate when said out loud. Maybe you just
know when you're pregnant. Maybe your body feels
different? How the hell was I supposed to know?

The supply of tears had been replenished and

began to spill out again. 'I *know* I'm pregnant. I've known ever since . . .'

'*Please* tell me what happened, Sal. I'm your best friend – if you can't tell me, you're screwed . . .' I winced. 'Sorry . . . bad choice of words.' She half laughed at my bad joke, but then shook her head and looked at me sadly.

'Please . . . you have to understand. I just can't.' I felt like I'd failed some sort of test – probably the most important test our friendship would ever face. If only I'd said the right thing I could have got her to open up to me. Instead, I'd put my foot in it as usual, making a joke of something that was *so* not funny.

I practically begged her to tell me, but she wouldn't budge. And I couldn't help but feel a seed of resentment planting itself within me. I'd told her my deepest, darkest secrets; shouldn't it be a give-and-take sort of thing? I looked away and gazed out the window. The rain had finally stopped.

Sal took hold of my hand. 'Don't be angry with me, Grace. I couldn't bear it if you were angry with me.'

'I don't know what you want me to say. How can I help you if you won't even talk to me about it?' I *was* angry, but I didn't want her to know it.

'It doesn't matter what happened. I don't want to think about it. Please don't make me think about it.

I don't want you to hate me or think I'm any more stupid than you must do already. I just need you to be here for me.' She was pleading with me now. Scared and vulnerable and sad. My anger faded.

'Why would I hate you? Why would I think you're stupid? Stuff like this happens. I mean, it's a bit of a shock, but it's OK. I'd never think any less of you, you daft cow. You know me better than that. But if you really don't want to tell me, then I suppose I'll just have to get over it, won't I?' *Tell me tell me tell me NOW!*

Sal seemed grateful that I didn't push it any further. She stood and yawned. 'God, I'm *so* tired. Mind if I just have a little sleep? Just for a few minutes.' She curled up on the bed, kitten-style.

'Er . . . Sal, don't you think there's things we should be talking about?' *How can she be thinking of sleep at a time like this?*

'Later, Gracie. Later, I promise.' She sounded so exhausted that I decided to leave it – for now. *Maybe she'll be more rational after a bit of shut-eye.* I lay down next to her and stared at the ceiling until I heard her breathing relax into sleep.

So, my sweet and innocent best friend was pregnant. Or at least she seemed pretty sure she was. There was a *baby* growing inside her. An actual real, live baby/foetus/whatever. This was bad bad bad. Couldn't get

44

much worse in fact. First things first though. I had to make Sal get a pregnancy test, just to be sure. It would be annoying to be stressing this much over a false alarm.

I couldn't even begin to imagine *who* she'd slept with. Sal wouldn't have sex with just anyone – she's too damn choosy for that. *Oh God, maybe someone raped her. That could explain her reluctance to tell me what happened.* I wanted to wake her up right that moment and ask her. But she looked so serene and peaceful – I just couldn't do it.

I decided that a cup of tea was probably in order. Nothing like a cuppa in a crisis. So I went down to the kitchen and put the kettle on. Leaned against the worktop and sipped my tea. My mind was racing – it couldn't seem to stay on one topic for five seconds before flitting on to something else. *How could this have happened? And why the hell hadn't she taken the morning-after pill? And where was I when this was all going on? Easter. It had to have been at Easter. If I'd been here, maybe this wouldn't have happened. My fault?*

❦

Now there's a coincidence. There I was talking about having a cuppa, and guess who walks in? Ethan: Man of Mystery, bearing a mug (white) of steaming hot tea.

He set it down in front of me, carefully placing it in the corner of the table, far from the paper I've written on. Quite a pile now. Looks like it could turn into a pretty hefty tome. It's already longer than any of the several false starts I've had at writing The Novel. Maybe this should have happened to me sooner. There are too many distractions in the real world, always some reason not to write. If only that was the case here.

The tea is good. Scalding hot, and not too strong. It's the first cup of tea I've had since I've been here. Maybe Ethan was saving it as some kind of reward? I huddle over the mug, with my fingers wrapped around it. It feels like a crackling fire. Or a hug. I could do with a hug. Arms to wrap around me and make all the bad go away.

Finished now. And I've just realized that I missed the perfect opportunity to take Ethan by surprise. I should have chucked it in his face and made a run for it.

Could I have done that?

Could I do it next time maybe?

I don't know.

Why am I being so pathetic? Got to get out of here somehow . . . don't I?

Do I have to get out of here? Why would I want to go back to the colossal pile of crap that is my life? Nothing will have changed. I wonder how they're feeling now. I bet they're glad I'm gone. Probably makes it a lot easier on them. They might (pretend to) be upset for a bit, but I reckon they'll get over it before too long.

Ooh, I wonder if I'm in the newspapers? I must be, unless they reckon I'm too old. 'Missing seventeen-year-old' just doesn't have the same ring to it as a missing toddler, or even a twelve-year-old. I probably just made it into the local rag on the first day or so. I hope it was the front page, but I really really really hope they didn't use my last school photo, cos I'd forgotten the photographer was coming that day and I'd slept in too late to wash my hair. Gross.

Mum probably had to ask Sal for a decent photo, given that we haven't used our camera for years. We haven't even got a digital one. Dad was the designated photographer in the family. There *are* photos of me at home. Eight albums full, in fact. All carefully dated and labelled, hidden in the cupboard behind the TV, under a battered Trivial Pursuit box. The (almost) complete childhood of Grace Carlyle. Mum'll be wishing she'd made more of an effort to keep them up to date now.

Maybe Sal gave them the photo she took when I was asleep on the way back from a gig. The paper

wouldn't print that one though – I look like a corpse.
If corpses drool, that is. But she wouldn't do that to
me, would she?

Who am I trying to kid?

Fingers crossed it's the one from Kirsty's party. Sal
caught me by surprise, calling my name to make me
turn around and then snapping away. She thought it
was the funniest thing ever, cos she knows I hate having my picture taken these days. I grabbed the camera
and looked at the little screen on the back, ready to
DELETE DELETE DELETE. But the truth is, I looked
kind of OK. My hair looked awesome (but only cos
Sal had worked her magic on it earlier) and my eyes
looked all twinkly and amused somehow. I looked like
someone who good things were going to happen to
(someone to *whom* good things were going to happen.
Sorry). Plus, the top I was wearing actually made my
breasts look big, which is a feat in itself.

Yes. The newspaper will have used that one. Unless
they thought I looked a bit slutty. Dammit! I bet they
went for the school one. Urgh. That would be enough
to put anyone off their cornflakes in the morning. Let's
hope they printed it really small.

I don't reckon I'll be in any of the national papers.
People my age go missing all the time, don't they?
Everyone probably thinks I've run off with some guy I

met on the Internet. Maybe Mum's done one of those appeals on local telly, begging me to come home, and saying that I won't be in any trouble.

Nope. I bet she's actually gone on holiday, or swanned off to London to buy even *more* clothes she'll never wear. Seriously, how many pairs of shoes does a woman her age really need? I mean, I like shoes as much as the next girl, but there has to be something wrong with a woman who buys three pairs the same and hoards them in the back of the wardrobe.

No one is looking for me. That's the truth.

day 12

Slept well. Ethan brought me fresh fruit for breakfast – papaya and melon and mango and pineapple. He didn't speak to me, and I returned the favour. He came back when I'd finished eating to take away the bowl. He always seems to know when I've finished eating. I never have to deal with congealing leftovers, which is good, because bad smells make me gag. I've looked around for hidden cameras or peepholes, but there's nothing. Although I saw this TV programme once where there was a camera hidden in the end of a ballpoint pen. So maybe he's watching after all, but I DON'T CARE. It doesn't make a difference. I don't even care if he reads this. Perhaps I should let him, and then maybe he'd realize that I'm slightly unhinged and he really ought to let me go.

Back to the saga of Sal, I think.

So who on earth had Sal had sex with? It's a big world, and Sal is gorgeous, so pretty much the entire male population could be under suspicion. But Sal is fussy, like REALLY fussy. I was always pointing out hot boys to her, and sometimes she'd half-heartedly agree, but most of the time she'd look at me sceptically. It was frustrating.

I knew she still pined over that boy Chris, so there was a potential suspect. She *definitely* would have told me though. We'd certainly talked about him often enough. I knew so much about that boy he could've been my specialist subject on *Mastermind*. He has his lip pierced (gross times three, but Sal obsessed over it). He defied all the usual school cliques . . . a little bit emo, a little bit skater boy, a little bit Mr Popular, even little bit geek (he was into physics). He wore glasses that were nerdy but cool. Sounded to me like he was suffering from some kind of identity crisis, but each to their own. Sal showed me a picture of him at a school ball. He *did* look fit, I suppose.

Sitting at the kitchen table, staring at the tea stains, I decided to rule out Chris. There was just no way on earth she wouldn't have told me. Even if she was embarrassed about not using a condom. We've all been there. OK, maybe we haven't *all* been there. But I have. It's not exactly something I'm proud of, but at least I'd admitted it to Sal (who'd gone on to give me a ten-minute lecture, bless her).

Next, and pretty much the *only* other suspect I had, was Devon.

I've known Devon Scott for eight years, but before Sal came along I'd only talked to him a handful of times. He just didn't really cross my radar. Sal sits next to him in History, and it was obvious from the first day they met that he worshipped the ground she walked on. Sal told me this, not because she was making fun of him (in fact she thought he was quite sweet), but because she thought he had potential. She always said that in a couple of years he would grow into his looks and be fighting off girls with a stick. I wasn't so sure. He's sort of skinny and his clothes aren't great, but he's got a nice, honest sort of face, I suppose.

Sal sometimes talked about him – almost like she was coming round to the idea. He never asked her out, and I can't blame him. Girls like Sal don't usually go out with boys like Devon. Plus, she still obsessed over Chris. She didn't listen when I told her to get over him. Surely even with her shiny happy optimism she could see that nothing was ever going to happen there. Long-distance relationships are for idiots.

So . . . maybe Devon had finally worked up the

courage to say something to Sal. Or maybe he just got her really drunk during a little literary get-together and made his move. She might not have told me if it was Devon. He was a sort-of-possibility.

The only other option was a complete stranger, but it just didn't seem like a very 'Sal' thing to do. She believed in true love and romance and all that crap. She would NEVER have sex with a stranger.

And the thought that she might have been raped . . . well, that was just too much for me to deal with.

I gulped down the dregs of my tea and left the mug in the sink. The lack of dishwasher is a constant bone of contention between Mum and me. Washing dishes is *not* character-building. We had a dishwasher in the old house. We had a LOT of things in the old house.

I crept up the stairs and paused in the doorway of my room. Sal was still fast asleep – now with one arm flung above her head, bent at the wrist against the headboard, the other arm hanging off the side of my bed. She was even snoring – a tiny, snuffly, cute little snore. She was completely out of it.

I knew what I was going to do. She'd probably kill me, but it would be worth it.

I wrote a note and propped it up on the pillow next to Sal. Didn't want her waking up and thinking I'd abandoned her. I grabbed my purse, crept out of the room, down the stairs and out of the front door. It had stopped raining, and the air was fresh.

I hardly ever go to the chemist's down the road; the make-up selection leaves a lot to be desired and they don't even have any decent nail-varnish colours. They definitely cater to the somewhat more mature lady. A bell rang as I opened the door, and the girl behind the counter looked up from her book. *NO NO NO NO NO!*

I was expecting some kindly old dear who smelled like lavender, with glasses hanging on a gold chain around her neck.

Not Sophie Underwood.

Sophie Underwood. Seriously, it could have been almost ANYONE but her. Sophie and I go way back. We used to live on the same street – of course she still lives there, while I'm stuck in suburban terraced-house hell. We were friends in primary school, and in the first year of secondary too. Until I started to realize that maybe she wasn't the kind of friend I wanted to be lumbered with for the rest of my school days. Harsh, I know.

She's always been perfectly lovely and friendly and funny, but not too funny. But she's just so *good*. Never has a bad word to say about anyone, which is fine and makes her a much better person than I am. But twelve-year-old me just ran out of things to say to her. Sophie started hanging round with a group of nice but not-so-popular girls, and somehow I edged my way towards the popular lot. And so we just drifted apart, the way lots of friends seemed to in those first couple of years. You decide who you're going to throw your lot in with and just hope for the best.

Neither of us ever said anything about the gradual death of our friendship. We'd still say a vague 'hi' when we passed each other in the corridor.

It was just one of those things. One of those things that makes you feel like a horrible human being.

And now she was standing in front of me, with a look of mild surprise on her face. What the hell was she doing working *here*? She lived on the other side of town, for Christ's sake. *Hmm . . . awkward.* I gave her a little wave – nice and nonchalant – and headed straight for the shampoo display. At least there I could have my back to Sophie while I figured out how to play this.

There was no way I could get away with saying nothing. No point in playing the old 'It's not for me, it's for a friend' card, because a) she probably wouldn't believe me, and b) if she did, she would know it was for Sal because who else could it possibly be?

So I'd just have to say it was for me. *Brilliant*.

A few furtive glances around the shop confirmed my suspicions: the pregnancy tests were behind the counter. I took a deep breath and headed towards Sophie.

'Hey, Soph, how's it going?' She looked at me with a half-smile, one eyebrow raised, as if to say, 'When was the last time you called me *Soph*?'

'Hi, Grace. Exams going OK?'

'Yeah, y'know, the usual. How 'bout yours?'

Sophie rolled her eyes. 'Nightmare. I didn't even finish my chemistry exam yesterday.' *Yeah, right*.

'Er . . . Soph. This is really awkward, but I'm sure you get stuff like this happening all the time, working here. The thing is . . . I need a pregnancy test. This is really embarrassing and I don't want anyone to know, and I know I can trust you not to say anything . . .' *Babble babble babble*. If anything, Sophie looked the more awkward and embarrassed of the two of us. A flush of red came to her cheeks – more on the left side than the right, I noticed.

'Oh. Right. Of course. I would never . . . I would never say anything. Are you OK?' She looked genuinely concerned. She reached across the counter as if to touch my arm, and then pulled back at the last second. Obviously remembered that we weren't friends any more, and that touching me would be a weird thing for her to do.

I shrugged. 'Yeah, I'm fine. I just want to get this over with. It's probably nothing. I'm just being paranoid.' I briefly considered giving her some sob story, but reminded myself that it's always best to keep things simple when you're lying.

Sophie turned her back to me and scanned the shelves. 'We've got this digital one, if you want to try that. It's a bit more expensive, but it says it's ninety-nine per cent reliable. Or you could just go with the old kind. I think that's good too . . .'

'I suppose I'll take the digital one. How much is it?'

Sophie picked a box from the shelf and put it on the counter. Her face was still blotchy. She told me the price and I handed over the cash. She tapped away at the till and handed me back my change, avoiding eye contact. She handed me the box and asked if I wanted a bag.

I just looked at her.

Sophie winced. '*Of course* you want a bag. Sorry. This is just, well, it's a bit weird, isn't it? Listen, if there's anything . . . well, you know . . .' She trailed off into silence while she fumbled to find a bag under the counter.

The bell on the shop door rang again, and we both

jumped. It was just a little old man, stooped and shuf-
fling. I knew a chance to escape when I saw one. I took
the bag, said a quick but sincere thanks to Sophie, and
scarpered.

I hurried back up the road feeling weird and wistful and sad. Pushed all that to the back of my mind to
focus on the task ahead.

I unlocked the front door and pushed it open. Sal
was standing right in front of me, eyes bleary, hair all
over the place.

'And where do you think you're going . . . ?'

'I . . .' she faltered. Sheepish, big-time.

'You think I'm just going to let you do a runner?
Wearing my jeans too – the cheek of it!' I grinned
at her, grabbed her shoulders, turned her round and
marched her back upstairs. Once we were back in my
room, I sat Sal down on the bed and launched into
my spiel:

'Right. Here's the deal. You *think* you're pregnant.
You don't *know*. You can't possibly know till you've
done a test. Sooooo, I got you one.' I could see Sal was
about to interrupt, so I carried on speaking as quickly
as possible. 'Now I know you're scared, but you know
as well as I do that you have to be sure. Let's just find
out one way or the other and then we can get on with
things. I'm here now. You don't have to go through this

by yourself. We can deal with whatever happens – I promise you.'

The seconds seemed to stretch forever while I willed her to give in. I started drumming my fingers on the dressing table, partly because I was anxious, but mostly because I knew it was the one thing that drove Sal mental. She HATED it.

'That's not going to work, you know.'

'What's not going to work?' I asked, the picture of innocence.

'You're not going to irritate me into doing what you want.'

'It's hardly what I *want*, now, is it? You know you've got to do this. C'mon, Sal, you're the sensible one, remember? That's how it works: I do something stupid, and you tell me how to put it right. If you carry on like this, it's going to upset the delicate balance of our friendship. The repercussions could be serious!'

That managed to raise a teeny-tiny smile from Sal, which seemed like progress. So I took the box out of the bag and opened it. A quick scan of the instructions was enough to tell me what I already knew. I handed Sal the stick/wand/thingummyjig. She stared at it like it was going to explode, or at the very least bite off her hand.

'Now, off you go. You know what to do. There's

none of that blue line malarkey to try and decipher. It'll tell us in words and everything – the marvels of technology, eh?'

Sal got up and took a deep breath. I hugged her hard, and whispered, 'It's going to be OK. We can do this.' She left the room, and I heard the bathroom door shutting. I flopped down on the bed and stared at the ceiling. The wait was hellish.

I heard the toilet flush and before I knew it Sal was back in the room. I bolted upright, making my head spin.

'I can't look, Grace. Will you . . . ?' She handed me the test. Her thumb was over the little screen. I took it from her without looking.

'OK, so it says you could get a result within a minute, but let's just wait a little bit to be sure.'

We sat facing each other on the bed, my hand wrapped tightly around the test. So this was it. In a few seconds we were either going to be going crazy with relief (in which case we were going to get seriously wasted – exams or no exams), or . . .

I grabbed Sal's hand and squeezed it, as much to reassure myself as to reassure her. Then, when there was really nothing else to say or do, I looked down at the screen.

day 13

So last night was weird. Yet another dream about Ethan. He was my doctor and he was examining me as I lay on a hospital bed. He listened to my heartbeat with a stethoscope, looking worried. Then he shone a light in my eyes and shook his head. And then I woke up. My leg must have kicked out, and my foot touched something that was definitely not bed.

Ethan was sitting at the end of the bed, watching me. I freaked out.

'What the hell are you doing?! You need to watch me sleep now? Jesus! What is *wrong* with you?' I grabbed the duvet and cocooned myself in the corner of the bed, as far away from him as I could get. Ethan just looked at me, cool as you like. His face was half lit by the light streaming in through the open door. The open door! Maybe this was my chance to get out of here. I had to think fast. First of all, I had to try

not to look at the doorway. I didn't want Ethan realizing his mistake until it was too late. I had to calm
down. My heart was drum-drum-drumming loud as
anything.

We sat in silence for a little while. I got a chance
to look at him properly, while doing my very best to
ignore my escape route. He looked different. Not only
was he wearing a proper colour for the first time, he
was wearing *my* colour – my favourite green. It was a
fitted shirt with the sleeves rolled up to the elbows.
The top three buttons were undone, and I could see
his pale smooth chest. I wondered if he knew it was
my favourite colour. Of course not. How could he?
He was wearing his usual jeans – frayed and faded, and
his feet were bare. *Aha!* That could be a considerable
advantage, if there was going to be some kind of chase
scenario. Until I remembered I was in bed, and definitely not wearing a pair of super-fast running shoes.
Idiot.

'Were you dreaming, Grace?' he asked.

'What's it to you?'

'You looked like you were dreaming.'

'I don't remember.' I didn't want him to know that
I'd been dreaming about him. And had been doing so A
LOT over the past few days.

He sighed. 'I like dreaming. It's my favourite part of

the day. Have you ever noticed that dreams can change the way you feel?'

I just looked at him, saying nothing. If he wanted to go off on one, he was welcome to. I was still trying to work out how to make a run for it.

'Well, you might think one way about something, or someone, and then you dream about it. And it's completely different to the way you thought it would be. You wake up, and everything has changed.' I had no clue what he was going on about.

His eyes were intense, darker than usual. 'The door is open, Grace. The door is always open.' I turned my head towards the door, but it was closed. And it was dark. And Ethan wasn't there. The old dream-within-a-dream situation. *Bastard. WAKE UP!*

I got up and padded quietly towards the door. It was locked. Of course it was locked. I started to cry.

I need to not be here.

I need to see the sky.

I need to run.

❧

Ethan brought me an early breakfast. At least I *think* it was an early breakfast. There's really no way of knowing. All I know is that I was still snivelling after that dream. It felt early though, like no one else in the world was awake yet. Ethan was not wearing green. He was wearing a black T-shirt and grey jeans. He looks exhausted today. It's the first time he's looked slightly less than perfect since I've been here. Maybe his conscience is keeping him awake at night.

He asked me if I had slept well. Not particularly, I said. I told him he looked tired and then mentally kicked myself – I didn't want him thinking that I cared.

He seemed a bit startled that I had noticed. He paused and said, 'It's not easy, is it, Grace?' I shook my head, not quite understanding. He smiled a cute, sad little smile at me and left the room.

I jumped in the shower straight after breakfast. I like the water to be almost scalding – it clears the fuzz out of my brain. I stood there for some time with the water streaming down my shoulders. I held my arms out in front of me; the scars stood out against the rest of my ruddy skin. I scratched my fingernail down my left forearm. Again and again. Harder and harder. I couldn't make it bleed, but the pain felt good. I felt more awake. More alive.

Now my arm is covered in ugly red scratches. Never mind.

But I don't want Ethan to see. I don't think he'd like it.

๛

Sal was pregnant. That was the turning point – when everything turned to shit.

It didn't happen straight away. Everything was *kind of* OK (in an awful sort of way) for a while. Of course, Sal was devastated. There were a lot of tears and late-night phone calls, but somehow the two of us managed to stumble through our exams without screwing up. Sal had to run out of an English Lit. exam to be sick, but she'd already finished the paper so it was no big deal. She blamed it on food poisoning from Gino's. Not exactly fair on Gino.

It was a bad time for Sal, but there was something about it that made me feel sort of good. That sounds awful. But for maybe the first time in my life, I felt useful and . . . I don't know . . . needed? My best friend was going through the worst thing imaginable, and I was, in some strange, perverse way, *enjoying* myself. How bad is that? I dunno, maybe 'enjoying' is not quite the right word, but there *was* a certain amount of excitement from the drama of it all. I felt beyond awful for Sal, and I truly would have done anything in my power to change the situation. But all I could do was help her through it the best I could – be the sort of best friend she deserved. And that's what I tried to do.

I covered for her with her parents, as and when it was called for. When Devon came sniffing around because he'd 'sensed' something was wrong, I put him off the scent. I went with her to the doctor's – it had taken weeks for me to persuade her to go. Sal maintained that she wanted to get her exams out of the way first. I pestered her and pestered her, but she wouldn't budge.

Of course there was no question what Sal was going to do: there was no way she could keep the baby. We didn't even discuss it as an option. Nothing like those cheesy TV programmes where there's a lot of angsty decision-making, and heart-to-hearts about how it might be OK for a schoolgirl to raise a baby on her own. And how the baby was a part of her now and blah blah blah blah. Nope. Sal didn't want the baby, and that was that.

I still wanted to know who she'd had sex with. As far as I was concerned, she simply wasn't playing fair. It should be tit for tat (I'll tell you mine if you'll tell me yours). Still, I tried my best to ignore the resentment that was starting to fester inside me.

Sal didn't actually want me to go with her to the doc's, but I insisted. It's not that I didn't trust her to go on her own – I just felt I should be there. The doctor talked Sal through her options, but I could tell she wasn't listening. When the doc had finished, Sal calmly explained that she'd already considered all her options in great detail (lie), and that she wasn't stupid (truth) and knew that she wasn't ready for the responsibility (also truth). She was eerily composed. It was almost like she wasn't quite there, or like she was watching the whole thing happen through a pane of glass. An opaque pane of glass.

The bad news was that we shouldn't have waited those extra couple of weeks. If Sal had gone to the doctor's sooner, she would have been given some pills to take to terminate the pregnancy. It wouldn't have been pleasant, but she wouldn't have had to go through the trauma of going to a clinic. I felt like I'd let Sal down. I should have made her listen. Should have *forced* her to see a doctor sooner. Maybe I'd been too busy relishing the drama of it all. *Maybe*.

It was strange; we'd both accepted the idea of an abortion until we found out that she shouldn't have needed one in the first place. I don't know why, but having to have an actual operation seemed way worse than taking some pills, even if the end result was the same.

Something changed in Sal then, I think. We left the surgery, having made an appointment for her to go to the clinic the following week. I suggested we head to a greasy spoon I knew for a cup of tea.

We sat opposite each other at the back of the cafe. The table had more chips on it than the menu did. The tea was bitter and strong. Sal was distracted, but that was hardly surprising. I was yabbering on about how it was all going to be OK, and that she'd soon be able to put it all behind her and hadn't the doctor been nice?

Sal interrupted. 'Grace, can you just stop please?'

'Stop what?'

Sal looked at me like I was being particularly dense. 'Can we just . . . ? I can't do this right now. I have to go.' She pushed back her chair. It made a horrible scraping noise on the lino.

'Where are you going? What's up?' I was baffled. I knew she was upset – but she was supposed to want to be upset *with* me, not off by herself somewhere. This wasn't the way it was meant to go.

Sal had tears in her eyes and her voice was shaky when she said, 'Just . . . nothing. I have to go home.' Then she legged it out of the cafe before I even knew what was happening. Leaving me to pick up the bill. *Nice.*

I paid and rushed outside to catch up with her. I figured she'd be just around the corner, ready to apologize for being such a drama queen. She wasn't, so I

called her. Her phone went straight to voicemail. *Odd.*
Sal never turned off her phone. Never ever. We'd made
a deal.

~

The scratches on my arm are fading.

A broken biro works better than fingernails.

Blood on my pyjamas.

Red. White.

~

Another visit from Ethan. The real one, not the dream
one – I think. He saw the blood straight away, probably
because I didn't try to hide it. 'Give me your hand,' he
said, so softly I wasn't even sure he'd said it out loud. He
gently prised the broken biro from my hand and put it in
the pocket of his jeans. 'I'll get you some clean clothes.'

A couple of minutes later he was back with another set of pyjamas, identical to the ones I was
wearing. 'Do you want me to help with that?' He
nodded towards my bloody arms. I shook my head,
which felt all woolly and slow.

'Make sure you clean them up well. There's anti-
septic under the sink.' I nodded, took the clothes from
the bed and went into the bathroom. I felt like I was
walking underwater.

When I came out about ten minutes later, Ethan was sitting on the bed with the bloody biro in his hands. He didn't seem to mind that he was getting my blood all over his fingers. 'Should I take the pens away?' His tone was neutral.

'No, please, don't. I . . . I have to write. It's all I can do.'

'You can't keep doing this, Grace. You know that, don't you?'

I was starting to panic now. If I couldn't write, I really might start losing it. 'Please, Ethan. I won't do it again, I promise.' He looked up, and I felt like he was really *seeing* me. I held his gaze for as long as I could bear before looking away. He knew I was lying. I couldn't make a promise like that.

I've tried and failed before.

Ethan stood and walked to the door, leaving me staring into space. As he opened the door, he said, 'Sometimes it's hard for us to understand why people do the things they do, isn't it?' I waited for the familiar snick of the deadbolts. When I heard that, I whispered a quiet 'Tell me about it' to the empty room.

I sat down on the bed and rolled up my sleeves. Looking at my arms, criss-crossed with scars, old and new, I was struck for the very first time by the thought that it's a strange thing to do to yourself.

day 14

That makes it an even fortnight. Two whole weeks here and nothing's changed. Actually that's not strictly true; today I cleaned the bathroom. That was a bit of a surprise. It was starting to look not so white any more. And for some reason that bothered me. If by some miracle, a knight in shining armour does rescue me (and I can't exactly picture volunteers lining up for the job), I don't want him thinking I'm a total pig.

Sometimes I catch myself in a lie. The truth is I don't want Ethan thinking I'm a total pig. There. That's better. I don't know why I care, but I do. Mum would be proud. It's only taken two full weeks in captivity to finally get me to do some chores.

There's bleach under the sink.

I wonder what it would be like to drink it.

Ethan brought my lunch while I was on my cleaning mission. He poked his head round the bathroom door and grinned at me. Before I could stop myself, I grinned back. Neither of us spoke. Lunch was a salad. I ate it all up in about ten minutes. Scrubbing must have given me an appetite. I didn't write this afternoon; I exercised. Some sit-ups, a few stretches, nothing too hardcore. I paced from wall to wall one hundred times.

I couldn't get hold of Sal the evening after we went to the doctor's. Her mobile was still switched off, and no one was home either. Or at least, no one was answering the phone. I could just picture Sal hovering over the phone, rolling her eyes at the fact that I just wouldn't give up. I'll admit it: I was seriously worried. I had no idea what was going on.

The next few days were not much fun. I left countless messages on Sal's phone and a couple on her home number. The one time I spoke to her dad, he said she was out. I didn't want to hound her too much at home though – didn't want to raise any suspicions. Maybe she just needed some breathing space, a bit of time to think about next week.

Eventually I decided that she'd get in touch when she was good and ready. And when she was, I'd be there with all the tea and sympathy she could ever wish for. I tried to ignore that fact that I was annoyed about how she'd acted in the cafe. And annoyed that she was ignoring my calls. And still annoyed that she'd refused to tell me who she'd slept with. Quite a lot of annoyance really, but I was willing to put it aside. For now.

I was sure she would contact me before next week. And there was no way I was going to let her go through that nightmare by herself. So I waited, and waited some more. Nothing.

The day before Sal's appointment, I tried one last time. I left a pleading message on her mobile, telling her she HAD to call me, and that I knew things had been tough, but I was going to be there for her tomorrow, no matter what she said. A few hours later I got a text back: 'Meet in the park at 9 – by the swings'. Short and not so sweet. No 'sorry', no 'xxx', no nothing. Still, at least she'd finally agreed to see me.

I arrived at the park ten minutes early and meandered towards the swings. Sal was already there, much to my surprise. She was *never* on time. She had some kind of mental block about it. I've seen her *try* to leave the house in good time, only to realize she'd misplaced her keys or her phone or her bag, or oh wait . . . these weren't the jeans she wanted to wear today cos it looks like it might rain later. So seeing her there, swinging back and forth, was slightly disconcerting.

Sal saw me coming. I waved. She didn't. *Okaaaaay*. I sort of wanted to turn around and head home, but that wasn't really an option. I approached cautiously and sat on the swing next to her. She didn't look at me.

'Where have you been, Sal? I've been worried.'

'I haven't been anywhere. I just wanted some space.' She looked up at me. She looked, I don't know, sort of haunted.

'Fair enough, I can understand that. But you could have just *told* me that.'

Sal shook her head. Her hand was at her belly, gently rubbing.

'Talk to me, Sal. Please?'

'What do you want me to say?'

'Well, for starters, do you want me to come to yours tomorrow, or shall I meet you at the clinic?' I was perfectly willing to forget about the way she'd acted – at least until after the abortion.

'I don't want you to come.' There was a quiet determination in her voice that I didn't like one little bit.

'Don't be stupid – of course I'm coming! There's no way you'd let *me* go through something like this by myself. C'mon, Sal—'

'You're not listening to me. I don't want you there.'

'Why not? Is someone else going? Have you told

74

your mum?' A fleeting smile from Sal – so fleeting I wasn't even sure I'd seen it.

'Yeah, right.'

'So who then? Wait . . . have you told *him* . . . the boy, I mean?' This could be progress. If Boy X was facing up to his responsibilities, that could only be a good thing.

Sal shook her head, and tears welled up in her eyes. I reached for her hand and she flinched. She actually flinched! *WTF?*

'Sal, what is *wrong* with you? Jesus!' I got up from the swing and knelt down in front of her, forcing her to look at me.

'You really have no idea, do you?' She shook her head slowly as she spoke.

'I haven't got a scooby! Tell me. C'mon, you can tell me anything . . . you know that.'

She took a juddery deep breath, steeling herself for what she was about to say.

'This is all your fault.'

I couldn't speak for a moment or two. And when I finally managed, what came out wasn't even a proper word – more like an incredulous vowel sound.

'This would never have happened if it hadn't been for you.' Sal spoke quietly, but there was an underlying bitterness that I had never heard from her before.

I felt the first flickers of anger, spiked and hot. 'What the *fuck*? You're not serious, are you?'

'Do I look like I'm joking?' Now Sal was looking kind of angry too. *How can this be happening?* I was watching a bad play where the actors were getting the dialogue all wrong.

'How can this be my fault? As far as I can understand it, which isn't very far cos you haven't told me *anything*, you had sex with some random boy, didn't use a condom and . . . well, that's pretty much all I know, isn't it? Now explain to me exactly which part of that is *my* fault? C'mon, tell me. Sorry for being dense, if it's so fucking obvious!' I was standing now, not quite shouting, but sort of spitting the words. Dad always said I had a bit of a temper.

Sal said, 'You have no idea what the fuck you're talking about – as usual.'

The conversation was spiralling out of control, but there was nothing I could do to stop it. 'I don't know what's got into you. You're not even making sense any more. Sal, I've done nothing wrong and you know it!'

'Why do you think I'm in this situation?'

I felt like I was walking into some kind of trap, but I couldn't quite see how. 'Um . . . well . . . duh . . . let me see. I'm guessing it went something like this: you met a boy, there was probably a bit of kissing, he felt you up, you finally realized you didn't want to be the last virgin on the face of the planet and that maybe waiting around for your one true love was a complete waste of time after all so you let him shag you. Probably lasted about two minutes, and then you went boo hoo hoo all the way home.' As soon as the words were out of my mouth, I knew I'd made a terrible mistake.

Sal looked like I'd just slapped her in the face. I tried to backtrack. 'Shit, Sal, I'm sorry. I didn't mean that. I just got all . . . well, you know how I get some-times – mouth runs away with me. I don't know what I'm talking about.' I reached out to touch her arm and she looked at my hand as if it was some kind of mutant insect.

'Don't touch me,' she said in a hollow voice. 'You remember that Friday night we went out just before Easter? You pulled like three or was it even four boys in that club, leaving me sitting on my own in the cor-ner?'

'Yeah, I remember. I *said* I was sorry. Don't see what that's got to do with anything though,' I said sulkily.

'You were completely off your face when we got back to mine. No surprise there. Do you remember what you said to me in the kitchen?'

I mentally rewound to the night in question, but it was no good. I shook my head.

Sal mirrored my head-shaking, muttering, 'Typical,' under her breath. 'You said that if I didn't lose my virginity soon, you were either going to have me signed up to join a convent, or you were going to choose a boy yourself to do the honours.'

Ouch. That *did* sound like something I would say.

Sal continued, 'You said that pining over Chris was a waste of time, that I was "deluded" for thinking that something could ever happen there, and that I was "waaaaaaaaaaay too picky for my own good". Sounding familiar now? Ringing any bells?'

'Is *that* what this is about? I say something stupid when I'm pissed, and you go out and shag some boy because of it. Now, tell me exactly how that works.'

'You really have no idea what a bitch you can be sometimes, do you?'

'For Christ's sake, I was *joking*, Sal. I was wasted! This is ridiculous.' I turned away from her.

'It wasn't just that night, Grace – there were constant little digs about it, all the time. Maybe you don't remember, but I do! If your best friend says something to you enough times, you start to believe it. I wouldn't have slept with anyone if it hadn't been for you – I wasn't ready! That might be difficult for you to understand, Little Miss "Oh, I've only known you for five minutes but of *course* I'll have sex with you. It might make me like myself a little bit more and finally prove I'm actually worth something, instead of just being some freak who cuts herself in a pathetic attempt to get sympathy from people—'"

I slapped Sal square in the face, hard.

Sal was shocked, and so was I. I'd never hit anyone in my life. I walked away, leaving her standing there gawping after me.

I felt numb. How could this have happened? Our friendship was over – that was for sure. There'd be no coming back from this. All this time I'd thought Sal cared about me . . . and then to hear her spouting that poison?

I started to run. As fast as I could. Far away from Sal. Far away from everything.

But no matter how fast I ran, I couldn't outrun my tears.

day 15

More dreams. Some that seemed to go on forever, and some that were just snapshots. There's only one that I can remember clearly though; the others fade every time I try to focus my mind. Maybe I'll remember later. I'm not one of those people who think that dreams necessarily *mean* anything, but I suppose I'm open-minded about the whole thing.

Last night I dreamed I was having sex with Nat. Everything about it was just right. His smell, his touch on my skin, the movement of his taut sinewy back muscles under my hands. We weren't in his bed or mine – we were in Sal's bed. The sex was good, maybe even better than it ever was in real life.

And then the old dream-morphing trick happened again, and suddenly it was Ethan on top of me. But it was still Nat too. A kind of Ethan/Nat hybrid of gorgeousness.

Afterwards, I lay with my head on his chest. It was definitely all Ethan now. His chest was so very pale.

I lay there for what seemed like hours. Until I noticed that I couldn't hear his heartbeat. His chest wasn't moving up and down the way it should – he wasn't breathing. I bolted upright to look at his face. And he just smiled a peaceful smile at me and said, 'What's the matter, Gracie?' I told him I couldn't hear his heartbeat and I'd thought he was dead. He smiled again, shaking his head as if I was overreacting. 'Maybe you're just not listening hard enough? Listen carefully and you can hear the ocean.' I pressed my ear against his chest and there *was* a heartbeat, faint but definitely there. And I *could* hear the ocean – the tide flowing in and out, in and out. I smiled.

And then I woke up – half horny, half puzzled. Dreams are tiring.

Something's changed in me, I think. I can't pinpoint exactly *when* it changed, but it definitely has. I've stopped questioning why I'm here. I just am. This is the way things are. I don't know how it's going to turn out, but maybe it doesn't matter.

But I still want to know about Ethan. I *need* to know about Ethan. What does he do all day? Where does he sleep? Does he ever go outside? Is he happy?

I'm going to try to speak to him, properly. No more petulance, no more tears.

I start today.

&

After lunch, Ethan brought me some grey trackie bottoms and a couple of white vests. Some underwear too. Everything fits. When he handed over the neatly folded pile, I looked at him quizzically.

He blushed. 'For when you exercise, I thought you'd . . .' I thanked him, noticing a couple of black hair bobbles nestled on top of the pile. He'd obviously really thought about this. It's only now that I'm wondering how he knew I'd started exercising. And how did he know that it wasn't just a one-off?

It felt good to be out of those pyjamas for a while. Felt a bit like me again. It was good to get some exercise – to do something else besides remembering. Even tried to do some press-ups, before I realized that was a tad overambitious after hardly having moved for two weeks. I'm going to have to try to do a little bit more every day if I'm going to stay healthy.

Ethan came back later this afternoon. I was lying on the floor, my heart beating wildly. I'd been running on the spot for ten minutes, which normally wouldn't even make me break a sweat. I was exhausted. I heard the door open behind me. Ethan loomed over me, his face upside down.

'Hi,' I croaked.

'Hello,' he said. 'How do you feel?'

'Bloody knackered,' I replied. I heard rather than saw him move over to sit on the edge of the bed. I stayed where I was, on the floor, one arm flung across my forehead. This was my chance. 'Is Ethan your real name?'

'Do you think I would lie to you, Grace?'

'I don't know. Maybe. It's one of my favourite names, you know.'

'Is it? I'm glad.' He smiled.

'Do you have a last name?'

'Doesn't everyone?'

'You're very confusing, you know.'

'Isn't everyone?'

I laughed at this. 'OK, what do you do all day then? You can't just spend all your time cooking and doing the washing. How boring is *that*? Do you cook my meals?' I was determined to get something from him.

He paused. 'It's not important.'

I sighed. This wasn't exactly going to plan. 'You look tired.' It was true. Dark circles shadowed his eyes, and his skin was sallow.

'You shouldn't worry about me, Grace. How is it going?' He gestured to the desk.

I manoeuvred myself up onto one elbow, conscious that he was getting a more than decent view of my breasts. 'I'm not sure. It's hard. It hurts . . . to think about things.'

Ethan stared at me for a few seconds. 'Maybe hurt isn't always a bad thing.' He got up and stretched, stifling a yawn. 'I'll leave you to it. It's getting late.' He closed the door behind him and I was left wondering exactly what he meant.

It's not getting late.

Is it?

～

After my fight with Sal, I ran all the way home. Three miles went past in a blur. The tears had dried by the time I got to the front door. I hardly slept that night. Instead I replayed the conversation in my head, again and again – trying to make sense of it. It was hopeless.

The next day was even worse. Knowing what Sal was going through, alone. Every few minutes I looked at the clock on my phone. An hour before Sal's appointment, I couldn't take it any more, and called Sal's number. Straight to voicemail. 'Sal, it's me.

I . . . I don't really know what to say. I hope it goes OK today. Last night was . . . I think we need to talk about it. Ring me.'

I didn't hear anything from Sal – that day, or the next. I knew she must have gone ahead with the abortion. There was no question about it. I felt awful that she'd had to go through it by herself, but I was so angry about what she'd said.

I couldn't get over the fact that Sal had clearly harboured these feelings about me for some time. What I had said to her was stupid, no doubt. But to blame me for her getting pregnant? That was a step too far. This was Sal – the most sensible, intelligent, grounded person I knew. It made no sense at all. Still, it didn't stop me feeling like the lowest of the low for what I'd said – in the park *and* that night after the club. Idiotic in the extreme, but Sal knew me. I *thought* she knew when to take me seriously and when to just ignore me. Everything had been fine between us before the visit to the doctor, hadn't it?

Days and days went by – a blur of angry tears and confusion. I cut. Even after what Sal had said.

I went a bit too deep with one of the cuts in my arm. The blood oozed out so fast I thought it would never stop. I tasted a drop. It was warm on my tongue.

Mum knew full well something was up. She even

tried talking to me. I ignored her. I was so lonely — absolutely desperate to talk to someone. But not desperate enough to talk to her.

I briefly considered calling Sophie. I was actually a little bit annoyed with her. I thought she might have called to see how I was. After all, as far as she was concerned I could have been pregnant. I knew I was being ridiculous because a) I had dropped that girl like a particularly heavy brick and didn't deserve her concern, and b) I'd lied to her about the pregnancy test. So my indignation was hardly righteous.

I called no one, and no one called me. I was suffocating with loneliness. The pain was almost physical. I felt like tearing myself apart. I wanted to escape from my own skin.

And then one night everything changed. I'd spent the evening in my room, drinking, trying to forget. Listening to depressing music. Being such a *teenager*. It even struck me at the time: I was a cliché, and not even a good one.

I decided to get up off my arse and do something. I changed into my leggings and an old T-shirt, put on my trusty trainers and bolted out of the house. Running while inebriated: I can thoroughly recommend it. I flew through the streets. Yeah, there was a bit of stumbling here and there, but other than that I'd say the alcohol was more of a help than a hindrance. It wasn't long before I felt that same rush that running always gives me. I could have run forever. It didn't even bother me when it started to rain. I just pounded the pavement even harder.

I didn't mean to end up at Sal's house. Not consciously anyway. But sure enough, that was where I found myself. Leaning against a lamp post, looking up at her bedroom window like some kind of crazed stalker. I stood there, trying to catch my breath, wondering what to do. I didn't feel drunk any more, that was for sure. It wasn't that late; Sal's light was on. The curtains were drawn. I was *so* close to striding up to the front door and ringing the doorbell. I was torn. Part of me wanted to grab Sal, give her the biggest hug in the world and pray that everything could go back to how it had been before. And part of me wanted to grab her and shake her and shout and scream, 'How could you say those things to me?!' I wanted to do both of those things and neither of them. I did nothing.

I turned my back on Sal's house and slouched off down the street. Suddenly the idea of running all the way home didn't seem so appealing. I felt sick, and just . . . sad. I headed for the nearest bus stop without a second thought. There was a boy there, sitting in the bus shelter in the dark. The light must have been broken. I sat at the other end of the bench; I didn't have the energy to stand. I leaned my head back against the glass and closed my eyes. I breathed – in and out, in and out, trying to empty my head of everything. It was raining again. I could hear it pattering against the roof of the shelter, and the slick sound of car tyres on wet tarmac.

I knew the boy was watching me. You can feel it sometimes, can't you? With a sigh I opened my eyes and turned towards him. He looked away quickly – guiltily. And then back at me, to see if I was still looking. I was. He looked away again. And then back again! I treated him to my trademark eyebrow raise.

He stuttered, 'Sorry. I . . . Sorry.' I said nothing, just looked at him. He was kind of hot. Scruffy, short-ish blond hair, a bit unshaven. Nice strong face with a good straight nose. I couldn't tell what colour his eyes were. Clothes-wise he was going for the T-shirt over a long-sleeved T-shirt look – it worked for me. Even in the darkness I could make out a pair of bright white trainers peeking out from the bottom of his jeans. I wasn't looking him up and down, you understand. I took in this information in a millisecond (or maybe two).

'Can I help you?' I said, but not in a mean way.

He looked embarrassed. 'Er, no. Sorry.' Then he looked away – again! He was a shy one all right. I closed my eyes again, not really caring if he took the opportunity to look me over. I wasn't in the mood.

I opened my eyes when I heard a bus pull up. The bright lights of the bus dazzled me as I approached the surly-looking driver. And realized I didn't have my purse. *Idiot.*

'I . . . Sorry. I seem to have left my purse at home.'

The driver looked at me sceptically, even going so far as to use my very own eyebrow trick against me.

I was indignant. 'It's true! Please. I need to get home. I'm cold, I'm wet. Come on . . .' The driver just shook his head. He'd yet to utter a word.

I felt a tap on my shoulder. Bus-stop boy stepped around me and stood in front of the driver. 'Two singles, please,' and I heard the jangle of money dropping into the money-collecting tickety machine thing. Without even a look over his shoulder, he hurried forward and up the stairs.

The driver smirked. 'All right for some.'

I walked past him, saying nothing.

I was so relieved. My legs were leaden. Maybe drinking and running hadn't been such a stellar idea after all. I trudged up the stairs. The bus was half full in that irritating way – every double seat had a single person on it. I spotted bus-stop boy towards the back. Normally I like to sit as near to the front as I can. When Dad used to take me to the park I would run up the stairs as fast as I could, praying that the front seat would be empty. I liked to pretend I was driving the bus. I was very good at pretending.

I slid onto the seat next to the boy and said thank you. He looked up and smiled, and for the first time I got to see his eyes. They were blue, and framed by the longest eyelashes I have ever seen on a boy. He was quite pale, and looked as tired as I felt. I suddenly realized what a sight I must look. I pushed a stray bit of hair behind my ear and tried to surreptitiously check out my reflection in the window. It was no good – he was in the way. No make-up and sweaty running clothes: there was no way he would be interested. And I wasn't interested either. *Who am I kidding? I'm* always *interested.* It had been a crappy day, I was probably still a bit worse for wear and I was sitting next to a (sort of) fit boy.

'That was really nice of you, paying my fare.'

'No worries. I couldn't just leave you stranded there, could I?' He smiled again. Nice smile, good teeth (very important). 'Not the nicest night for a run,' he said. The raindrops streaked along the window next to him.

'Yeah, it was a spur of the moment thing. Went out a bit too hard, I suppose. Need to pace myself a bit better next time.' I shrugged.

'Or bring your bus fare with you?' We smiled at each other. *Hmm, I like.*

'I'm Grace, by the way.'

'Nat. Nice to meet you.'

'You too. So do you make a habit of rescuing damsels in distress then, Nat?'

He smiled a quick smile, but it didn't quite reach his eyes. 'I wish.'

I waited for him to explain, but he shook his head and said, 'Never mind.' I let it go.

So we talked. That is, I asked a lot of questions. And he answered them in a perfectly polite, friendly fashion. He asked me stuff too, but I could tell that he wasn't *that* interested. I mean, he was kind of interested, but I wasn't getting the right signals. Something was slightly off, and my radar was screaming GIRL-FRIEND ALERT! GIRLFRIEND ALERT! So I asked THE question.

Nat shook his head and said no. I believed him, but there was something a bit weird about the way he said it. I couldn't put my finger on it, so I ignored it.

Things I learned about Nat on the bus

1. He was nineteen.
2. He'd just finished his first year at uni and was home for the summer.
3. He was studying medicine (clever as well as pretty – yay!).
4. He'd bought the trainers that day and was embarrassed about their shiny white obvious newness.
5. He was working part-time in some crappy pub in town.
6. He'd spent three months last summer doing some kind of charity work in Nepal. Obviously the caring, sharing type.
7. He was yummy.

He also admitted – very reluctantly – that he still hadn't passed his driving test. Hence the need to get buses everywhere. He was embarrassed about that; he was really cute when he was embarrassed. His eyelashes made him look all coy and sweet.

For the first time in ages I was enjoying myself. It just felt so *normal* – talking to a boy, trying to work out if he liked me or not. Not-so-subconsciously mirroring his body language (trickier than it sounds on a cramped bus seat). To be perfectly honest, I was so bloody lonely that I think I'd have jumped at the chance to talk to *anyone* that night. But lucky for me, it was Nat. Luscious, butter-wouldn't-melt, too-good-to-be-true Nat.

My stop was coming up a lot faster than I'd have liked. I toyed with the idea of staying on the bus with Nat, but I was knackered. Plus, it's always better to play hard to get in these situations. Assuming the boy actually wants to get you, of course.

'Listen, my stop's coming up. Thanks again for coming to my rescue. I'd like to pay you back somehow.' I let that hang in the air for a moment before pressing on, 'Could I maybe buy you a drink to say thanks?' Pleasepleasepleasepleaseplease say yes.

Nat looked at me for a couple of seconds. I think he was a bit taken aback, poor love. And just when I was sure he was going to say, 'Thanks, but no thanks,' he said, 'That would be nice' instead! It seemed a bit of an effort for him to get the words out, but I wasn't going to dwell on that. I gave him my number, since I didn't have my mobile on me (duh!). He promised to call, and I believed him. I practically skipped down the aisle. A quick glance back at the top of the stairs, but he was looking out of the window. *Huh. Two can play the hard-to-get game, I suppose.*

That night I slept better than I had in ages. Of

course I hadn't forgotten about Sal — not even close. But at least now I had an alternative to think about. Whenever Sal popped up inside my head, I re-routed my brain down the path to Nat. It worked, sort of.

day 16

The exercise is definitely doing me good. I really went for it today. I was running on the spot, sweating like a bastard, when Ethan came in. I stood there, hands on hips, breathing hard, waiting for him to speak first. 'Don't stop,' he said. So I got down on the floor and started some sit-ups, watching Ethan as he took a seat at the table. He made no effort to look at the stack of paper there. His eyes never left mine. I counted thirty sit-ups, with us staring at each other the whole time. It definitely wasn't normal.

Just when I thought I couldn't take any more staring, Ethan's head drooped down to his chest. He'd fallen asleep. It was a moment or two before the realization fully kicked in. Ethan was *asleep*. There was nothing to stop me walking out the door. My heart thumped wildly. But then, maybe he was faking – testing me to see what I would do.

I sat on the floor, straining to hear the sound of his breathing above my own. A snore or two would have been helpful. Maybe a little bit of drooling, just to be sure. I scooted over to him so that I could a get a better look at his face. His hair had fallen in front of his eyes, but I could see that they were closed. This was my chance. I could just make a run for it. Or rather, a creep for it. It could all be over in a matter of minutes, assuming the building wasn't some kind of mad fortress.

So what was stopping me? I wish I knew. Instead of scarpering, I sat back on the floor, with my legs tucked underneath me. And then I don't know what possessed me, but I rested my head on Ethan's thigh. I'd clearly lost my mind, but it felt . . . right. Ethan moaned a little bit and shifted his leg. I held my breath, certain that he would wake up. He didn't.

I don't know how long I sat there – maybe twenty minutes? I couldn't believe he'd fallen asleep. It was bizarre. I mean, I've fallen asleep on the night bus a couple of times, but what kind of half-arsed kidnapper falls asleep, allowing the perfect opportunity for escape? And what kind of screwed-up girl has the perfect opportunity to escape but just sits there like some kind of lapdog?

I came to my senses. Carefully, quietly, I stood up

and backed towards the door, keeping my eyes on Ethan with every step. When I got to the door, I paused for a second, readying myself. I reached for the door handle and turned it. And then I was suddenly overwhelmed by a blast of pure panic. My heart slammed in my chest, and I felt hot and cold and shaky and weird. I couldn't get enough air into my lungs. There wasn't enough air in the room. I thought I was dying.

My stomach flipped. I ran to the bathroom and puked in the toilet, coughing and spluttering and choking. And then I lay down on the cold floor and cried. I didn't know what was happening to me. I didn't know how I felt about anything any more – why hadn't I been able to leave? I didn't want to be here . . .

. . . did I?

Eventually I dragged myself out of the bathroom and onto the bed. Crawled under the duvet and lay watching Ethan, trying to ignore the bitter taste at the back of my throat. After a while, Ethan stirred. He raised his head, put his hands up to his face and rubbed his eyes. He turned towards me and blinked.

'You're still here,' he said. I couldn't tell if he was pleased or disappointed. Maybe both.

'Where else would I be?'

He nodded towards the door.

'What's out there?' I asked.

'Everything.'

Christ! All this Man of Mystery crap is really starting to grate.

'Grace, why didn't you leave? What are you afraid of?'

I thought for a moment. 'Everything.'

It's true.

～

Ethan sat a little while longer, saying nothing. I felt my eyelids get heavier and heavier, until I couldn't resist. Sleep came. I don't remember any dreams as such, just a few random images that I can't piece together. Dad's funeral in the rain. Sal sitting on a park bench, holding hands with a shadowy someone. And Devon, looking like he hadn't slept in a week – sad and worried, slouched in an uncomfortable-looking chair.

～

Nat called me two days after we met. I'd been kicking myself for not getting his number, and starting to doubt that he'd ever call. Maybe I'd been a bit full on? Not full on enough? I'd spent most of my time staring at my phone, willing it to ring. Picturing Nat taking a deep breath before punching the numbers into his phone. I was desperate for a distraction from my craptastic life – anything I could lay my hands on. And I was definitely more than a little bit keen to lay my hands on Nat. When he finally did ring, I was not quite as cool as I wanted to be. We chatted for a bit, with me saying things so stupid I had to physically restrain myself from whacking the phone against my head. Still, I managed to pin him down to go out for a drink that night.

That first night I thought I had no chance. He was friendly and sweet and funny, but in a brotherly sort of way. But I wasn't after a brother, or a friend. I *really* wanted him. Somehow, in just a few days, he'd transformed from 'sort of hot' into 'Hottie McHotterson, fittest boy in the history of the world – EVER' in my mind.

At one point in the evening, Nat even went so far as to say he had a friend he thought would be perfect for me. And here was me thinking that I couldn't have made it any more obvious how I felt. Well, not without jumping the poor boy in the middle of the pub. And I don't think the rest of the clientele would have been best pleased about that. Looking back, I'm not sure if I would have gone after him quite so determinedly if it hadn't been for all the crap I'd been going through. I mean, I probably would have still been interested, but I would have tried to maintain at least a nugget of dignity. No boy is worth looking like a fool for.

We said goodbye at the bus stop. He really was my bus-stop boy. We hugged, and I was just about to turn and leave when I thought, 'Fuck it,' and decided to take the bull by the horns/the boy by the balls.

'Listen, Nat, I've been dropping hints all night, and I'm not sure if you don't get it, or you're not interested – which is fair enough, by the way – but I like you, and I'd like to see you again. And not as a friend.' *There. Said it. Eek.*

He looked awkward. 'I like you too, Grace. But there's someone—'

I jumped in. 'OK, I get it. I wish you'd told me before. I did ask. That's fine. I . . . I'll see you around.' And then suddenly I was fighting back tears – beyond ridiculous! I'd only just met the boy. It's not like he meant anything to me. I think it was just the *idea* of him that was so appealing. I was desperate for someone to take care of me. To tell me everything would be OK. To hold me and touch me and make me feel better.

I turned away in embarrassment. Nat touched my shoulder just as I was about to make a run for it.

'Hey,' he said softly. 'Hey, come on now. I don't have a girlfriend, if that's what you're thinking. There was just someone who I thought . . . I don't know . . .

I liked her. And I thought that something could happen there. But it didn't work out like that and I'm trying to forget about it. And I don't want to use you to do that. I think you deserve better than that.' I could feel his breath on the back of my neck. He was so sincere, and so completely and utterly desirable right at that moment. I turned back to him. His face was inches from mine. He smelled really, really good.

'Why don't you let me be the judge of that?' I whispered. Then I kissed him, just a little bit. He kissed me back. God, that kiss . . .

And so began the one and only relationship in my life that ever meant anything.

day 17

Aargh. More bloody dreams. And this time one of them was *actually* rather bloody. Nat and I were at the park, sitting in the den at the top of the climbing frame. For some reason we couldn't talk – it wasn't allowed. We just looked at each other. Nat wasn't wearing a shirt. He had scars criss-crossing his arms. I was surprised I hadn't noticed them before. I wanted to ask him about them, but I couldn't.

As I watched, the scars turned from white to red, and blood started to drip down his arms. It soaked into his jeans. Blood splashed onto the floor. I tried to reach out to him, but my arms wouldn't move. I tried to scream, but no sound came out of my mouth. Nat started to laugh, and the laughter turned to tears, and he turned into Ethan. And Ethan was sobbing and looking at me imploringly, and I knew he was trying to tell me something but I couldn't understand.

I woke up sweating and shivering, all tangled up in the duvet. I jumped in the shower and stood under the hot spray, willing the pounding water to drum the images out of my head. Afterwards, I wiped the steam from the mirror and stood looking at myself. I ran my fingers down the inside of my left arm, and the girl in the mirror did the same. The skin was ridged where it should have been smooth. It will never be smooth again.

I was nervous the first time I undressed in front of Nat. I'd never really cared that much before. Boys were usually too drunk to notice, and when they occasionally did, I'd find some way or other to distract them (which never proved too hard). But this was different. I didn't want Nat to think I was a weirdo. It felt like what Sal had said was now tattooed on my brain . . . some freak who cuts herself in a pathetic attempt to get sympathy from people. Each of those words cut deeper than a blade ever could. If Nat felt the same way, I didn't know what I would do.

It was maybe the third or fourth time we'd been out. Up until then, Nat had been the perfect gentleman. But I was gagging to do more than just kiss him. I'd never met anyone like him before. My mind was really starting to run away with itself – already wondering if he could be THE ONE. Ridiculous. But he was thoughtful, and clever and caring. I felt a twinge of sadness that Sal wasn't around to talk to about him. Maybe it was just as well though – I'd probably have bored her to tears with 'Nat said this . . .' and 'Nat did that . . .' and 'Oh, he's just sooooo dreamy'. Well, maybe not the last one. I would never actually *say* 'dreamy' . . . but I might think it.

I met Nat at the pub where he was working a lunchtime shift. I'd never normally be seen dead in a place like that, but sometimes you've got to compromise. I sat at the bar and chatted to him while he worked. He was brilliant with the customers, even the crazy old muttering man at the other end of the bar. Nat just has this kind of easy manner that makes anyone who talks to him warm to him immediately. He's completely comfortable talking to *anyone*. Not that he's cocky or anything – that would be gross. He just knows how people work and exactly what to say to put them at ease. Back then I could picture him as a doctor, maybe breaking the news to someone about the death of a loved one. (And then coming home to tell me all about it. Like I said: my mind was really starting to run away with itself.)

Every so often, Nat would catch my eye and smile that beautiful smile. Tonight was going to be the night. Mum was away for the weekend (again), so the coast was clear. I'd taken extra-special care shaving my legs that morning, put on my hottest underwear (black, of course) and even changed the sheets on my bed (maybe the second time I had ever done that in my life). I was nervous and excited, which made a nice change.

Nat got off work at six, and we went back to my house. We cracked open a bottle of red wine and cooked a meal together. I chopped the tomatoes while Nat set to work on the onions. The onions made him cry a little. I laughed and kissed him on the nose. It was so perfectly domestic and comfortable. For a fleeting moment, I imagined that this must be what it was like to be married. *Get a grip.*

There were candles on the table. The food tasted great. The wine was luscious and warm. And Nat . . . well, he was hot hot hot. I'd never wanted someone more. I liked listening to him talk about the things that interested him. He'd get so passionate and his eyes would twinkle and shine. After dinner, we sat on the sofa. I was pleasantly tipsy – just tipsy enough to ask him about that girl he'd been interested in.

Nat shook his head. 'I don't really want to talk about it, Grace. I'm here with you now.' I wanted to know more, but Nat used my old trick of distraction. He kissed me, with a new kind of urgency. I soon forgot all about Mystery Girl and sank back into the moment. Before long, Nat was on top of me, and I was pulling him closer to me. One of his legs was between mine, and I squirmed against it. I could feel the heat of him through his jeans. He started to paw at my T-shirt, and it took all the willpower I had to half whisper, half pant, 'Not here . . . upstairs.'

'OK, I'll give you a head start.' He grinned a wicked grin.

I ran up the stairs two at a time, with Nat close on my heels, swiping at my bum. Both of us laughing like idiots. He caught me at my bedroom door and manhandled me around to face him. Pushed me up against the door frame and kissed me again. I pulled his T-shirt up, and it got stuck going over his head. I kissed him through the white cotton and then pulled the T-shirt the rest of the way off. His hair was all mussed up, and he looked better than ever. Better than anyone. I raked my fingers over his chest. It was just hairy enough not to be too boyish, but nowhere near gorilla-hairy (thank God). We stumbled over to the bed and I pushed him down and straddled him, kissing his chest. He lay back, and I pulled off my top.

This was it.

No more hiding. Nat was going to see.

The only light in the room was streaming through the open door. Still, it was enough to illuminate me.

Of course, Nat *was* a boy, and so his eyes (and hands) immediately fixed on my breasts. It was only when he started to run his hands over me that he noticed something wasn't quite right. His thumb was tracing a path down the inside of my arm. 'What's this?' he murmured, in between kisses. 'Nothing,' I said, and found his mouth with mine. But he pulled away and I rolled off him, steeling myself for what was to come. 'What happened to you?' Genuine concern.

I lay back on the bed with a sigh, hardly able to look at him. He sat up and took hold of my arm. 'God . . .' he whispered. 'This looks like . . . you did this, didn't you?' I nodded, still looking away. I could feel his eyes roving over me, taking in the most recent cuts, which had yet to heal. *Sal's right. I am a freak.* Shame, uncoiling and wrapping itself around me.

'Look at me, Grace.' I did – reluctantly. 'Do you want to talk about this?'

I shook my head. He nodded, leaned down, and kissed me perfectly. 'You're beautiful,' he whispered. And I believed him. He kissed me all over and ran his tongue over the scars, which didn't seem creepy or weird. It was as if he was trying to kiss them better.

He didn't have any condoms with him (clueless), but didn't mind that I had a small stash in my bedside drawer. Some boys can be funny like that. Boys are stupid, mostly.

And so we had sex. It was OK, not mind-blowing. It was sweet and tender, and (dare I say it?) something close to loving. A new experience for me. Afterwards, we lay face-to-face, our legs intertwined. I nuzzled against his neck, and he stroked my back.

'Now can we talk?' Nat said after a while.

'Mmm?'

'About this?' His roaming fingers had found some scars.

I tried to distract him, but he was having none of it.

'Grace, talk to me.'

I sighed. 'There's nothing to talk about. It's just something I do sometimes. It's embarrassing and stupid and I bet you think I'm a freak and . . .' He silenced me with a kiss.

'I don't think you're a freak. I want to understand.'

I lay back and stared at the ceiling. 'I don't really understand it myself. All I know is that it makes me feel better when things are bad.'

Nat pushed himself up onto one elbow so that his face was above me. He rested his left hand on my stomach. It felt warm and comforting.

'Do you think you can stop . . . hurting yourself like this?' I said nothing. 'Do you want to stop?'

'I don't know. I've never tried.'

'Would you try for me? Go on . . . let's make a deal. You stop hurting yourself and I'll . . . er . . . I'll give you plenty of red hot lovin' whenever you so desire.' He wiggled his eyebrows at me and I burst out laughing. His hand moved lower and lower and my breath caught in my throat. Maybe this deal could work after all.

Nat stayed with me that night. And the rest of the weekend. There was a lot of talking and laughing and just being together. The sex got better, which was a relief. The whole weekend was practically perfect. We didn't talk about the cutting. I began to think that maybe I could forget about what Sal had said, after all.

Nat dropped a bit of an interesting bombshell on Sunday night. We were lying in bed, talking about our families. I think we'd both realized that we didn't actually know that much about each other. I'd told Nat a bit about Dad, and how things were with Mum, and he'd been unbelievably great about it. And then he started telling me about his brother.

'He's a good kid. I love him to bits, but he's so

highly strung. Way too sensitive for his own good. It all gets too much for him sometimes, you know?' I nodded.

'Dev gets so depressed. I worry about him a lot – that he might do something stupid one day.'

'Dev?' I said.

'Yeah, Devon. He got the short straw when our parents were deciding on names. I mean, Nathaniel's not so great, but it beats Devon any day of the week.' Nat noticed me looking at him strangely. 'What?'

'Devon's your *brother*?'

'You don't *know* him, do you? Seriously?'

'He's in my year at school.'

'Shit, I should have thought. I forget we're not the same age. Dev seems so bloody young, and you . . . well . . .' He eyed me up approvingly.

'How come you didn't go to my school then? I'm sure I would have remembered someone like you.'

'Our parents split up about nine years ago. My dad scarpered with one of Mum's friends – what a gent, eh? Mum had a complete breakdown. Couldn't cope with me and Dev. And I didn't help matters much. I played up quite a bit – just to get attention, really. Not something I'm particularly proud of. Anyway, lucky old me got sent to boarding school. Dev would have gone too, but Mum didn't think he could cope. I was well pissed off at being sent away while "Mummy's little prince" got to stay at home. But looking back on it now, getting away from here was the best thing that ever happened to me. No offence.'

'God,' I said. It was a lot to take in. I couldn't believe I was going out with Devon's brother. *Mental*. How could I not have known about him before? If I had, I'd have been a lot more friendly to Devon, that's for sure.

'Listen, Grace. I never would have said anything about Devon if I thought there was even a remote chance that you knew him. Clearly I'm a complete retard. Promise you won't say anything about what I told you – about Dev.'

'Of course I won't say anything. I don't really know Devon that well, anyway. He's more a friend of a friend. Don't worry your pretty little head about it.' I kissed Nat on the forehead and we lay in silence for a while. I was wondering whether Sal had ever met Nat. I knew she'd been to Devon's house a couple of times, but surely she'd have told me about him if she had? I was dying to ask if Nat had met any of Devon's friends, but I didn't feel ready to get into the whole Sal thing yet.

Over the next few days, I found myself thinking about Devon quite a bit – about his depression. It just showed that you can never tell what's *really* going on with people. Beneath the shiny surface they present to the world.

I wondered if Devon ever cut. *Probably not. More of a girl thing, I guess.* It's in all the magazines. I find it sort of shameful to be part of such an *obvious* teenage statistic. I like to be a bit more original if I can.

Those first few weeks with Nat were pretty great. For the first time in my life I was perhaps eighty per cent happy. And the missing twenty per cent was all Sal. Probably more than that, if I'm honest. I thought about her a lot, and nearly picked up the phone a hundred times. But as distractions go, Nat was more than adequate.

We had been going out for about a month when I decided to pay Sophie a visit. I'm not entirely sure why. Anyway, I popped into the shop on the off-chance and, sure enough, there she was behind the counter. The shop was busy. A yummy mummy with a screaming baby in a bizarre sling-type thing. Two old ladies gossiping and trading stories of ailments. A shifty-looking boy wearing skinny grey jeans and a black T-shirt emblazoned with the name of some band I'd never heard of. He was lurking in the condom section. *Bless.*

I waited until the old dears were the only ones left in the shop. They were oblivious to everything, not to mention slightly deaf. At least I assumed that's why they were talking so very loudly about haemorrhoids. *Grim.*

I headed up to the counter, and Sophie and I exchanged cautious hellos.

'How are you, Grace? Is everything . . . ?'

'Fine, thanks. Oh, yeah . . . it was a false alarm, by the way.'

'You must be relieved.'

'Uh, yeah, just a little bit.' I forced a laugh, but Sophie didn't laugh with me.

'So listen, Soph . . .' I began, trying not to be put off by the guarded look on her face. 'I've been thinking . . . I don't suppose you'd like to go out for a drink one night, would you? Celebrate my lucky escape from the nightmare of nappies and sleepless nights?' I was kind of nervous, much to my surprise.

'Er . . . I don't know. Maybe.'

'Steady! I've heard that too much enthusiasm can seriously damage your health.'

'Well, it's just a bit weird, that's all. We haven't spoken in God knows how long and suddenly you want to go for a drink with me.' Sophie was picking at the edge of the counter with her thumbnail.

'Well, when you put it that way, I suppose it *is* a bit weird. Still, I just thought it might be a laugh . . . but if you don't want to, that's cool.'

'What about your partner-in-crime?' I hated when people called Sal that. I'm not sure why it bothered me so much. Looking back, it was actually sort of cool. Like Batman and Robin or something. Except they're partners-against-crime. And Robin is *so* gay.

'I do have other friends, you know. Sal and I aren't joined at the hip, believe it or not.' Much to my surprise, Sophie laughed. Sophie Underwood was laughing at ME!

'Yeah, whatever. You're like Tweedledum and Tweedledee. Or maybe the Chuckle Brothers.' She definitely had a glint in her eye now. This was something I hadn't seen before.

'Hey!'

'Aw, come on, Grace. You know it's true!' She paused and then said, 'I suppose a drink would be nice. Tonight?' Nat was working that evening, so that was good. Not that I'm one of those pathetic girls who has to spend every minute of every day with their boyfriend. Sophie and I arranged to meet in Bar Code, a quietly cool bar in town – with a seriously crap name.

As soon as I got home, I headed to the kitchen and grabbed the penguin jar off the top shelf. I'm tall enough to reach it without standing on a chair now. Just like always, the jar had a few tenners in it. I took three – enough for a semi-decent night out.

I can't even remember when I first started taking money from that jar. Mum MUST have known, but she never mentioned it. Like some sort of unspoken agreement: I wouldn't call her on being a terrible mother, and she wouldn't call me on being a sneaky little thief. I always looked on it as a sort of payment for babysitting myself, and maybe she did too. That's why she kept topping it up every few weeks. I've never really thought about it before, but it was kind of decent of her. She could have cut me off completely, but she didn't.

Mum cooked an early tea, which I could barely stomach. I was weirdly nervous. We had a half-proper conversation for the first time in ages. She even asked me what I was up to that evening (like she cared). I twirled some spaghetti round my fork, watching the orange globules of fat from the sauce swirl round the plate.

'I'm going for a drink with Sophie.' I looked up in time to see her perfectly plucked eyebrows rise in surprise.

'Sophie?'

'Yeah,' I muttered like the moody little cow I am.

'God, I haven't seen her in . . . well, it's been a long time. I didn't know you two were still friends.'

'We're not. I mean, I just ran into her and we decided to catch up tonight.' I shrugged, like it was no big deal. Which it wasn't.

'Is Sal going too?'

'No, why would she be?'

'No reason. I just haven't seen her around in a while.' Mum was looking down at her plate now too. I got the feeling she'd been waiting to ask about this for some time.

'So?'

'Have you two had a falling-out?' I swear to God, the way she said it made me want to hit her. *A falling-out?!* Like I'd pulled Sal's pigtails, or she wouldn't share her toys with me.

I gave her my most withering look, which, I have to say, is pretty withering. 'No, we haven't had a "falling-out", but thanks for asking.'

Mum pretended to ignore my tetchiness. 'It's just, well, you know I'm here, if you want to talk about anything. You do know that, don't you, sweetie?' I could have choked on my garlic bread! First of all, saying that I could *talk* to her? And second of all, calling me *sweetie*? Had she been watching some kind of How To Be A Parent programme on TV?

I looked at her for a few moments. Her hair highlighted to within an inch of its life. Her face strangely lacking in wrinkles or emotion or love or anything. I was supposed to believe that she suddenly cared? *Yeah, right. Nice try.*

'Thanks, *Mother*,' I said as sarcastically as was humanly possible. 'I'll let you know when I feel the need to share.' I stood up, chucked my napkin on top of the congealing spaghetti and left the table without another word. When I turned to head up the stairs, I saw her framed by the kitchen doorway, coolly sipping her glass of water and staring into space.

The bus dropped me off just over the road from Bar Code. There was a bouncer outside, but it was still early so there was no queue. Inside, the bar was all retro chic – shabby leather sofas and weird curvy chairs. I looked for Sophie, not an easy task given all the nooks and crannies. It's like when you're at school, scanning the canteen for your friends – and trying to look as if that's the *last* thing you're trying to do. I embarked on a quick circuit of the bar, as nonchalantly as possible, and eventually spotted Sophie secreted in a booth in one corner. She was tapping away on her phone, playing with her hair at the same time. No drink on the table in front of her.

'Hi, sorry I'm late,' I said, knowing full well that I was exactly on time. Sophie was even worse (or better, depending on how you feel about these things) than I was when it came to punctuality.

Sophie put down her phone and said hi. I asked if she wanted a drink, and she nodded. 'Vodka and coke . . . a double if that's OK?' I managed to hide my surprise. *Little Sophie Underwood . . . drinking doubles? My, my.*

When I came back with the drinks I slid into the booth opposite Sophie. A quick 'Cheers', a swig of vodka, and my first chance to really check her out. She wasn't wearing her glasses, and was wearing (*shock, horror!*) make-up. Actual, proper make-up. I hadn't even bothered with any (well, the bare minimum, but that hardly counts). I had to admit, Sophie looked pretty good. I even recognized the top she was wearing. A rather cool little red number from Top Shop that showed off her breasts to full advantage. I suddenly felt self-conscious in my somewhat scraggy black-top-and-jeans combo. It was unsettling. I needed to re-establish the equilibrium, pronto. After a bit of small talk about exams and whatever, I started telling her all about Nat. Now, I really dislike girls who brag about their boyfriends, as if they deserve a bloody medal for having bagged a half-decent one. But I couldn't help myself.

Sophie listened politely while I talked, nodding in all the right places, saying all the right things. By the time I'd run out of steam, we'd both finished our drinks. Sophie went to the bar this time – probably grateful for a breather from me. When she came back, I asked her the killer question. *I am a bad person.*

'Not . . . not at the moment.' She opened her mouth as if she had something else to say, and then promptly snapped it shut again. I raised a quizzical eyebrow. She swirled her drink round and round, clinking the ice.

'Well, there is someone I sort of . . . well . . . kind of like.' Sophie exhaled loudly, as if she'd just made some kind of major confession, like she'd been shagging the whole rugby team or something. *This is more like it.* I felt more comfortable with Awkward Sophie

I pressed her to try to find out who the mystery boy was, but she kept shtum. Maybe it was something to do with the fact that I was being unbelievably patronizing . . . As if I was her big sister, teasing her because she was finally getting interested in boys. I apologized and changed the subject.

We talked about school for a bit, but there really wasn't much to say. We might as well have gone to different schools entirely for all the common ground we shared. But after a while and a couple more drinks, the conversation flowed a lot more smoothly. Sophie had a surprisingly dry sense of humour. She hadn't had that when we'd been friends, had she? She must have grown it or bought it off the Internet or something.

As the evening progressed, the inevitable reminiscing began. Like the time we'd scared ourselves shitless, climbing in the window of the old deserted house at the top of our road. I'd somehow become obsessed with the idea that a creepy bald man with bloodshot eyes and no eyelids lived there, lying in wait for the neighbourhood children. The crack addicts who were hanging out in the attic actually gave us a bigger scare than anything my overactive imagination could ever have come up with.

Sophie was handling her drink a lot better than I would have expected. I couldn't help thinking that you don't build up that kind of tolerance by sitting in your room every night, studying like a good little girl.

'I have to say, Soph, you're pretty hardcore. Most people would be on the floor by now.'

'Don't look so surprised!'

'Well, I kind of am,' I admitted, a tad sheepishly. 'I suppose I didn't think . . .'

'What? You didn't think that I was "that sort of girl"? More an "in bed by ten, cuddling a teddy bear and reading a book" sort of girl? Is that it?'

I shrugged. 'Welllllllll . . .' We both laughed.

'Oh, Grace, you really have no idea, do you?' I noticed a slight edge to her voice, but we were both still smiling. 'We haven't been friends for five years . . . Do you not think that maybe, just maybe, I might have changed a little bit in all that time?'

'Er . . . course. I was just . . .' I stammered.

'Just what?' Sophie looked amused at my discomfort.

'Nothing.'

'You know, I bet I could tell you a thing or two that would surprise you.' Her words weren't exactly slurred, but she was definitely tipsy.

'Oh yeah? Like what?'

'You think I'm going to spill out all my deepest, darkest secrets just like that? Not a chance.'

'Well, maybe if we did this again some time? I think that would be . . . cool.'

She looked at me, weighing up the truth of my words. 'Really?'

'Yeah. I've had fun. Haven't you?'

'Yeah.' She paused and then went on: 'You've fallen out with Sal, haven't you?'

'What makes you say that?'

Sophie shrugged. 'You should sort it out.' Now this was all turning a bit strange. I had half a mind to tell her to fuck off and mind her own business.

'No offence, Soph, but I'd rather not talk about it.'

'Fair enough, but don't just give up on her. It's easy to do that when things get hard.' She stood up, a little unsteady on her feet. 'Sometimes you need to dig a bit deeper and find out who someone really is instead of walking away.'

'Are we talking about you or Sal now?'

She shrugged again, and laughed. 'Who can say? I'm wasted . . . Don't listen to me! Right, I've got to run or my mum's going to kill me. You're OK to get the bus on your own?' I nodded dully. 'OK. I'll see you soon?' Another nod from me. And then she was gone. *Bizarre. And what's with the not-so-cryptic words of wisdom?*

When I got home I had a sudden drunken desire to look at old photos. So I dug out my photo album from under my bed. I'd put it together a few years ago, decorating the cover with a collage of cat pictures for some unknown reason.

The first few pages were filled with pictures of a little me. Quite cute, bad hair and a gappy smile. Then there was one of me and Sophie in the back garden, arms slung around each other, mischief in our eyes. You could just make out my dad in the background, tending to the barbecue, can of beer in one hand, tongs in the other. He loved that barbecue. Any opportunity to cook outside (and it didn't even have to be summer) and he'd be out there, blowing on the white-hot coals, explaining to me the finer points of marinating meat. I would ask question after question, just happy to listen to his voice. Not really understanding, not really even caring, just wanting to spend time with him.

I wonder if it will ever get easier – thinking about him. You'd have thought that I'd have got used to the idea of him being gone. *If only*. My two favourite words when I'm feeling sorry for myself.

If only he was still here.

If only Mum could understand.

If only I could stop hurting myself, punishing myself.

Useless words.

Anyway, looking at the photos made me feel sad and happy at the same time. I slipped a picture of Dad out from its plastic sleeve. It was a photo I had taken one Christmas. There was wrapping paper strewn everywhere. Dad was sitting in the middle of it with sparkly baubles dangling from his ears. I remember directing him where to sit and oh-so-artfully hanging the baubles. In the photo he's laughing hard and his eyes are squeezed shut. My mum's slippered foot sneaks into the bottom left-hand corner of the frame.

I kissed the photo and put it under my pillow. Then I phoned my perfect boyfriend and left a long, rambling message that didn't make a whole lot of sense (as he took great pleasure in telling me the next day).

day 18

I feel good today. Slept well, no dreams to speak of. Mum reckons she never dreams, but what would she even dream *about*? Row upon row of shoes as far as the eye can see?

Ethan was sitting on the bed when I emerged from the bathroom all ruddy and wrapped in a towel that just about covered everything a good girl would want covered. There was a chocolate croissant and a big mug of tea on the table. I tore off a bit of croissant and popped it into my mouth, licking the oozing chocolate from my finger.

'Want some?'

Ethan quickly shook his head.

I shrugged and continued to eat, saying nothing. When I'd finished, and sucked every last bit of chocolate from my fingers, I sat down next to him on the bed. The towel just about managed to hang on for dear life.

'Cat got your tongue?' I teased him.

'Good morning, Grace. You look . . . different to-day,' he said.

'Most people do without their clothes on.' He looked confused. His eyes frantically searched mine, as if he could look deep enough and see the truth of me. I held his gaze. The dark circles under his eyes looked like bruises.

'Ethan, I . . .'

He brought his finger to my lips to silence me. He tucked a few damp strands of hair behind my ear and whispered, 'Drink your tea.' And then he was gone. Just like that.

I flopped back on the bed and sighed. Confused and frustrated.

Then I did as I was told.

I lay on the bed for most of the morning, not really thinking about anything in particular. Not unhappy. Just sort of being. Before I knew it, Ethan was here again with lunch. I was strangely ravenous for some-one who had done fuck-all. When he came to take away my plate, I was licking the last drops of gravy from my knife. Mum would be appalled. Ethan seemed pleased. 'Was that good?'

'Mmm. Roast chicken is my favourite. You can't beat a proper Sunday lunch.' A memory popped into my head of Mum dishing up roast potatoes at the table. She always gave me and Dad loads, and only took a couple for herself. And every week, without fail, Dad would say, 'These are the best roast potatoes I have EVER had,' and Mum would roll her eyes and say, 'But you say that every week, Jim!' And you could tell she was secretly pleased. And you could tell that he really meant it. And you could tell they really loved each other.

Ethan was saying my name, and I knew from his tone that it wasn't the first time. And just like that, the memory was gone.

'What?' I said, annoyed. My brain wasn't exactly brimming over with happy memories like that one.

'I was asking about your family.'

'Why?'

'I'm curious.'

'Why?'

'I'd like to know why you are the way you are.'

'And you think that's the answer? My family? What about *your* family? What's made *you* the way you are?'

He looked at me with those stormy eyes and said softly, 'We're not talking about me.'

'Why not? Why do we have to talk about *me* all the time? I'm not that interesting, you know!'

'Oh, I wouldn't say that, Grace.' He sounded as if

he hadn't slept in a thousand years. And then he looked me square in the eye and said, 'Do you miss your father?'

'Every day. I miss him every day.' I swallowed, determined not to start bawling. Ethan must have realized that I wasn't really in a sharing kind of mood. He said nothing more, just cleared up my plate and left. But not before he'd given my shoulder a reassuring (fatherly?) squeeze.

It wasn't until the door closed that I realized I haven't told Ethan about Dad. How did he know? How could he possibly know?

Why am I the way I am? What a weird question. Why is anyone the way they are? Nature or nurture? A bit of both? Maybe for some people it's neither. Maybe they were supposed to turn out a certain way, but then something terrible happened. And maybe nothing was ever the same again. Maybe.

day 19

At least, I *think* it's day 19. It must be by now. I can't sleep. I can't sleep. I can't sleep. I CAN'T SLEEP. I've tried every trick I know: reciting all the kings and queens of England (but I always get a bit mixed up with the Henrys), trying to remember the names of everyone in my class at junior school (but I got stuck on the name of the boy with the permanently snot-encrusted nose). I've even stooped so low as to try counting sheep. I don't know who thought that one up – it turns out I can count pretty high.

May as well get on with this as long as I'm up. It's not as if I can pop downstairs for a glass of hot milk. Hot milk? Gross.

~

Things were good with Nat. But I was sort of waiting for something to go wrong. Something *had* to go wrong. It was surely only a matter of time. I could never fully shake the feeling that I didn't deserve him. He was too good for me. And too good *to* me. He listened to me when I talked, instead of just waiting for his turn to speak. He bought me a little green monster finger puppet, which made me laugh. He put his arms around me and I felt right.

I went round to his house for the first time one afternoon. His mum was at work and we were messing around in his bedroom. We still had most of our clothes on, and I was trying to determine just how ticklish he was (very, as it turns out). I had him pinned down on his bed, both hands above his head, gripped by one of mine. We were both giggling like maniacs, Nat begging for mercy. And the door flew open and there was Devon – clearly not expecting to see me there. He stuttered an apology, and Nat said something like, 'It's OK, Dev. Wait a minute!' But Devon legged it, his face flushing bright red. I laughed and resumed my assault on Nat. But he wasn't laughing.

'Grace, stop for a minute.'

'What? Why? It's no big deal!'

'I know. It's . . . I don't know. It feels a bit weird.' He sat up and pulled on his shirt. 'Let me go and talk to him.'

A suspicion suddenly dawned on me. 'You *have* told him about us . . . haven't you?'

Nat's silence said it all. 'Shit! Why haven't you told him? No wonder his eyes nearly popped out of his head!'

Nat had the good grace to look ashamed. 'I'm sorry. I just . . . I wasn't sure if he'd be OK with it. You know . . . cos you two know each other.'

'So *what* if we know each other?' I said, with added sulk.

'Well . . . I just didn't want him worrying about us talking about him. That's all.'

I weighed this up while straightening my top. 'So it's not cos you're embarrassed to be seen with me?' This came out a little more poutingly than I'd intended.

'As if! Just look at you!' He pulled me towards him for a deep, long kiss.

'Flattery will get you everywhere, Nathaniel. But not right now. Come on. You've got some explaining to do. Go and talk to him. I'll wait here.'

'Are we OK then?'

'Yup. Now scoot!' Nat jumped up from the bed and left the room. I lay back and stared at the ceiling. There was a crack in it. I tried to tell myself that it was OK. Nat's reason for not telling Devon was perfectly plausible. And anyway, I hadn't told my mum about us either. But that was different. You need to be in the same room as someone for more than five seconds to have a conversation. And I'd made sure that hadn't happened since her little attempted heart-to-heart the night I'd met up with Soph.

As I lay on Nat's bed, surrounded by Nat's things, wrapped up in Nat's world, I couldn't help but think that this might be it – the first tiny little crack I'd been waiting for. A crack that would widen into a great big gaping fissure, which I would tumble into – never to be seen again.

Nat came back after a few minutes and sat on the side of the bed.

'Well?'

'He's gone out. He's pretty pissed off and I can't really blame him.' Nat sighed and stared at the floor.

'Hey, come on now. You haven't done anything wrong. So you didn't tell your little brother about your new girlfriend? It's hardly the crime of the century.' I reached out and stroked the back of his neck, where his hair was short and fuzzy. He twisted his head away.

'Don't, Grace.'

'Don't what? Come on . . . Devon's gone out. Let's just . . .' My hand crept up his thigh as I spoke.

'Stop it!' Nat leaped up from the bed and paced away. I was too surprised to say anything for a minute or two. He stood against the wall, his fist at his forehead.

'Okaaaay, I'm just gonna go.' I hastily stood and started to gather my stuff together, telling myself that I wasn't going to cry I wasn't going to cry I wasn't going to cry. I was halfway to the door before Nat turned to face me.

'Grace, I'm sorry. I'm so, so sorry.' He took a step towards me, put his hands over his face and exhaled loudly. When his hands slid down, he looked at me sadly. 'I'm sorry for being such a twat. It's just that things with Devon are kind of . . . complicated. They always have been. I just need to speak to him properly, and I'm sure it will all be fine.' Nat came closer, and reached out for my hand with his. His fingers wrapped around mine and squeezed them gently. I looked up into his eyes and searched for the truth in his words. I wasn't sure if it was there or not, but he looked so sad and so hopeful that it didn't seem to matter. I hugged him.

'Talk to Devon. Call me whenever. It's fine.' I was very impressed with myself for being such a big person about it. I felt terribly mature.

'You sure?'

'Yup.' Breezy as breezy can be. I kissed Nat quickly on the lips, said a cheery goodbye and left his room without looking back.

I was at the bottom of the stairs when Nat called to me, 'Grace!' I looked up and saw his face peering over the banisters.

'Thanks for being so amazing. I mean it. You're really . . . I really care about you. I just wanted you to know that.' I wanted to run back up the stairs and show him just *how* amazing I could be, but I was ever so taken with the 'new mature me' (even if she was only temporary), so I rewarded Nat with a winning smile and a quiet 'I know'. And then I was gone, out the front door and down the street. Trying my hardest to remember Nat's parting words, rather than the weirdness that had gone before.

Managed to get back to sleep for a while after all. It must be early though. Ethan hasn't been in with my breakfast yet. I'm starving. I hardly ever eat breakfast at home, much to Mum's annoyance. When I was fifteen I tried starting the day with a cup of black coffee. I must have been going through a 'disaffected youth' phase. I hated the taste; it was all I could do not to grimace each time I took a sip. It was worth it though, cos it annoyed Mum so much. She was all 'Breakfast is the most important meal of the day' and 'A girl your age shouldn't be drinking that'. Which was clearly the wrong way to go about getting me to do what she wanted. Mothers can be so dense. Just act like you approve of what we're doing. We'll soon do the exact opposite, just to spite you.

Anyway, I'm just going to have to ignore my gurgling stomach and try not to think about crispy bacon on white bread, splattered with ketchup and dripping with fat. Or a boiled egg and soldiers . . .

*

The day after the Devon Debacle, something surprising happened.

Sal texted me: 'Need to talk to you. Please?'

I had no idea what to make of it. The message filled me with hope and dread and everything in between. I had half a mind to let Sal sweat for a couple of days, but since I was being so very mature I texted her straight back, with a simple 'OK'. I certainly wasn't going to give anything away if she wasn't. I only had to wait a couple of seconds for a reply: 'Thanks. At the swings? Nine?' God knows why she wanted to go back there again.

It had been almost two months since our fight.

It was hard to believe that I hadn't even laid eyes on her since that ridiculous night. I'd always kept an eye out for her when I was out and about, especially when I was with Nat. Half hoping that she would see how happy I could be without her. And half hoping that just being face to face with her again would magically fix what was broken.

It was only just starting to get dark by the time I went to meet Sal. A few people lingered in the park, playing Frisbee, drinking beer and pretending they weren't getting cold. A couple of fourteen-year-olds were on the swings, ramming their tongues down each other's throats. *Nice.* I sat on a bench a little way away, looking at my watch every couple of minutes. 9.09 and still no sign of Sal.

And then there was a tap on my shoulder and a quiet 'Hey'. Sal rounded the bench and sat down next to me. I returned her 'Hey' and studied her in the fading light. She looked different. She'd had her hair cut, and it really suited her. But she looked so thin. She wasn't wearing any make-up and the dark circles under her eyes stood out a mile. I was shocked at the difference a couple of months could make. I was pretty sure I just looked like the same old Grace to her – apart from a mammoth spot that was threatening to erupt on my chin any moment.

I was the first to speak. 'So . . . how have you been?' I couldn't help but laugh nervously at the absurdity of the question. Sal even cracked a smile. 'I mean, well, I suppose I don't really know what to say.' I scuffed my trainers on the gravel under the bench, waiting for Sal to say something.

'Grace, I'm so, so sorry.' Well, that was a start at least. I waited for her to go on. 'This has all been a complete nightmare. I can't tell you how many times I've wanted to pick up the phone and ring you . . .' She trailed off and I could tell that she was fighting back the tears – unsuccessfully, as it turned out. 'I've missed you.'

And she looked at me with those Bambi eyes brimming with tears and quietly said, 'Do you think we can ever . . . ?' before trailing off again. She stared at the ground, not bothering to wipe the tears from her face. I just wanted to hug her and tell her everything would be OK. But I couldn't bring myself to do it.

'I don't know.'

'Grace, you *have* to believe me. I was an idiot. I don't have any excuses, but I was scared and angry and I didn't know what to do.'

'So you took it out on me?' It had to be said.

Sal nodded. 'I just wanted someone to blame, and somehow that ended up being you. I don't know why.

You were the one person who was there for me and I messed it up completely.'

'Why now?' I found it hard to look at her.

'What do you mean?'

'It's been two months. Why are you coming to me now?'

'I just . . . I thought you wouldn't talk to me before. Especially after what I said. About the cutting.' As if I needed reminding. 'Grace, I didn't mean it. You know I don't think that. I just lashed out with the first thing I could think of.' She reached out for my hand. I didn't pull away. 'It was a terrible thing to say and I know how it must have made you feel.'

'I don't think you do. When the person you love most in the world says something like that . . .'

'But it's not true!' Sal squeezed my hand.

I shrugged. 'Maybe it is.'

'Don't be stupid, Grace. If you did it for attention, do you not think that maybe you wouldn't hide it quite so well?'

Another shrug from me. I wasn't going to make this easy for her. 'And the boy stuff? You as good as called me a slag.'

'I didn't mean it. Just because we feel differently about the whole sex thing doesn't mean we can't be friends.' She paused. 'You know, you said some pretty harsh things too.'

I pulled my hand away from hers. 'Well, I was feeling pretty fucking defensive, wasn't I?! It's not every day I get blamed for someone getting pregnant, especially since I seem to be lacking the right equipment for the job!'

We sat in silence for a while. Sal had stopped crying and was picking at a hole in her jeans.

'I had the abortion.' Her voice was flat.

'Was it awful?'

'I don't know. It was weird. It was a relief, I suppose. I thought it would all be OK afterwards, and maybe it would have been if I hadn't pushed you away.'

'Did you go by yourself?'

Sal nodded, and I felt some of the bad feeling between us slip away into the night.

'I wish you'd have let me be there.'

'So do I.'

We looked at each other and I thought that maybe (just maybe) it was going to be all right for us. Maybe things could get back to normal. I wasn't going to forget the things she'd said. And she probably wasn't going to forget what I'd said – or the fact that I'd slapped her good and proper. But maybe there was a chance to move beyond all that.

'I've missed you loads as well, you know.' We smiled shy little smiles at each other. 'Come here, you.' I grabbed her in a hug. Now it was time for me to start blubbing, and Sal blubbed right along with me.

Eventually, I pulled away and looked at her. Tear-shiny, puffy face. 'Wow. I hope I don't look as bad as you!'

Sal laughed. 'Well, you do. Unless you think blotchy is a particularly good look . . . ?'

'I've always been quite partial to it myself! Listen, do you want to come back to mine. We can have a proper catch-up. It's . . . It's been too long.'

Back at home, I grabbed a bag of crisps and some salsa and we headed up to my room. Within a few minutes we were back in our all-too familiar positions – me propped up against the headboard with some pillows, Sal sitting opposite me cross-legged, food in the middle.

'So . . . have you seen your favourite would-be stalker recently?'

Sal looked up a little too quickly. 'I take it you mean Devon? Nah, haven't seen him since . . . Haven't seen him for ages.'

I was sceptical. 'Really? What kind of rubbish stalker is he if he can't even follow you around properly? He'll have to give his night-vision goggles back at stalker school.' Sal ignored my pathetic attempt at humour, and I felt a twinge of guilt about taking the piss out of Devon.

Sal munched on a crisp before casually asking me if *I'd* seen him. I thought for a split second that maybe Devon had managed to do a bit more than stalk Sal after all. And then my thoughts speedily bounced back to little old me, as per usual. I'd kind of wanted to keep the stuff about me and Nat to myself until I was feeling one hundred per cent about Sal. But I was up to a good seventy-five, and the comforting familiarity of the circumstances was hard to ignore.

I traced a finger over the pattern of the duvet cover, suddenly all coy. Not like me at all. But somehow this was different.

I cleared my throat and avoided eye contact. 'Er . . . I have seen him actually. I'm sort of . . . well, I'm seeing his brother.' I looked up shyly to see Sal's reaction. Not the one of complete gleeful surprise I was hoping for. More like a head-nodding 'Huh, interesting' sort of look. *Disappointing.*

'Really?' That was the best she could do. I tried not to show that I cared.

'Yeah. You didn't tell me Devon had such a fit brother! Wanted to keep him all to yourself, did you?'

'Don't be ridiculous. I . . .'

'Sal, I was *joking!*' Neither of us was laughing.

Then Sal said, 'I'm really happy for you. Tell me EVERYTHING.' I looked at her, trying to gauge her actual interest level, but it was hard to fault her. Her eyes were bright and her grin was firmly back in place.

'Well,' I started, with fake reluctance, 'he's just . . . great. I've only been seeing him a few weeks, but it feels, I don't know, different. There's something about him. I think I could fall in love with him.' I paused. 'In fact, I think I already have.' I could not believe I'd just said that. But the words sounded right.

Sal looked at me disbelievingly. 'You're kidding, right?'

'Er . . . no. Why is it so hard to believe?'

'It's not. I suppose it just doesn't sound like you. Don't get me wrong, I think it's great. I just thought you didn't buy into all that love stuff.'

I shrugged. 'Maybe I've changed. He really is different, you know. Those other boys were, well, they were losers, weren't they? Nat makes me feel like I'm worth something. I didn't think I'd meet someone like that. Part of me thinks that he's going to realize what I'm really like and run a mile.'

'You deserve this, Grace – someone to treat you properly.'

'Whether I deserve him or not, I'm hanging on to him for dear life!' We both laughed. 'I can't wait for you to meet him. You're gonna love him – though not too much, I hope! The three of us should go out one night. It'll be great. God, I hope you do like him. I'm sure you will. And he'll definitely like you. You've got loads in common. Jesus, I'm wittering, aren't I? Just tell me to shut up.'

Sal smiled, happy to indulge me. 'You don't have to shut up! So what is it that makes this one so special?'

'I suppose it would be too lame to say "EVERY-THING"?'

'Yes, that is *definitely* too lame!'

I sat back and thought a little. 'He makes me feel giddy. He's incredibly hot, but I don't just want to have sex with him – I want to be his friend. I want to talk to him and find out what he thinks about things. And it feels like he sees something different in me . . . Maybe I'm not explaining it very well. He makes me feel good about myself. And I feel safe when I'm with him.' I looked up at Sal, certain she was going to chuck a pillow at my head for being so cheesy, but she had a faraway, wistful look in her eyes. I suddenly realized that maybe this was the last thing she wanted to be talking about right now.

'Sorry, Sal. I'm going to shut up now. Enough Nat chat! Let's talk about something else.'

Sal refocused her eyes on mine and smiled. 'I don't have much to say, I'm afraid.'

I saw the opportunity to say something I felt needed to be said. 'I know you probably don't want to talk about this, but I just want you to know something. If you do want to tell me what happened and who you slept with, I'm here to listen. I won't judge you, or think any less of you, no matter what you say. You're my best friend and I love you. You can tell me anything.'

There was a bit of an awkward silence before Sal said, 'Thank you. That means a lot. I just need you to understand that I don't want to talk about it.'

'Fair enough.' I shrugged, hiding my frustration fairly well. I'd sort of hoped that Sal would open up after I'd bared my soul about Nat. Except it wasn't really the same thing, was it?

I wish I knew what time it is. I'm exhausted. Today has been dullsville. Ethan eventually appeared with my breakfast. He asked if I was hungry and seemed to be genuinely sorry when I said that I was starving (slight exaggeration, but my stomach *was* making some rather fetching gurgling noises).

After my breakfast had settled, I ramped up the exercise a bit. Two hundred sit-ups, some random stretches and running for (I guess) thirty minutes. It felt good. No wonder I'm so knackered though.

There's not much more to tell about the Great Sal and Grace Reunion. After a couple more hours of inane chatter, and A LOT more of me mooning about Nat (despite my best intentions not to), Sal and I fell asleep. I woke up the next morning sprawled diagonally across the bed, still in my clothes. Sal was curled up at the bottom of the bed, her hair covering her face.

I sat up and reached for the glass of water I always keep by my bed, but my coordination was clearly a bit off and I ended up side-swiping the glass onto the floor. I swore loudly, and Sal woke up. She stretched, groaned a little and turned to give me a sleepy smile. In that moment, I'd have bet money that we were thinking the same thing. Something along the lines of: 'Maybe things can get back to normal after all.'

Or perhaps that was just me.

day 20

Funny dream last night. I was in the bathroom, brushing my teeth. I bent down to rinse out my mouth, and when I straightened up and looked in the mirror, I saw Ethan instead of me. I looked down at myself, to confirm that I was in fact me. And I was. But when I looked at my reflection again, there he was, looking back at me in puzzlement. I reached out to touch the mirror, and the Ethan-in-the-mirror did the same. I touched my finger to my lip, and he traced his finger down his silvery scar. I wasn't entirely freaked out. Some part of my mind just accepted it, and I carried on washing my face, brushing my hair, looking in the mirror pretty much the whole time. Mirror Ethan was wearing jeans and a green shirt that I felt I'd seen him in before. I was sorely tempted to take off my pyjamas, just to see if Mirror Ethan would do the same. But it didn't seem the right thing to do.

I turned to leave the bathroom, and then quickly

spun back round to face the mirror. I didn't know what I was expecting to see, but it was still Ethan, looking like I felt – a little bit stupid and shifty. When I came back into the bedroom, Ethan was asleep in the bed, wearing my pyjamas. I leaned over him and listened to him breathe. His breathing was laboured. Suddenly he opened his eyes, scaring the life out of me. He whispered, 'Wake up, sleepyhead,' and reached for my hand.

And then I woke up. I felt a bit strange. Almost peaceful. Serene and accepting. The dream only came back to me later, after Ethan had been here. Before then, I'd just felt like I'd had a really good night's sleep and I was somehow ready to tackle the day ahead, whatever it might bring. Even though I knew full well it would only bring three square meals, an enigmatic kidnapper and not a whole lot else.

When Ethan came in after lunch I was sitting at the table staring into space, trailing my fork back and forth across the plate. He perched on the edge of the bed, which was starting to become a regular occurrence. He said nothing, merely tucked his hands under his thighs as if to keep them warm, and then looked at me expectantly. I *did* have something on my mind.

'How do you know what foods I like?'

Ethan said nothing.

'Seriously, how come everything you've cooked for me or brought me is something I like?'

He shrugged.

'I mean, I don't want you to think I'm not grateful or anything, cos I am. I just think it's kind of weird. You'd think that you'd have got it wrong once or twice. But there hasn't been any fish, or broccoli, or nuts, or Brussels sprouts for that matter . . .'

'Grace, *no one* likes Brussels sprouts.'

'Huh. Good point, but still, you know what I mean.'

'What do you want me to say? That I've been secretly spying on you for months, carefully noting down all your food preferences? Would that make you feel better?' He was mocking me and I didn't like it.

'No, I just want you to tell me the truth. And it would be nice if you tried not to be too sarcastic while you're doing it.'

'We like the same things, Grace. Haven't you noticed?'

'Er . . . no. I haven't.' I sighed. 'Whatever. It doesn't matter anyway, does it? None of it matters.'

'Don't be like that. It all matters. *All* of it. When are you going to see that?'

Now I was getting really quite annoyed. Yes, enigmatic can be sexy, but it can also just be plain irritating.

'Do you mind leaving? I've got stuff I want to do.'

'If you say so, Grace.' He didn't seem to mind my rudeness. Just gathered up my dishes and left without another word.

After Ethan left, I thought about our conversation. There's something I've noticed about the way he talks. He says my name A LOT. I think it's a little strange. I mean, it's normal to say someone's name a bit, but saying it over and over again is kind of creepy. I wonder why he does it, or if he even realizes he's doing it. I have this vague idea that maybe he's trying to remind me who I am. In case I forget in this weird room of whiteness.

Dad used to say my name a lot too. I think he liked the way it sounded. Sometimes he called me Graciebear. It made me cringe, but I let him get away with it, cos it was just Dad being Dad. I think he stopped calling me that about the same time I went to secondary school. I didn't notice or anything. I suppose he must have just phased it out – a small concession to the fact that his little girl was growing up. I'd give anything to hear him say it one more time. Or to hear him say anything. Or just to see him, sitting in his shabby old leather chair, frowning at the crossword.

I'd give anything.

day 21

Yesterday was pretty much a write-off once I got all maudlin. I cried and cried and cried. Ethan came in at one point. At least I think he did. It was all pretty blurry and hazy, but I think he sat with his hand resting on my shoulder while I lay sobbing on the bed. Or was that a dream? I can't remember. Hmm. Losing touch with reality = not good.

I saw Nat a couple of days after me and Sal made up. I'd never even mentioned Sal to him before, which was a little bit weird, granted. But it was too messy to explain, and it didn't exactly show me in the best light. And I definitely wanted him to see me in the best light (all soft focus and angelic . . . but not *too* angelic).

I hadn't called or texted him after the thing with

Devon. The ball was well and truly in his court this time. The waiting was agony. I'm not exactly the most patient person in the world. I prefer to go out and get things, rather than waiting for them to come to me. Plus, I'm never completely convinced that things are going to come to me anyway, so I like to make sure. But this time I was determined to wait. It was such a relief when he texted. I guessed that he and Devon must have sorted things out.

We agreed to meet in a pub in town after his shift. The pub was quiet when I arrived. Nat was sitting in the far corner, a pint in front of him, staring intently at the phone in his hand. His right leg was jiggling up and down under the table, and he was wearing the trainers he'd worn the night we met. They'd lost their shiny white newness. He looked good.

I walked over and touched his shoulder. He jumped a little, before jamming the phone in his pocket and standing to kiss me. His mouth tasted beery, but in a nice way. It had only been a few days, but I had missed kissing him. He got me a drink from the bar without me asking.

I took a sip. 'Is this a double? Are you trying to get me drunk, mister?'

He wiggled his eyebrows at me. 'Why? Would that be a problem?'

'As long as you make sure to take advantage of me later, I'm fine with it.' I leaned across the table and kissed him again. 'So, what was so fascinating on your phone? It had better not be naked pictures of some other girl. Or naked pictures of some boy, for that matter.' I mock-grimaced at the thought.

'Maybe it was naked pictures of you.'

'You don't have any! And don't try and say you took one while I was asleep, cos I know you'd do nothing of the sort. You're too much of a gentleman.'

'That's what you think . . . Nah, it was just a text. Nothing important.'

I was curious about the mystery text, but I didn't want to come over all psychojealousgirlfriendy, so I let it go. Nat told me what he'd been up to the last couple of days, while I listened, intertwining my fingers with his and generally gazing at him adoringly. Urgh. I HATE girls like that.

After a couple more drinks and a rather heated debate about the merits of various universities compared to others, I told him about Sal. I was so excited about them meeting each other.

'Oh yeah, Devon mentioned some girl you were mates with.' Nat didn't seem all that interested, which kind of hurt a little bit. But I suppose it was fair enough. He wasn't to know, was he?

'She's not "some girl", she's my best friend. We sort of fell out for a bit. It was just before I met you actually. Anyway, it was stupid, and everything's totally cool now.'

'Why didn't you mention her before?' Nat was looking at his pint glass, slowly turning it in his hand.

'I dunno. Didn't see the point, I suppose. I didn't think Sal and I would ever be friends again and . . . I felt a bit stupid and sad about it all. And I didn't want it to put a downer on how things were going with us.'

'You could have talked to me about it, you know.'

'I'm sorry. I should have, but let's just forget about it. Sal's dying to meet you, so we'll have to sort something out soon. You're going to love her!'

'Sounds cool. I'm going to get more drinks in.'

While Nat was at the bar, I went through the conversation in my mind. So, he was a bit annoyed with me for not telling him. And he didn't exactly seem wild about the prospect of meeting Sal. But he was a boy, and boys just don't get excited about the same things we do. I was sure he'd be fine about it soon.

A bit later, Nat asked me why I'd fallen out with Sal. Maybe he *was* interested after all. I had no intention of telling him the truth – Sal wouldn't have thanked me for that. I didn't exactly feel happy about lying to him, but sometimes honesty isn't the best policy.

'It was stupid really. Just some ridiculous argument that snowballed out of control. And we were both too stubborn to apologize.'

Nat looked sceptical. 'So it wasn't even serious?'

'Nah, not really. It seemed that way at the time, but it's all in the past now.'

'Man, girls are weird.'

I smiled. 'Hey! Watch what you're saying!' I punched him gently on the shoulder. 'Haven't you ever fallen out with any of your mates?'

'Yeah, I suppose. Sorry.' He looked thoughtful.

'Hey, it's all right.'

'Yeah, sorry. I was just thinking . . .'

'What?'

He shook his head slightly and said, 'Nah, it doesn't matter.' He picked up his pint and took a few gulps, then reached across the table and squeezed my hand. He gave me *that* look. 'Listen, let's get out of here. There's no one home at mine.'

'Thank God for that, cos my mum's actually in for once. And although I'm sure she'd LOVE to meet you, I don't think tonight is the night . . . considering what I've got in mind for you.' I leaned across the table and brushed my lips against Nat's ear, whispering the filthiest thing I could think of. It had the desired effect. I barely had time to grab my bag before he dragged me out of the pub.

Nat flagged down a taxi and we clambered into the back seat. We couldn't keep our hands off each other. Managed to refrain from taking things too far, but it took more than a little bit of willpower. Plus, I wasn't keen on the looks I was getting from the taxi driver in the rear-view mirror. The thought that he was getting a free show was kind of distracting. I pulled away from Nat and looked into his eyes. *Beautiful*. And he wanted me. He really, really wanted me. In that moment, I felt so lucky. And, in a weird way, sort of powerful. He was lost in his lust. It felt like I could have got him to do anything I wanted. Luckily for Nat, all I wanted him to do was me.

The sex was unbelievable. Nat was different – he was definitely the one in control this time. Made a nice change. Afterwards I lay beside him, my body pressed against his side, my left leg comfortably nestled between his legs.

I was happy.

&

This is getting harder. I want to put down the pen and tear up all this paper into tiny little pieces, throw them in the air and let them fall like snow. I could turn this room into one of those tacky snow globe things. A snow globe for a giant. Let the bath run and fill the room to the ceiling with water. I would drown, but that might be nice.

day 22

Ethan's here. Every time I look up, he's there, staring into space. He came in to take away my lunch stuff and then returned a couple of minutes later, just as I sat down to write. He seemed a little jumpy. I looked up at him expectantly. 'Hi, again.'

'Hello, Grace.'

I waited for him to say something, but he seemed reluctant to do so. I sat with pen poised, and he stood with his back against the door.

'Do you need anything?' I wanted him to say something – it was getting a little bit weird.

'No. I . . . would you mind if I stayed for a while? I won't disturb you.'

I hesitated, and Ethan continued, 'I just want to be here.'

Now this *was* interesting. I didn't really know what to say, so I just nodded dumbly. He said a barely audible 'Thank you' and settled himself on the floor in the corner nearest the door.

And so here we are, sitting in a sort of companionable silence. Ethan has his back to the wall, with his legs drawn up in front of him and his arms wrapped around them. His chin is resting on his knees. He looks like a little boy – a lost little boy. His feet are bare, his toes just peeking out from the bottom of his frayed jeans. Every so often he absentmindedly rubs his right wrist with his left hand, before going back to hugging his knees to his chest.

I wonder if I should say something, or go to him.

I won't.

I can't.

꙳

Sal and I got our exam results. Even with all that craziness going on, Sal had managed to blitz them. I did too. Neither of us was surprised – maybe just a tiny bit relieved, but that was all.

I saw Sophie in the school hall. She was talking to Devon. I had no idea that those two knew each other, but it was hardly surprising. Not to be mean or anything, but they were both sort of geeks. And I mean that in the nicest possible way. I tried to catch Sophie's eye, but she was too busy leaning close to Devon, looking at the piece of paper in his hand. Those two certainly had nothing to worry about when it came to exams.

Tanya was holding court in a corner with her usual cronies. She saw me and waved me over. 'Grace! You and Sal fancy coming to mine tonight? My folks are in Barbados and the house is practically begging me to have a party in it!' A couple of years ago I'd have jumped at the offer. But not any more. It's weird how things change.

'Nah, can't. Sorry, Tan. Got plans.' *Which don't involve shagging some stranger in your parents' bedroom.*

'God, G. You're so BORING! You never come out and play these days.' She pouted for a moment and then laughed. 'Whatever. Congrats on your results, anyway. Hear you aced them.' I stayed and chatted for a minute or two before heading back to Sal. The idea of going to Tanya's party appealed to her about as much as it did to me.

When we got outside, I texted Nat to tell him my results. I kind of wanted to impress him. He *was* studying medicine, after all. The boy had probably never had so much as a B in his entire educational career. Mind you, me neither (well, I'd had two, but who's counting?).

We went back to Sal's for lunch. It was cool to see her parents and little brother again. Sal's family always seems so normal. It was nice to be a part of that for a while. They didn't question the fact that they hadn't seen me for a couple of months, which was a relief. God knows what Sal had told them. It must have been awful for her, trying to hide what she was going through. I don't know how she did it. It's easy enough for me, with a mother who's nowhere to be found more often than not. I could probably have given birth to triplets and raised them at home without my mum noticing. But with two parents who actually *care*? And a nosey little brother too. That was seriously impressive.

Sal's parents were dead pleased with her results, and seemed almost as happy about mine, which was sweet of them. They even cracked open a bottle of champagne in our honour. I made a mental note to call home later and tell Mum how I'd done. Of course, I'd probably have to remind her that I'd taken some exams first. Sal and I went up to her room to polish off the champagne and get ready. The plan was to have a *proper* night out – our first since the Badness had all kicked off. I was looking forward to it.

When Sal was finished getting ready I eyed her up approvingly. She looked hot, no question. I felt a twinge of jealousy, but no more than that. This was

Sal's night. I was determined that she was going to forget about everything that had happened. And not just cos I was intending on getting her blind drunk. Don't get me wrong – I was *fully* intending to get her blind drunk, but the purpose of the evening was to have a laugh. And if Sal happened to get a cheeky snog from a fit boy or two, then all the better.

'Jesus, Sal, you look amazing!'

She looked all coy. 'You think?'

'Oh yes. You're going to be in trouble tonight.'

'What do you mean?'

I laughed. 'Don't look so worried! I mean, you are going to be getting A LOT of attention . . . particularly wearing that top . . .' She had *major* cleavage going on.

Sal hurried over to the mirror behind her bedroom door and quickly examined herself from every possible angle. 'Do you think it's a bit much?'

'If anything, I'd say it's not enough!'

'I'm going to change it.' She started to pull the top up over her head. I jumped up from the bed and pulled it right down again.

'Don't you dare! You look wicked. Right, we're going. Come on, get your coat, love, you've pulled.' I winked at her, and she looked at me sceptically, before reluctantly straightening her top and taking one last look in the mirror.

'Grace, I'm not on the pull tonight, you know.'

'Yeah, but you never know, Prince Charming might be just around the corner, or more likely propping up the bar. Never say never . . .'

'It's too soon, OK? I'm not ready for anything. You do understand that, don't you? Please tell me you do, otherwise we might as well stay in.'

I sighed. 'Yeah, I understand. That's totally cool. You just let me know when you are ready though, cos I am going to find you an amazing boy. I can't promise he'll be as amazing as my one, but I'll see what I can do!'

Sal was looking too thoughtful so I dragged her out the door, hoping to leave whatever bad thoughts she was having far behind us. We said a hurried goodbye to Sal's family. Her dad wolf-whistled at us in that classic embarrassing dad way. Sal rolled her eyes at me, and we both laughed.

On the bus into town, I felt my phone vibrate in my bag. It was a text from Nat: 'Hey, you! Big congrats, clever girl. Want to meet up and celebrate? x'

Sal was busy staring out the window as I considered how to respond. Tonight was supposed to be a girls' night. It was about me and Sal. *Hmm. But maybe later on we could hook up with Nat . . . Sal won't mind, will she?* She *was* dying to meet him. Well, I thought she was – I suppose I'd kind of just assumed. I texted back: 'Thanks! Am tied up at the mo, but let's meet at Bar Code at 9ish? xxx'

I felt a brief pang of worry before I hit send, but I did it anyway. I checked my watch. It was coming up for six o'clock now. Plenty of time for me and Sal to hang out before he arrived. Seemed like the perfect opportunity for them to meet. It was a much better idea than a proper, pre-planned thing. Spontaneity rules, right?

I decided not to tell Sal that Nat was coming later. I didn't want her to be pissed off that I was spoiling the whole 'girls' night' thing. I'd probably tell her after we'd had a few drinks. Or maybe I'd let it be a surprise. I wasn't exactly sure why I hadn't told Nat I was out with Sal. Perhaps I didn't want him stressing about having to impress my best friend. And maybe I was just curious to see their genuine reactions to meeting the other. And what better way to get a genuine reaction than to spring a surprise on them? I silently congratulated myself on my cunning plan. What could possibly go wrong?

❧

I forgot Ethan was here, he's been so quiet. But now he's humming softly to himself. I've heard that song

163

somewhere before, I'm sure of it. What the hell is it? It's driving me crazy.

❧

I asked Ethan. He looked up me, sort of dazed, as if I'd woken him from a dream. I had to repeat my question.

'What song?'

'Er . . . the one you've been humming for ages.'

'Oh.'

'Well? What is it? You must know.'

He shook his head slowly. 'I didn't even realize I was doing it. Sorry. Was it bothering you?'

'No, not really. It just sounded really familiar.'

'I wonder where you've heard it?'

'Well, you're the one who was humming it! It'd help if you could remember.' I was frustrated. I don't know why; it was just a stupid song. Why did it suddenly feel so important?

'I'm sorry, Grace.'

I sighed. 'Fuck it. Who cares anyway? It doesn't matter.'

'Are you sure?' Ethan was suddenly looking all intense.

'It's only a song. How could it possibly be important?'

'Everything's important, even the little things. And sometimes they're the most important things of all.'

He got up and gave me one last meaningful look (well it would have been meaningful if I'd had a clue what he'd been on about) before he left the room.

That was about twenty minutes ago, and that stupid tune is still whirling round my head.

I want it to stop.

~

Another dream.

I was lying on my bed in my old house, flicking through the pages of a magazine. I vaguely heard Mum yelling that dinner was on the table. I ignored her for a couple of minutes, carried on reading. Then I heard Dad pipe up, 'Dinner time, Grace!' I knew I had to go downstairs, but I didn't want to. If only I could stay in my room, everything would be OK. Another minute or so went by and Dad popped his head round my bedroom door. 'Gracie, if you're not at the table in the next thirty seconds, I'm going to start eating your roast potatoes. And then I'm going to start on the Yorkshire puds too . . .' I looked up from my magazine, smiled and said, 'No way! I'll race you downstairs!' Dad said, 'You're on!' and disappeared from view.

Just as I was about to jump up from the bed, I took one last glance at my magazine. Except it wasn't a magazine any more. It was a copy of the local newspaper. There was a picture of Dad on the front page. I tried to read the headline, but it didn't make any sense. All the words on the page were just wiggly lines. They writhed like worms. I panicked. Why couldn't I read it? I knew how to read. Maybe if I put my glasses on? There was a pair of glasses on the bedside table, but I didn't wear glasses, so that was weird. I picked them up. They were Dad's reading glasses, but I put them on anyway. One of the lenses was cracked. I looked around my room, and everything was cracked and broken and ruined. I was going to be sick.

I woke up curled into a little ball against the wall, my skin slick with sweat. I only just made it into the bathroom before the contents of my stomach rose up through my throat. I coughed and spluttered and choked. Tears rolled down my cheeks and I lay shivering on the bathroom floor. The dream had seemed so, so real. Dad was there, alive and laughing, his eyes all crinkly at the edges from smiling. There was a dull ache in my chest. I swear my heart felt bruised or something. I lay my head against the cool ceramic tiles. I could hear the blood rushing round my brain, feel my pulse racing like mad, feel my stomach convulse again. I wondered if I was going to die. And then I must have passed out.

Next thing I knew, I could hear Ethan's voice calling my name, faintly, as if he was at the other end of a long tunnel. I couldn't speak at first. Then his voice got closer and closer and closer, and I opened my eyes to see him peering down at me. There was a blinding light all around him. It hurt my eyes, so I shut them tight again. I could feel Ethan's hand against my cheek. It felt soft and warm and comforting. I tried opening my eyes again and this time it was better, darker. He helped me prop myself up against the sink cabinet. I looked down at myself. There was vomit down my vest and all over the floor. I could feel it on my chin and taste it in my mouth.

I was vaguely aware of Ethan wiping my mouth with a wet towel, then pulling my vest over my head, all the while telling me that I was going to be OK. He helped me over to the bed and undressed me. I felt too dazed and sick and strange to feel even a little bit embarrassed. I got under the covers and Ethan pulled the chair over to the bed and sat down. I stared at the ceiling and started to cry. The tears trickled down the sides of my face, tickling my ears and wetting my hair. He held my hand.

After a while, Ethan said, 'Do you want to tell me about it, Grace?'

'I don't know what's happening to me. These dreams – there's something about them. I feel . . . I don't know . . . I feel as if I'm on the edge of something.'

'What do you mean?'

I sat up, swiped at my teary face and cocooned myself in the duvet, before continuing: 'I wish I could explain it better. I feel like I don't know what's real any more. All I have is this room, and you. And that's all that makes sense to me. Being here seems right somehow, but how *can* it be? I should be doing my homework or going out with friends – that's "normal". But that all seems so far away that I almost can't believe my life used to be like that. And I sit here, day after day, writing and writing and writing about it. But what's the point? Why am I even bothering?' I laughed a short, hollow laugh.

Ethan leaned forward in his chair. 'Grace, what did you mean just then, when you said you felt you were on the edge of something?' He spoke deliberately, as if he was taking great care to choose the perfect words.

'Oh, I don't know. I didn't mean anything.'

He looked disappointed.

'You have to try harder, Grace. Just be honest with me. That's all I ask.'

'I don't know what you mean. I *am* being honest. I don't know what you want me to say.'

'You're so close.'

'OK, now you're freaking me out a bit. Tell me what this is all about. Why am I here?'

Ethan shook his head slowly. He got up from the chair and pushed it back under the table. I felt like I'd failed in some way.

As he headed to the door, I said, 'I'm sorry. Please don't be angry with me.' The words sounded pathetic and whiny, and I wasn't quite sure why I'd said them.

Ethan turned to me. 'I'm not angry with you, Grace. But I just wish you could be honest – if not with me, at least with yourself. What is it that you feel you're on the edge of?'

And before I'd even thought about it, the answer was out of my mouth:

'The truth.'

❧

So that was a little bit weird. It was obviously the right thing to say, because Ethan smiled and nodded before he left the room. And even if he hadn't, I *knew* it was the right answer.

I hope he comes back later. I think I miss him a bit. Talking to him makes me feel strange though – it's not like a normal conversation. Sometimes I feel it's about as much use as talking to myself.

One thought keeps bouncing off the edges of my brain like a pinball: the truth about *what*?

THE TRUTH ABOUT WHAT?!

I never was any good at pinball.

day 23

Ethan didn't come back. And I'd been so sure he would. I had a rubbish sleep: too many dreams and nightmares and little snippets of things that didn't make any sense. And throughout it all, threading together the scenes of weirdness, was that bloody song that Ethan was humming yesterday.

I've tried humming it myself, but it doesn't sound right. Mum always said I was tone deaf. Of course she has a beautiful voice. She used to sing to me when I was young. Like if I'd just woken up from a nightmare, she'd come and sit beside me on my bed, stroking my hair and singing softly. Her voice was like honey, maybe mixed with a little alcohol or something; it never failed to soothe me and make me sleepy again.

And then one day the singing stopped.

When Sal and I arrived at Bar Code, it was already starting to fill up. There didn't seem to be anyone from our school though. The popular lot would be at Tanya's by now, and the rest were probably at the lame pub round the corner from school. We managed to snag a booth in a quiet corner – the same one Sophie and I had sat in. Sal offered to get the first round in, and I watched as she headed to the bar. Two blokes standing there immediately started nudging each other and glancing in her direction. She was utterly oblivious, completely focused on the (admittedly very important) task at hand. While the barman was getting our drinks, one of the guys moved closer to Sal. His mate gulped from his pint glass, trying his best not to look. I could see Bloke Number One's lips move as he spoke to Sal.

He was quite cute, in an obvious kind of way. A bit cocky, and wearing one of those ridiculous 'distressed' T-shirts. Fifty quid for a piece of crap covered in paint splatters and tiny little holes? *Bargain*. His jeans were just as self-consciously worn and ragged, but the look didn't extend to the shoes. They were black and shiny and a bit pointy. All in all, not the best look in the world. I knew Sal would feel the same way. She didn't even turn to face him when he spoke to her. She must have said something though, cos the guy kept talking to her, leaning further forward on the bar, trying his best to get some eye contact. Sal glanced at him briefly, before resuming her intense stare at the barman's back. When she eventually got the drinks, Sal left the bar without a backwards glance, leaving the poor guy staring after her. He shrugged his shoulders as casually as he could and then turned back to his mate, who was shaking his head and grinning widely.

'So what did he say then?' I smiled at Sal as she put the drinks on the table, careful not to spill a single precious drop.

Sal looked confused. 'What did who say?'

'Er . . . duh! Mr Smooth at the bar. I was watching.'

She sat down and took a big swig of her drink. 'Him? Nothing much – you know.'

'He was trying it on though, wasn't he? Did you check out the shoes on him? Still, he was quite fit though.'

'You think?' She turned back to the bar, where the two guys were laughing. Distressed Boy didn't look *too* distressed after his knock-back.

'Yeah. Nice body, pretty decent face, shame about the clothes, but I'm sure you could have had them off in a matter of minutes . . .'

'Grace!' Sal pretended to be horrified.

'I'm just saying! You could probably have any boy in here, if you wanted. And I'm sure at least *some* of them *have* to have decent taste in footwear.'

We both laughed.

'So what do you say then? Want to try any of them on for size?'

Sal shot me a look that said 'Don't go there', but I decided to go there anyway.

'You're allowed to have a bit of fun, you know? And I know that you've been through a lot, but maybe this is just what you need. A bit of fun with a nice, or even not-so-nice, boy. It's good for the ego. You don't have to *sleep* with anyone . . . just enjoy yourself.'

'That's easy for you to say. You've got Nat.' I couldn't read Sal's expression. I wasn't sure if she was getting annoyed or if it was OK to carry on down this path.

'I'd have said the same thing before he came along, and you know it.' I reached out and grasped Sal's hand between mine. 'Look, all I'm trying to say is, you don't have to take this boy malarkey too seriously. You've had one terrible experience, and I don't know what happened there . . . Did I mention that I'd quite like to know?' I shot her a cheeky glance to show I was only joking. 'But things don't have to be like that. If you want to kiss a random stranger, then just go and kiss a random stranger. He doesn't have to be The One, or even anything remotely close to The One. Just do whatever you feel like doing. Don't let what happened ruin things for you. It's in the past.'

Sal said nothing.

'Er . . . lecture over. Sorry. I just want you to be happy. You know that, don't you?'

Sal sighed. 'I know you do, and I appreciate it. I wish it was that simple. We can't always get what we want though – life isn't like that.'

'What *do* you want?'

'I dunno. Turning back time would be a good place to start.' Sal smirked.

'I'll drink to that!' And so we did. I was relieved. I hadn't meant for things to get so serious – and on our first drink as well!

A couple more drinks down the line and we were having a grand old time, laughing and bitching and generally reassuring ourselves that things were back to normal between us. It was lovely to see Sal looking happy and normal after everything that had happened. She was halfway through telling me some story about a teacher at her old school with a penchant for getting it on with sixth-form boys when I did something inexplicable. I suppose it had been bugging me for a long time. Still, I don't know why it popped into my head right then, when everything was going so well. But it did, and it went straight from brain to mouth in less than a millisecond.

'Sal, did someone . . . did someone rape you?' And then there was silence between us. The bar and everyone in it disappeared. There was only Sal and me left. I wanted the earth to open up and swallow me for my complete and utter lack of anything approaching tact. I didn't say anything. Neither did Sal. She just looked at me, eyes slightly narrowed. She didn't look all that shocked, or even mildly surprised. If anything, I was the shocked one – still shocked after seventeen years at my capacity to ruin everything just by opening my mouth.

Sal was the first to speak, after taking a tiny sip from her drink. 'Why?'

I shook my head.

'Why would you ask me that? Why now?' Her voice was calm, unreadable.

'I don't know. I honestly don't know.'

'Why would you think that . . . *that* had happened to me?' She couldn't even say the word that had spilled so readily from my mouth.

'I don't think that.' I paused, frantically trying to work out exactly what it was that I wanted to say, and not wanting to make a bad situation any worse. 'I suppose I've just been trying to understand what happened. I want to understand – no, that's not quite right – I feel like I *need* to understand. Maybe it all boils down to the fact that I just can't imagine you going out and shagging some random.'

Sal shook her head.

A barmaid appeared out of nowhere, cleared our empties and wiped the table. She seemed to take ages, making sure every last inch was sparkly clean. When she finally left, Sal said, 'What does it mean anyway?'

I was confused. 'What does what mean?'

'Rape.'

I could hardly believe what I was hearing. '*What?*'

'I just mean that sometimes things aren't that simple. It's not all black and white.'

'Er . . . yeah, it is! Why would you say something like that? Just tell me what happened. I can help you. If someone did . . . rape you, we can go to the police. It's not too late. You can get counselling or something.'

Sal was shaking her head and I was beginning to get annoyed. 'Stop that! Come on, Sal, tell me.' She shook her head even harder, like she was trying to shake thoughts right out of her brain.

'No, it was nothing like that. I don't know why I even said that. I was just being stupid. Right, my round.' There was a fake brightness in her voice and a slightly manic look in her eyes.

'Sal, wait . . .'

'No. There's nothing more to say. No one did . . . that to me. You know, maybe we're more similar than you think.' Before I could reply, she'd scarpered off to the bar.

The lads from before were still there, and Sal went right up and elbowed her way in between them, sandwiching herself into the non-existent space. Not that the boys seemed to mind, of course. I watched as she laughed and joked with them, touching Distressed Boy on the arm to emphasize what she was saying. He clearly couldn't believe his luck, raising his eyebrows at his mate behind Sal's back. His hand moved down to her bum and stayed there. Sal didn't even flinch. When the barman handed her our drinks, Distressed Boy couldn't get his wallet out fast enough, brandishing a tenner with a flourish. *Loser.* Sal made a move to leave the bar, and this time Distressed Boy really did look distressed . . . well a bit put out at least. Sal put the drinks back on the bar and grabbed him by his T-shirt, pulling him towards her almost violently. And then she proceeded to snog him as if her life depended on it. She was properly going for it – it was quite a sight. Distressed Boy's mate looked over at me hopefully, but I just shook my head and looked away.

It was so obvious that the whole show was for my benefit. *What is she playing at? Trying to prove she's just like me? We both know that's not true.* She could get off with every bloke in the bar (and even the girls . . . why not?), but I still wouldn't believe it. What the fuck had happened to her? I was more determined than ever to get to the bottom of it.

Sal came and sat down, looking like the cat that got the cream. Not that the cat had even wanted the cream in the first place; the cat had been trying to prove a point, in a painfully obvious way.

'Nice show you put on there.'

'I don't know what you're talking about.' Sal replied airily, with a look of mock innocence. That really pissed me off, but I held my tongue. After all, she'd been doing exactly what I'd advised, hadn't she? So I should have no complaints. Still, our previous conversation had left me with a nasty, niggling feeling that I just had to bury. *For now, anyway.*

'So, you gonna get his number then?'

'His? No chance. His technique needs a bit of work.'

I snorted into my drink. 'Really? It didn't *look* like you had any complaints.'

'Well, he did pay for our drinks, didn't he? I thought he deserved a little reward.'

'Yeah, Sal, you're all heart.' We giggled and chinked our glasses together, downing the contents. I wasn't buying her new attitude AT ALL, but it did no harm to play along. Anything for a quiet life.

A little later, I noticed the bar had filled up considerably. I checked the time – Nat was late. While Sal was in the toilet, I texted him: 'Babe, where R U? Getting busy here. In booth behind bar – far right. x'. I thought I might as well make it easy for the poor boy. He had no idea he was walking straight into The Best Friend Test (fail it at your peril).

When Sal returned, I headed to the toilet. I wanted to be back in the bar by the time Nat arrived. Hmm. What is it they say about the best-laid plans? I took time to make sure my make-up was OK, hair was passable, etc., and then somehow got embroiled in conversation with a wasted girl about whether she should break up with her boyfriend.

I eventually escaped the ladies' with a sigh of relief, only to reverse it into a sharp intake of breath when I saw a distinctly Nat-shaped boy standing at our booth. *Damn.* I could only see the back of him, and his body obscured Sal from view, preventing me from spying on this unexpected turn of events from afar. I snuck up behind Nat and put my arms around him, encircling his chest. To say that I surprised him would be something of an understatement. He whirled around to face me, eyes wide.

'Grace! You made me jump.' I went to kiss him, but he turned his head slightly so my lips met his cheek. *Huh.* I grabbed his hand and scooted into the booth, pulling him in next to me. Finally I faced Sal expectantly. 'So . . . I suppose you've met Nat?'

Sal nodded. 'Yeah, I suppose I have.' She smiled at Nat, and he smiled back awkwardly.

'No need for lame introductions then – excellent!' I turned to Nat with a stern look on my face. 'Haven't you got something to say to me?' He looked back at me, and was it my imagination or did he look just a teensy bit panicky? His eyes flitted between me and Sal, as if he'd be able to find the answer written on our faces.

'Er . . . I don't *think* so.'

'Come on – I'm waiting!' I thought I'd better help him out. 'Er . . . the reason we're all here tonight . . . ? Does that ring any bells? Celebrating your girlfriend's complete geniusness? Or rather, her being a bit of a jammy cow at exams.'

Nat slapped his forehead. 'How could I have forgotten?! You are indeed a genius!' He gave me a swift hug, and I raised my eyebrows at Sal over his shoulder. She looked on in amusement, quietly taking it all in. Nat was quick to ask Sal how she'd done too. *Good boy. Obviously knows how to make a decent first impression.* I listened to the two of them talk for a bit, congratulating myself that my plan was back on track, despite the initial setback.

Suddenly Nat banged his hands down on the table. 'Right, you two. This deserves a celebration. How about a little champagne for the two geniuses . . . er . . . genii . . . er . . . dead clever girls?'

'Now you're talking! Thanks, hon.' *Wow. He's really going for broke.* And here I'd thought all students were supposed to BE broke. Still, it was a lovely gesture – even if it was just to show off in front of Sal.

Nat headed off to the bar (and ended up standing next to Distressed Boy, I noticed) and I turned back to face Sal, dying to quiz her on her first impressions of my beautiful boy. But Sal did not look like a particularly happy bunny. Far from it, in fact.

'What the hell do you think you're playing at?'

I feigned innocence. 'What do you mean?'

'I thought this was supposed to be a girls' night out. Just the two of us . . . remember?'

'I know, I know. I'm sorry. It was going to be, but then Nat texted me to go out and celebrate, and

I thought it might be fun.' I paused, checked to see that Sal was still looking seriously unimpressed, before continuing, 'Look, I'm sorry, Sal. I totally should have checked with you first. I just really wanted you to meet him. And this gets it out of the way for both of you without any awkwardness.'

'Yeah, cos this isn't awkward *at all*, is it? God, this is just so typical of you. Sometimes I wish you'd just think about things a bit more. I was really looking forward to tonight.'

'I know you were. I was too, but it'll still be fun – I promise. And we'll go out next week, yeah? You and me – just like the good old days . . . well, not *exactly* like the good old days, but you know what I mean.' I couldn't wait any longer; I just had to ask. 'Sooooo . . . What do you think of him anyway? Isn't he just . . . no, OK, I'll shut up now.'

Sal rolled her eyes, but she looked a little happier at least. 'He seems nice.'

'*He seems nice?* Whoa, careful there, Sal – don't go overboard.'

'Sorry, I mean, I like him. And buying champagne certainly works for me.' We both laughed.

I looked over in Nat's direction. He was tapping his hand against his thigh in time to the music while the barman cracked open the champagne.

'He is *so* hot, don't you think?' I was determined to get more than faint enthusiasm out of Sal.

'Er . . . yeah, I suppose. He's your boyfriend, Grace – not mine!'

'Ha! Yeah, hands off! I guess he's not really your type though, is he? No bizarre piercings or anything like that.'

'Very funny.'

'And he doesn't exactly look like Devon, does he? Hard to believe they're from the same gene pool.'

'Maybe, although Devon's . . .'

'Devon's what?'

'I just . . . I dunno. I kind of wish you wouldn't take the piss out of him so much. He's been good to me.'

'Really? I thought you hadn't seen him in ages?'

'No, no, I haven't. I meant before.'

Before I had time to mull this over, Nat was back, plonking a bucket in front of us. As he was passing round the glasses, I said, 'Thanks, babe. I was just saying to Sal how weird it is that you and Devon are brothers. Not much family resemblance, is there?'

'Oh, you know Dev? I didn't realize.' There was a forced casualness in the way Nat spoke. Or maybe I was just imagining it. 'Anyway, let's get stuck into this before it gets warm.' He raised his glass, gesturing for us to do the same. 'Cheers, you two. May all your exams be this easy!'

We all clinked glasses and took a swig of fizz. I nudged Nat, stage-whispering, 'Not as easy as I'm gonna be tonight if you play your cards right!' He raised his eyebrows at me and looked at Sal somewhat uncomfortably, before taking another gulp of his drink. *Some people are so easily embarrassed.*

And then silence – the strangest silence. Sal coughed, and turned away to look at the bar. Nat twisted the stem of his glass between his fingers. And I . . . well, I was looking at the other two. The silence probably only lasted a few seconds, but it seemed like close to forever to me. I couldn't think of a single thing to say. Luckily Sal jumped in with, 'So, Nat . . . Grace tells me you're going to be a doctor?'

'Um, yes. That's the idea anyway.' And they were off, talking about Nat's course. But there was something not quite right. I couldn't put my finger on it at first, but then I realized that they were both using that fake voice that you use when you're talking to someone else's parents – you know, when you're utterly polite and on your best behaviour. Sal was suddenly talking like a sober person, and Nat was looking oh-so-earnest. Neither of them seemed comfortable AT ALL. I sat back, puzzled.

The rest of the evening passed – uneventfully, I suppose. Things improved for me with each and every drink. I started to think I had imagined the strangeness of earlier. Maybe I'd just been a bit paranoid, because I was so anxious for the two of them to like each other. I got pretty drunk.

Things I can remember about the rest of that night

1. Kissing Nat while Sal was at the bar. Once again I told myself the weirdness was just my imagination: he WAS as into it as I was. He did NOT pull away from me like he'd just got an electric shock from my lips.

2. Asking Nat if he had any fit friends for Sal. She looked daggers at me, and Nat avoided answering the question.

3. Coming back from the bar with a tray of shots and thinking that Sal and Nat were getting on a lot better.

4. Drinking shots until everything blurred. Someone telling me to slow down. Nat or Sal? I don't re-member.

5. Being sick in the toilets and then feeling much better.

6. Nat putting me in the back of a taxi and handing

me a tenner. Did I beg him to come back with me? I *think* I did, but he said something about having to get up early next day.

7. Er . . . that's pretty much it.

Ethan hasn't had much to say for himself today. Maybe yesterday was just a little bit intense for both of us. I feel empty and hollow. My throat hurts too.

I'm tired of thinking so hard.

I'm tired of remembering.

day 24

Lunch was good today – a perfect sandwich can be a thing of wonder. When Ethan came in to take away my plate, we chatted for a couple of minutes. It was almost like a normal conversation. And then I had to go and ruin it.

'Ethan, can I ask you something? Something serious. And I don't want you to answer me with a question, or with some weird cryptic answer. I just want you to be honest with me. Please?'

He weighed that up for a moment or two. 'I can try.'

I took a deep breath. I was finally ready to ask the question I'd been too afraid (or stupid) to ask before now. 'Are you ever going to let me go?'

He looked at me curiously. I managed to hold his gaze, even though I wanted to cry. I was scared to hear the answer.

'That's not the right question, Grace.'

I snapped. I launched myself towards him, my chair clattering to the floor. I punched him in the mouth, then shoved him back against the wall. He offered no resistance; it was like he wasn't even there. Or maybe my rage gave me extra strength. I was screaming in his face, my hands clenched into fists, grabbing the material on the front of his shirt. My face was inches away from his, and as I shouted and screamed and ranted and raved, my saliva spotted his face. A trickle of blood emerged from where I'd punched him, just under his nose. I must have caught him with one of my rings – and on the exact same spot as his scar too. The sight of the blood brought me to my senses. I stopped shouting and watched as it trickled down to his top lip, hanging there for a second before continuing its path towards the crease of his closed mouth.

My grip on his shirt loosened, but I made no move to step back. I looked up into Ethan's eyes, afraid to see the shock and anger that would surely be there. But of course this was Ethan, and there was no such thing. His beautiful eyes were untroubled and met my gaze as calm as you like. Neither of us spoke, but something suddenly dawned on me, something I knew with absolute certainty:

Ethan wasn't in the least bit surprised about what

had just happened. He had *known* I was going to attack him.

What the fuck was going on here? Why had he said what he did, if he knew how I was going to react? And more importantly, how could he have possibly known how I'd react?

For the first time in weeks, I was scared. I backed away from Ethan, shaking my head. Stumbled towards the bed, afraid to look away, even for a second. His eyes followed me across the room. There was no escape. I felt like he could see straight through me, as if I was fading away to nothing. I curled up on the corner of the bed, as far away from him as I could possibly get in this mad white room . . . this prison.

I closed my eyes. But it was no good. I could still *feel* him looking at me. I buried my head in my hands, pushing my palms into my eyes so hard that I saw stars.

After a minute or two, I spoke softly, my voice muffled. 'Who *are* you?' There was no answer. Silence in the room, except for my ragged breathing. I knew he'd heard me. He had to have heard me. So I looked up cautiously. Ethan had lifted up his vest, and was using the bottom of it to dab at his bloody mouth. My gaze flickered down to his perfectly toned stomach. I felt numb.

'Answer me! For fuck's sake, who are you?'

Ethan let his vest fall back into place. There was a lot of blood on it now. I was surprised, and a little bit disgusted, at the damage I'd done. He opened his mouth and started to say something, before stopping himself. He started again. 'You know who I am. You know me.'

I was too baffled to speak. A wave of exhaustion suddenly hit me, and I had to stifle a yawn. I had so many questions, but what was the point? I felt beaten.

Ethan said, 'You're tired, Grace. You should rest.' I nodded and buried myself under the covers. I heard the door opening and closing, and muttered to myself, 'I *don't* know who you are. I don't know a fucking thing any more.' And then . . . well, I know this is going to sound mental, but at least there are mitigating circumstances here . . .

I *heard* Ethan's voice inside my head. I didn't imagine it – I heard it. And he definitely wasn't in the room any more – I checked. I swear on my life that I heard him. And this is what Ethan-in-my-head had to say for himself:

'You know much more than you think. All you have to do is remember.'

What the hell?!

I'm losing my mind. It's the only explanation. I suppose there's only so much the mind can take before it starts to fragment; the pieces of the jigsaw puzzle falling apart. I should be grateful I've stayed sane for this long. Reckon it's only a matter of time before I'm sitting on the floor rocking back and forth, banging my head against the wall and drooling.

I can't think about being crazy any more – it's making me crazy. But I can't stop thinking about what I heard. So I know much more than I think I know, do I? Just where is this information supposed to be hiding? In some cobwebbed corner of my addled brain? Maybe alongside that fucking song I can't remember.

All I have to do is remember. Remember, remember, the fifth of November.

I could be dead by the fifth of November.

I slept all afternoon, I think. Feeling loads better now. I don't feel like a crazy person any more. Well, not a proper crazy person – just a slightly eccentric one, maybe. Just because I 'heard' Ethan inside my head, it doesn't mean anything at all. I'm so used to his stupid cryptic replies that I can fill them in for myself. It's kind of like with me and Sal, when we used to say the same thing at the exact same time and then both shout, 'Jinx!' You spend enough time with a person, you start to think a bit like them, don't you? Ethan's become so predictable to me that I *know* what he's going to say. I won't need to speak to him any more; I'll just hold the conversations in my head. They'll go something like this:

Me: How did you know I was going to attack you?

Ethan-in-my-head: How do you think I knew, Grace?

Me: Fuck off and die.

Yup, it's that simple. I know Ethan. And he knows me. We've bonded. We are one.

day 25

The morning after the big Sal/Nat meeting, I felt like death. Hardly surprising. My head was thumping, and when I licked my lips it felt like my tongue was twice its usual size and that all the moisture had been sucked out of it. I was sprawled across the bed starfish-style, fully dressed, make-up clinging on for dear life. All in all, not the prettiest picture – thank God Nat hadn't come back with me.

I got up gingerly, testing my body to see if movement was going to result in another bout of barfing. Luckily it didn't, so I headed towards the bathroom. The smell of frying bacon wafted up the stairs. Now, food smells can go one of two ways when you're that hungover. Either it's exactly what you need OR it'll have your head down the toilet again in no time. That morning, a bacon sarnie seemed just the ticket. But I was weirded out by the significance of the glorious bacon smell: it meant that Mum was cooking break-fast. Not so strange for normal human beings perhaps, but for *my* mum? She hadn't made breakfast in years. *Why now?*

And then I remembered – my results. *Shit!* Had I texted her last night? It was all a bit hazy in my head. I hurried back to my room and scrabbled through my bag to get my phone. Four missed calls, all from Mum. I checked my sent items, and sighed with relief when I saw that I had texted her after all: 'All As and Abs – piece of cake. Back late tonight. G'

Maybe not the nicest message in the world, but it did the job. The missed calls had been made about every half-hour after my text. *Hmm. This is not good.*

No time for a shower, so I gave my face a quick wash and brushed my teeth. As I trudged downstairs I was trying to figure out the best way to play this. It all depended on *her*. I was going to have to wing it.

I paused at the kitchen door. And there she was, standing in front of the hob, fish slice in hand. With an apron on! She looked a bizarre parody of a domestic goddess. The whole picture was wrong, and I realized why – she was sort of smiling. Just a little hint of a smile, as she flipped the bacon (as crisp as can be, just the way I like it) onto a plate.

I stood in the doorway, quietly surveying this scene of strangeness. Mum turned to face me, and the sort-of-smile even managed to stay in place. 'Grace! You're up at last. Just in time for breakfast. Here, you sit down and I'll get you some orange juice.' I did as I was told. Who was this woman and what had she done with my mother? Whoever she was, she poured me a glass of orange juice (freshly squeezed!) before making up the sandwiches. I didn't speak, for fear of breaking whatever voodoo magic spell was going on.

And then we were sitting opposite each other at the table, eating our sandwiches in silence. The sandwich was perfect.

I cleared my throat. 'I'm sorry I didn't answer my phone last night. It was in my bag – I didn't hear it.'

Mum looked me in the eye. I noticed that for once she wasn't caked in make-up. She looked better for it – lighter, younger. 'That's all right. Did you have a nice time?'

'Yeah, it was fun . . . from what I can remember.'

Her smile slipped a little. 'You shouldn't drink so much, you know.' I bristled, but didn't take the bait. Just munched on my sandwich.

'Congratulations on your results. I'm . . . you're so much brighter than I was at your age.' She laughed a dainty little laugh. 'I barely scraped through my

O levels. No, you certainly didn't get your brains from me. That's your dad's doing.'

The mention of Dad came as a shock. She NEVER talked about him. And every time *I* tried to talk about him, she changed the subject. I hated that.

Mum reached across the table and put her hand over mine. 'He'd have been so proud of you, Grace. You know that, don't you?' I nodded. My throat felt suddenly tight. I didn't trust myself to speak. I would *not* let myself cry in front of her. And then before I knew it, the moment had passed. It was like Mum suddenly remembered who she was.

'Anyway . . . I can't sit around here all day. There's so much to do. You have remembered I'm away tonight, haven't you? I'll be back Monday – no, maybe Tuesday,' she babbled, clearly uncomfortable. She started rushing around the kitchen, clearing away dishes and wiping the table.

I got up to leave. 'Thanks Mum. Breakfast was really nice.'

'Well, don't get too used to it. I expect you to be pulling your weight around here a bit more from now on. I don't see why I should spend all my time running after you . . .' and on and on and on and on. Oddly enough, I was sort of comforted by this. *Here* was the mother I knew and loved. Well . . . tolerated.

I spent the rest of the day in my room, feeling pretty crap about the way things had gone last night. I was annoyed with myself for getting so drunk in front of Nat. I justified it by deciding that if I was willing to be a drunken fool in front of him, maybe it showed I was feeling a bit more secure in the relationship. *Yeah, right.*

I called him, but he didn't pick up. This happened more often than I would have liked, and it was starting to annoy me a little. Still, I left a message which I thought was a nice balance of apology for being a drunken idiot and light-hearted flirtation.

Then I called Sal, which went better than expected. She accepted my apologies for springing Nat on her AND for being a drunken idiot with a minimum amount of grovelling from me. She didn't seem up for the usual post mortem of the night's events though. In fact, she seemed pretty distracted. Not distant, exactly, but certainly not engaged in her usual Sal-type way. I suggested another night out with Nat – I was determined that they would get to know each other properly. I got a vague 'Yeah, maybe' for my troubles. And she reminded me that Nat was off back to uni in a few weeks so it might not be easy to arrange. Like I needed reminding. Nat and I hadn't really talked about it. The future is a very scary thing, especially when you can't believe your luck at how the here-and-now is going.

It wasn't as if Nat was going to be at the other end of the country or anything extreme like that. A fifty-minute train ride is nothing, if you really think about it. And it would be cool going to see him in his flat. No chance of certain little brothers walking in on us. I saw no reason why anything should change between us. I could see him every weekend, and even during the week sometimes – I could just get the train back early in the morning. No worries. I wished Sal hadn't mentioned it though. There were still a good few weeks of maximum Nat time for me to enjoy, and I intended to make the most of every second. Since Mum was going away yet again (what's so great about London anyway?), I had the perfect chance for some quality time with him. It almost made me grateful that Mum was so useless. Almost.

I texted Nat, seeing if he wanted to come over the next day. I'd cook something special (or rather, something vaguely edible) and then we'd spend the rest of the weekend in bed. Nat could call in sick at the pub, and I'd have him all to myself for three whole days. The thought of it sent a shiver of anticipation through my body.

Nat didn't reply to my text for aaaaages. Mum

had already departed in her usual whirlwind panic, leaving nothing behind but a faint cloud of too-sweet perfume and a list of the ready meals she had ever so thoughtfully stocked up on. When it eventually did arrive, Nat's text was short and to the point – a simple 'OK, see you then.' Not quite what I'd been after. Maybe he *was* annoyed at me for being such an embarrassment last night. Or maybe he was just being a boy. They're just not all that communicative.

I got an early night and slept for a stupidly long time. Woke up feeling groggy and slow, so I decided to go for a run to kick-start the day. The first twenty minutes or so were hideous. My lungs felt like they would burst, and my legs didn't seem to want to go on at the pace I was demanding. I felt sure I would collapse in a sweaty heap on the pavement. But of course I didn't. I did what I always do – I ran through it. I started to relish the pain, to enjoy it even. And then it went away, and I was flying.

All I could think about was him. I loved him, I was sure of it. Nothing had ever felt this right before. Nothing had ever felt even *close* to right before. Being with Nat was so different to what I was used to, in every single way. I hadn't cut myself for weeks. Was I changing? Had this glimpse of what a normal relationship could be like actually altered me in some fundamental way? Maybe I could be one of those girls after all, living their shiny happy lives with their loving and supportive boyfriends always there to back them up and make everything right.

Before my default setting of cynicism could raise its ugly head, I stomped all over it with thoughts of Nat and how perfect he was. Of course, I knew full well, even then, that he wasn't *actually* perfect. There were tiny, little things that I would maybe change if I had the chance. Sometimes he could be a little too serious. And (a lot) more often than not it seemed like *I* was the one who made plans for us to spend time together. I was usually the first one to call. And there was the whole not-answering-the-phone thing. But that was OK – everyone has their strengths. I happened to be good at organizing things, and Nat happened to excel at being hot.

Should I tell him that I loved him? Or should I wait for him to say it first? This was all new to me. The nearest I'd ever got was having 'I'd love to do xxxxxxx (insert whatever pure filth you can think of here) to you' whispered in my ear. Not exactly *Romeo and Juliet* material. But this actual, real 'love' business was a whole different kettle of fish. It just . . . seemed like something he might like to know. And then he would say it back and we would kiss and have sex (even though

we'd just done it twice) and we would live happily ever
after in a cottage with a thatched roof and we'd have a
dog named Boy and no children because children are
annoying. The End.

But what if he *didn't* say it back to me? What if
there was an awkward silence? What if my saying those
three little words was the beginning of the end for
us?

By the time I threw myself down on the sofa,
panting like a dog (named Boy?), I was thoroughly
confused. There was only one thing left to do: ask Sal.
She'd know what I should do. She was nearly always
right. It was something we'd joke about: Sal was right
eighty per cent of the time, which meant that I was
right a measly twenty per cent. You can't argue with
numbers like those.

Sal answered after what seemed like a million
rings. 'Hey, you.'

'Hey, you, yourself. What are you up to today?'

'Not much. Don't suppose you want to do something tonight? I'm so bored.'

'Aw, Sal, I'd love to, but I've already made plans
with Nat . . . He's coming over later. Little does he
know I'm planning to keep him as my own personal
sex slave for the rest of the weekend.' I laughed, but
didn't hear anything at the other end. 'Sorry, sweetie, I

really would like to hang out with you. Let's do something early next week?' I thought for a moment. 'Or maybe you could come over on Sunday and hang out with us? You two could get to know each other better, and I promise to be less drunk.'

'Hmm, I don't know, Grace. I don't want to be a third wheel or whatever – watching you guys groping each other isn't exactly my idea of a fun evening.'

'C'mon, it won't be like that at all. I promise. Pleeeeeeeeeease. Say you'll come. For me? Go on, you know you want to . . .'

'Doesn't sound like I have much choice, does it?'

'Nope. That's settled then. It'll be awesome – you'll see.' I took a deep breath. 'Actually . . . there was something I wanted to talk to you about . . . I think I might tell him that I love him.' I breathed out in relief. *There. I've said it.* Silence down the line. 'Sal? You still there?'

'I'm still here.' Her voice was quiet.

'Well? What do you think? I need you to tell me what to do.'

'Do you love him? I mean, really.'

'Yes, I do. Really. He's . . . I dunno. He's just *right,* y'know?'

More silence from Sal. I wondered what she was thinking. 'Sal, should I tell him?'

She sighed. 'It's up to you. I can't help you with this one. You know that, right?'

'But what would *you* do? You're good at this stuff.'

'What stuff? *Love?* Are you joking? Do you even *remember* the last couple of months?'

'I meant you're good at knowing what's right, and you know me better than anyone does. What if he doesn't feel the same way? Do you think saying it could ruin everything?'

'I don't know. Things get ruined for all sorts of reasons.'

'Er . . . thanks for the positivity!'

'Sorry. You just . . . you never know what's going to happen. Look, Grace, I'm going to have to go – that was the doorbell. Good luck with whatever you decide.'

I barely had time to say goodbye and confirm our plans for Sunday before she hung up. Now I was none the wiser about the Nat situation. And confused about Sal. I hadn't heard the doorbell ring. And they had one of those stupidly loud chiming ones too.

Later, I hopped on a bus to the supermarket to stock up for the weekend. I roamed the aisles, waiting for inspiration to strike. *What can I cook for Nat that won't be a complete disaster?* Eventually I decided on steak. Surely I couldn't fuck that up *too* badly? And red meat seemed like a proper boy dish. I was baffled by the choice on offer: sirloin, rump, rib-eye, fillet. It was all just meat to me. After much pondering, I went for fillet.

'I wouldn't get that if I were you. Rump is better – much tastier.'

I turned around to find myself face to face with Devon.

'Hi! Um . . . thanks for the tip.' I felt uneasy. I don't like bumping into people in random places. I like seeing people in context: Devon in school, for example. It was weird to see him standing there, a basket swinging awkwardly by his side. I noticed that the basket was empty except for three different types of cheese.

'No worries. I suppose you're cooking that for my brother.' I couldn't quite read his tone, but I thought he might be mocking me somehow.

'Yeah, he's coming over later. I thought that he might like steak. Does he like steak? Or should I cook something else? Maybe chicken? Or lamb? Lamb is good.' I was babbling like a fool.

Devon smiled. 'Grace, I'm sure steak will be fine. Here, get these two.' He reached in front of me, brushing my bare arm with his. His touch made me feel strange. I almost forgot that he was my boyfriend's loser little brother for a second there. I shivered.

'Thanks. So . . . how are you? Do OK in your

exams? I saw you at school the other day. Sorry I didn't come over and say hi.'

He looked confused. 'What? Oh, no worries. Yeah, I did OK. I hear you did really well.'

'Did Sal tell you?'

'Er . . . no. Nat did.' This surprised me – the idea that Nat talked about me to Devon. Maybe Devon was OK with me seeing his brother after all.

'It must be a bit weird for you. Y'know, me going out with Nat.'

He shook his head and started to speak, but I interrupted. 'Yeah, it must be a little bit though. You being friends with Sal, me being friends with her, and now me and Nat. But we don't really know each other – I mean you and me.' *What am I on about?! Just leave it!*

'Well, maybe it took a bit of getting used to. It's fine though. Really.' He looked like he wanted to disappear.

'Maybe the four of us should hang out sometime?' Even as I said it, I knew it was the worst idea in the universe and it looked like Devon felt the same way.

'I'm not sure that's such a good idea. I don't think Nat wouldn't be up for it. Or Sal, for that matter.' I noticed for the first time that his eyes were remarkably

entangled

like Nat's. It was just harder to see them behind those god-awful glasses.

'Yeah, maybe you're right.' I mustered up my most casual, disinterested tone of voice. 'Have you seen much of Sal recently?'

'Not really, no. I saw her last week, but it was . . . I don't know.' He paused and looked at his feet, scuffing them on the shiny floor.

'It was what?'

'Nothing really. Look, I'd better get going. Enjoy the steak.' And then he was gone, rushing down the aisle towards the checkout with his basket of cheese.

I wandered aimlessly around the shop, feeling decidedly less contented than before. The encounter with Devon had left me a bit flustered and confused. Why had he made me so nervous? Why had I pushed the issue about me and Nat? And why had I never noticed before that he really was not bad-looking at all? All too weird for words.

Nat arrived twenty minutes late. This was getting to be a bit of a habit, and not one I was particularly keen on. Still, he smelled good and his just-washed hair was endearingly all over the place. I kissed him like I hadn't seen him in years. He tasted minty fresh, good enough to eat. I pulled him towards me and kissed him harder. I just wanted to get as close as I possibly could, maybe to reassure myself that I hadn't been attracted to Devon for a few moments of madness in the supermarket. Now that I had the real thing in front of me, instead of a (quite literally) pale imitation, I knew everything was OK after all.

I started to pull at Nat's T-shirt, running my fingers up and down his spine. He pinned me against the wall in the hall, pressing hard against me, exactly like I wanted him to. Just as things were getting interesting, he suddenly pulled back, breathing hard.

He looked at me and laughed. 'Er . . . don't you think we should maybe shut the door first?'

I looked over his shoulder through the open door, to see the neighbour's cat perched on the wall, quietly watching us in that supercilious cat way. Then I looked at Nat, belt and trousers undone.

'Be my guest. Don't want to give any of the neighbours a heart attack.'

Nat fixed his clothes, then shut the door and turned to face me. 'I brought some wine.' He nodded towards the bag he'd dropped in the face of my onslaught. 'And some flowers.' He reached into the bag and pulled out some rumpled-looking tulips.

'They're beautiful. Thank you.' I put the flowers on the coffee table and sat down on the sofa. 'Now get over here.' I patted the space beside me.

'Don't you want to put those in water first?' Nat said as he sat down.

'I reckon they can wait a few minutes. I, on the other hand . . .' My fingers crept up his thigh.

'Hey, hey, hold on a second. What's the rush?' He grabbed my wandering hand. 'Why don't we just talk for a bit?'

I laughed, and resumed my wandering with my other hand. He grabbed that one too, so now he had both my hands pinned on his thighs, achingly close to their intended target. I tried to wrestle them free, but Nat was too strong for me. He lifted my hands in the air and raised his eyebrows at me, as if to say, 'What are you going to do now, huh?' So I clambered on top of him, straddling his thighs where my hands had been moments before. I shuffled in really close and moved my pelvis against him. There was no way he was winning this battle – I could feel it working already.

'Hey! That's . . . cheating.' His voice was hoarse and his breath was hot on my neck. He let go of my hands and moved his own to my waist.

'That's better,' I whispered. 'Now, I've been waiting

for this for days, so be a good boy, take off your clothes and have sex with me. Right now.'

And so he did.

~

Later that night – much later – I cooked the steak. Nat helped, making sure I didn't burn it to a crisp. Devon had been right; the meat was tender and delicious.

I woke in the middle of the night to find Nat curled up facing away from me. I watched his back as he slept. God, I loved his back. And his neck. And his hair. And the back of his ear. And all the other bits of him that I couldn't see right that minute. I'd nearly said those three little words over dinner, but the timing hadn't been quite right. And I hadn't wanted to say it after we'd had sex on the sofa – that seemed too crass for words. I was beginning to wonder if I'd ever say it at all.

When I woke up in the morning, Nat was already dressed and downstairs, leaning against the kitchen work surface and munching on a piece of toast. I wandered over to him and put my arms around him, kissing his neck.

'What's with the early morning?'

'It's hardly early! It's eleven thirty and I'm going to be late for work.'

Crap. Forgot about that. 'Aww no . . . work? Really?

I was thinking . . . maybe . . . you could phone in sick. We could spend the day in bed,' I said in maximum-allure mode. I went to kiss him, snaking a hand around his waist. Nat moved his head at the last second, so I got a mouthful of cold ear instead. He gave me the slip and ended up on the other side of the kitchen, hands raised as if he was surrendering. But he wasn't.

'No no no no no. That's not going to work – not this time. I *really* have to get to work. I'm sorry – I know it sucks.'

'But, Nat . . .' Even *I* didn't like the whiny tone I could hear in my own voice.

'I'm sorry. I'll be back at about seven.'

I knew when I was beaten. I sighed. 'OK, but you'd better make it up to me later.' I was only half joking. I really was pissed off that he'd rather go and work in some poxy pub than spend the day with me.

'I will. I'll see you later.' He gave me a quick kiss on the forehead and was gone.

As I trudged upstairs, I caught a look at myself in the mirror on the landing. Petulant expression and a serious case of bed hair. No wonder he'd scarpered so quickly – who could blame him?

The best-laid plans turn to shit.

My mood didn't improve until I'd had a shower and dealt with the hair situation. I decided it was a good thing that Nat took his job seriously. It showed he was grown-up and responsible and lots of other things that I'm not. It didn't mean that he was a boring goody two-shoes who wouldn't know rebellion if it came up and spat in his face. And he wasn't going to be gone that long anyway. I just had to find something to fill my day – that was all. No big deal.

I wolfed down some cereal and spent a couple of hours watching TV, surfing a gazillion channels, trying to stay ahead of the adverts so that I never had to watch one. Then I headed upstairs and sorted out my nail varnishes, chucking out the ones that were too crusty for words. That took all of five minutes, but I did line them up in order of colour, which I found strangely satisfying. Then I downloaded some songs onto my iPod. Then I listened to them and wondered why I'd bothered.

Then there was nothing else to do.

That interminable Saturday afternoon, as the clock stubbornly refused to fast-forward the way I wanted it to, I did something inexplicable. I cut myself.

Ethan and I haven't spoken today. Not surprising really. He's been in a few times, but it's the same each time: he looks at me; I look at him; he looks away. The cut above his mouth looks bad, and the skin around it is swollen and tinged with yellow. It's hard to believe that I did that. I don't feel good about it, but every time I opened my mouth to apologize, something stopped me. You can't keep someone locked up for this long and not expect them to go a bit mental. He brought it on himself. Kind of.

After each Ethan visit I listened hard, in case I heard him inside my head again. I didn't. Then I realized what a fool I was being and laughed out loud.

day 26

Another day dawns, or maybe it doesn't. For all I know the sun has stopped shining and the world has come to an end. Maybe Ethan and I are the only ones left. Not a comforting thought. But if we *are* the only ones left then I'm going to have to talk to him at some point. Might as well start today if I don't want to die of loneliness. Besides, it might be down to us to repopulate the planet. Or something.

It's when I'm alone that the doubt sets in. It's been that way for years. As long as there are people around, I can pretend that everything's OK. But I need that audience to pretend *for*, otherwise it doesn't work. Alone, I'm not that easy to fool.

It's not that I mind being alone, not really. I can distract myself with silly fantasies and daydreams for hours, but in the end it always comes back to me. That's what I'm left with: just me. And that's what scares me more than anything. Me. The thoughts I try to purge by cutting. The memories that seem to get louder and brighter the harder I try to forget. The whys and what ifs. And always crouching somewhere in the background, waiting to knock me down whenever things seem OK for once, is the thought – the knowledge – that breaks my heart: my father would be ashamed of the person I have become.

Sometimes I used to feel glad he was dead, just so I didn't have to see the look on his face when I stumbled home completely off my face, clothes a mess, mouth red-raw from kissing some random. *She* never cared. *She* never waited up. Dad would have though, I'm sure of it. He would have worried about me and shouted at me and grounded me and told me I couldn't see those boys any more. And I would have cried and slammed my bedroom door and begged to be allowed out. But inside it would be different. Inside I would be secretly pleased, comforted by the knowledge that someone cared. I wouldn't go out every weekend. Sometimes I would stay at home and watch telly with him, even those crappy old sitcoms he loved so much. She might be there too, but we wouldn't care either way. It would be different. Everything would be so different. I might not have gone to the park that day, armed with a bottle of cider. That's where it all began – that's where I began.

I was fourteen and clueless. It was all down to Tanya. She sat next to me in English and we'd become almost-but-not-quite friends over the past few months. She was pretty (but wore too much mascara), clever (but could never be bothered to do any work) and bitchy as anything (but she was nice to me, so that was OK). One Friday in May, Tanya asked me what I was up to at the weekend. 'This and that, y'know' was my particularly eloquent answer, not wanting to admit that I was headed for another weekend in front of the telly. It was around the time that Mum had started going away and the TV was my constant companion – anything to stop the silence from suffocating me. But Tanya was having none of it. 'Fuck "this and that". Why don't you come out with us tonight?' The thought of going out with Tanya and her friends scared the crap out of me, but I found myself saying yes in spite of myself. She told me about an off-licence near the park that would sell to anyone, no matter how young they looked, and said everyone was meeting at the kids' play area at eight. I had no idea who 'everyone' was.

I nearly chickened out when I was getting ready. It would be so much easier to stay at home. I could take my duvet downstairs, curl up on the sofa and order a pizza. But I didn't. I changed into a shortish skirt and a pretty black top that I'd never worn before. I pulled on my boots and checked that my make-up was OK. My face looked different, maybe because I'd gone a little bit overboard on the kohl. I felt different too. Maybe this was going to be the start of something for me. These people didn't know me, not really. I could be different; I could be anyone.

Buying the booze was as easy as Tanya had said, and it wasn't hard to see why. The lady behind the counter was about a hundred years old, with the thickest glasses I'd ever seen. She asked if I was eighteen, and (surprise, surprise) I said I was. I'd never drunk much of anything before, so cider seemed like a safe choice: apple juice with a bit of a kick.

I approached the play area with caution. I could hear laughter coming from the den at the top of the climbing frame. Suddenly a bottle came hurtling out of one of the windows. It sailed over my head and smashed on the path behind me. I nearly bolted, but Tanya's head poked out right at that second.

'Grace! Hi! Come on up!' So I did as I was told.

It was a tight squeeze inside the den. There were seven people already in there: Tanya and two of her friends from school, and four boys I'd never seen before. I sat near the entrance and Tanya introduced me to everyone. I recognized Zoë and Kirsty, but of course they had no clue who I was. The boys had ridiculous nicknames that I found hard to remember. But the one next to me was Kez and I could remember that. His leg was pressed against mine in the confined space.

It was awkward at first. I could feel the judgemental stares of Zoë and Kirsty, but Tanya did her best to make me feel comfortable, talking at a zillion miles an hour about how I was one of the only cool people in her English class, and that if it wasn't for me she'd have died from boredom already. She passed me the bottle she'd been swigging from and I took a big gulp, which burned my throat as it went down. But it felt good; it made me feel strong somehow.

They'd all had a bit of a head start on the drinking, so I did my best to catch up. I cracked open my cider and passed it around. As the others joked and laughed, I mostly listened. One of the boys was clearly a loudmouth joker, and the others (Kirsty in particular) thought he was hilarious. I wasn't convinced. After a while it became clear that the girls weren't in the least bit bothered that I was there; they were one hundred per cent focused on the boys. That suited me just fine.

Later, it dawned on me why Tanya had invited me: I was there to make up the numbers. I felt stupid for not realizing straight away. Kirsty was with Loudmouth, Zoë was already snogging the nondescript one in the corner, and Tanya was clearly interested in the best-looking one of the bunch. I was there for Kez. That was my purpose. But I was sort of drunk, and I didn't mind one little bit. I turned to Kez and tried to look at him impartially, but things were already getting a little blurry. His hair was bleached blond and styled with a lot of gunk. The roots were starting to show through. He had a nice enough face, but a nasty patch of acne on his chin. Shiny white teeth that stood out in the darkness of the den. He looked to be quite slight, but it was hard to tell with us all squished together. Only now did I notice the way he'd been looking at me – sort of wolfishly. I was a lamb to the slaughter and I hadn't even realized. The sacrificial virgin.

One by one, or rather two by two, the others gradually disappeared. It didn't take a genius to figure out what they were doing. And then there were two.

Kez put his hand on my thigh and said, 'So, how come I haven't seen you round here before?' I turned to face him as his hand crept higher. Instead of answering his question, I kissed him, because that was what he expected. I'd kissed a few boys before – boys I'd been out with for a week or two – but this was different. Kez tasted like beer and oranges and something kind of musky and grown-up. Kissing him was strange. I felt like he was trying to eat me up, like he couldn't get enough. Not exactly unpleasant, but it took a bit of getting used to.

Before long I was lying on the floor with Kez on top of me. *How did that happen?* I didn't really care. Kez was kissing and touching and rubbing me and it felt . . . well, nice. He was breathing hard and starting to moan a little as he was grinding against me. I knew full well what was about to happen – unless I stopped him. I didn't stop him. I think he expected me to stop him.

I remember thinking something along the lines of . . . *So this is it? This is really it. I am actually having sex. Huh.* Yes, it felt odd to be so very close to someone I had barely said two words to. But it was also weirdly comforting – this strange, sweaty boy who wanted me so much. For those few minutes I felt like he *needed* me. And I needed him. He seemed so grateful too. It didn't last long. At the time I wondered if he'd been so fast just in case I changed my mind. Of course, now I know better. And of course it had hurt a bit, but it was a good hurt – a badge of honour.

Afterwards, we hardly spoke. I sorted out my clothes and Kez rifled through a plastic bag for a can of beer. He drank greedily and then swiped the back of his hand across his mouth. He watched me in silence. I didn't know what to say. What could we talk about? We didn't know each other. We had nothing in common, and probably never would. Suddenly I wanted to go home and snuggle up in my own bed – all alone, the way it was supposed to be.

Before I could move, Kez shuffled closer to me. He put his hand on my waist and kissed me, ever so gently. And everything felt good again, until he whispered in my ear, 'Tanya didn't think you'd be up for it. But I knew you would the minute I saw you.' I pulled away and asked him what he meant.

'I knew you wanted it. I could just tell.'

I could feel my face redden. 'How? How could you tell?'

'I dunno. Just a feeling, innit? Some girls, you can just tell. Don't look at me like that! It's a good thing, knowing what you want. Not like those girls who lead you on and on till you're ready to explode and then they change their mind. You wouldn't do that, would you?' He moved to kiss me again and I didn't stop him. I didn't think he was trying to hurt me with his words. In fact, the opposite seemed to be true: I got the distinct impression that he was trying to *compliment* me.

So I was one of *those* girls. It was official. And if I

hadn't been one before, I certainly was now. There was no going back for me.

⌁

I talked to Ethan. Asked him if his mouth hurt. He looked confused for a moment, and then he touched his fingers to the cut, as if to remind himself it was there.

'No, it doesn't hurt at all.'

'Good. Look, Ethan, I'm sorry. It should never have happened. I don't know what I was thinking. Well, I mean, clearly I *wasn't* thinking. I don't go round randomly hitting people, you know. I just . . . it's hard being here. There's too much time to think. Anyway, I'm sorry.'

'It doesn't matter, Grace.'

'Of course it matters! I attacked you! I'm clearly losing my mind in here.'

Ethan shook his head. 'You're wrong.'

Here we go again, I thought. I didn't have the energy to go round in circles with him. 'I'm sick of thinking about stuff. And I'm sick of writing it all down. Why am I even bothering? No one's going to read it.'

Ethan leaned against the door. 'Have *you* read it, Grace?'

'Er . . . no. I don't need to – I know what it says.'

Ethan shrugged his shoulders and raised his eye-brows. The meaning was clear: That's what *you* think.

I turned to the pile of scrawled pages beside me. It couldn't do any harm, could it? I started to read, and soon forgot Ethan was even there. I don't know how long it took, but eventually I reached the last page, about that night in the park with Kez. I sighed and looked up. Ethan wasn't standing by the door any more. He was sitting on the bed with his legs crossed.

'Well?' He looked at me expectantly.

'Well what?'

'How do you feel?'

'I dunno.'

'Grace . . .' He sounded like a teacher, disappoint-ed when his star pupil gets an answer wrong.

'Sad. I feel sad, OK? My life's a fucking mess and I screwed everything up and I'm a terrible person. Happy now?'

'It doesn't make me happy that you're hurting. Why would it?'

'Why else are you doing this to me then? You must be getting some kind of kick out of it.'

Ethan's next words were unexpected. 'You miss your father, don't you?'

'Dad? What's he got to do with this?' I said cagily.

'What was he like?'

223

I decided to play along. 'He was . . . just Dad. A typical dad, y'know?'

'Tell me.'

I decided to play along; what harm could it do? 'Well, he used to embarrass me *all* the time. He'd do it on purpose. Like in the supermarket, he'd start doing monkey impressions for no reason. And the more embarrassed I got, the louder and more embarrassing he'd be. He didn't care who was watching – he never cared what other people thought. Not like me – I was always looking around, worrying that someone from school would see me. It was all right when I was younger. I used to join in and we'd have such a laugh.

'He was so good with people. Everybody loved him and laughed at his stupid jokes. He was the only person who could make Mum laugh. She never laughs at stuff on TV, even when it's really funny. But Dad could make her laugh just by wiggling his eyebrows.'

I stopped talking, suddenly aware that this was the most I'd said about Dad for years. Even with Sal I'd always been vague, claiming that I couldn't really remember what he was like. She never questioned how blatantly ridiculous that was, and I was grateful.

'It sounds like you loved him very much.'

'He was my dad – of course I loved him.'

'That's good, Grace. You're doing really well.'

I shrugged, not really sure what he was getting at.

I told Ethan about Dad's terrible cooking and how he used to invent mad dishes by chucking a bunch of leftovers in the pan and adding Worcestershire sauce. I told him about going to the cinema with Dad and getting hotdogs and nachos and the biggest box of popcorn you've ever seen (and throwing up in the car on the way home). I told him things I thought I'd forgotten. Things I hadn't thought about for years and years. Silly, inconsequential things. But it felt good to say them out loud, to speak the words to someone who listened and nodded and smiled in all the right places. Ethan never looked bored or tried to change the subject or talk about himself. He let me go on and on and on, for God knows how long.

And then he stopped me in my tracks with one question. His voice was ever so quiet, his face the very picture of sympathy as he uttered six words:

'Tell me about how he died.'

Wasn't expecting that. No one ever asked me that. Nat never asked me.

'There was an accident. A terrible accident.'

'What happened?' Ethan spoke so softly it felt like he was inside my head again.

Deep breath. 'He was coming back from a business trip. It was my birthday . . .'

'Go on,' he coaxed.

'He . . . There was a level crossing. His car got hit by a train.'

'An accident,' he said.

I nodded.

'Grace, you can tell me the truth. You should tell the truth.' He knelt in front of me and held my hand. His hand was cold. 'I know you can do it. You're strong enough now.'

No point in lying now. 'He drove onto the train tracks and stopped his car. He did it on purpose. He killed himself.'

Ethan nodded. 'That must have been very hard for you and your mother.'

'Hard for *her*? It was her fault!'

'Why do you say that?'

That stopped me dead. Why *did* I say that? Why had I always thought that?

'It . . . She was a bitch to him.'

'Was she?' he said, and I was thinking the same question.

I hesitated. 'Yeah, she . . .' The words disintegrated in my mouth. She loved him. Completely. She did everything for him. That's the truth.

'You've always blamed her, haven't you? Why do you think that is?'

Whywhywhywhywhy?

'Because she was there.'

Ethan nodded. 'And he wasn't, was he?' His voice was hoarse.

Tears came. I was amazed that I'd fended them off for so long. 'He left me. On my birthday. On my fucking *birthday*! Why would he do that? How could he do that to me?' I was sobbing now. I got up and threw myself onto the bed. Too many thoughts and memories were crowding my head.

I felt Ethan sit on the edge of the mattress beside me. 'I don't know. I don't know how someone could do that.'

I spoke into the pillow, my voice muffled. 'He never thought about us. He left us with nothing. How could he be so selfish?'

'You're right, Grace. It was a selfish thing to do.'

A thought popped into my head. A thought I'd never had before. Not even when things were really, really bad.

The moment I thought it, Ethan said it out loud:

'I hate him.'

day 27

Nat got back from work, exhausted from changing barrels and being nice to people all day. I was feeling weird and embarrassed about cutting myself. How was I going to explain it to him? How could I have been so stupid?

We ordered a pizza and lounged in front of the TV, neither of us saying much of anything. Nat ended up with his head in my lap and I stroked his hair. It was comfortable. Well, it would have been if I hadn't been dreading him seeing what I'd done to myself. It got later and later and I could hardly keep my eyes open.

'Come on, let's get to bed, sleepyhead.' Nat's voice seemed far away. I opened my eyes and saw him clearing away the pizza box and our glasses. I rubbed my face and looked at the clock on the mantelpiece. It was past two o'clock.

Nat grabbed both my hands and hauled me off

the sofa. He kissed my forehead before steering me towards the stairs. Each step was a mountain I reluctantly climbed. But what else could I do? I couldn't stay downstairs forever. And I was so, so tired. When we got to my bedroom, I turned to Nat and kissed him. My heart wasn't really in it and he could obviously tell.

'Why don't you change into your . . . er . . . pyjamas or nightie or whatever, and I'll go and brush my teeth?'

Pyjamas? Nat wasn't supposed to know that I even *owned* pyjamas, let alone be able to see them – ever. *And* he was supposed to want to have sex with me at every available opportunity. Surely we hadn't gone past that stage already? But I was falling asleep on my feet, and at least it postponed the inevitable that little bit longer. Still, I hesitated before pulling my PJs from their hiding place in the bottom of the wardrobe.

When Nat came back, he laughed. 'You never struck me as a Winnie-the-Pooh sort of girl! Nice!'

I punched his arm, none too gently. 'Shut up! And anyway, they're not Winnie-the-Pooh – they're Eeyore. *Totally* different thing. Eeyore rocks, and I won't hear anyone say any different. You have been warned.'

Nat kissed me right then. It was the best kiss and I don't know why.

'You're full of surprises, Grace Carlyle. I wonder what other deep, dark secrets you've been hiding from me . . . Eeyore . . . Who would have thought it? Don't worry, your secret's safe with me. I think it's adorable.'

'Are you taking the piss?'

'Noooooo, I wouldn't dream of it. I think it's perfectly normal that my girlfriend has a thing about depressed donkeys . . .'

I flounced out of the room, pretending (and failing) to look indignant. It's hard to look indignant in pyjamas of any kind. In the bathroom I examined the cuts on my legs. They looked pretty bad. Rusty red raw and angry.

Nat was stripped down to his boxers when I returned. He looked amazing. All manly, but sleepy and rumpled. Suddenly I wasn't feeling so tired after all. I kissed him. He pulled back after a while and smiled that beautiful smile. 'Right, into bed with you. And no funny business, OK?'

I frowned. 'Why? Don't you want to?' I didn't quite know why I was pushing it. But I wanted it to be *my* decision not to have sex, not his.

'Of course I want to, but I'm knackered and so are you. We don't have to have sex *all the time*, you know? There's no law or anything.'

'Well, maybe there *should* be a law. Or a commandment or something . . . Thou shalt drop thy pants whenever I so desire.' I raised my eyebrow at him. He responded by throwing a pillow at my head.

So we both got under the covers and I scooted up to him, nestling in the crook of his arm. It felt weird and not quite right at first. I blamed the pyjamas, but there was no way I was taking them off now.

We talked about all kinds of things, half whispering in the darkness. It's always easier to say things in the dark. Our words trailed off after a while, and I thought Nat had fallen asleep. I snuggled closer to his chest and sighed a contented sort of sigh. I drifted into that deliciously dreamy halfway world, but was jolted out of it by the sound of Nat's voice, which was strangely loud. 'Are you awake?'

I made a sound which meant yes but came out more of a 'mmmhm'.

'Tell me about Sal. What happened with her anyway?'

I made another sound, which roughly translated into 'What do you mean?'

'Why did you two fall out?'

I was fully awake now. I opened my eyes and shifted to look at Nat's face. 'I told you: it was just something stupid. Not worth talking about.'

He was quiet for a few moments. 'I don't believe you.'

'What?! Why?' I sat up.

'You two are *so* close. I don't think you'd have fallen out over something that wasn't important. Why won't you tell me the truth? Don't you trust me?'

This was just plain weird. Why wouldn't he just leave it?

'Of *course* I trust you, but why does it matter? Everything's fine now.'

'It matters to *me*, Grace.' He sat up and took my hands in his. 'I want to know everything there is to know about you, from your Eeyore pyjamas to the way you eat a Creme Egg. I want to know if you had an imaginary friend when you were little. I want to know when you learned to raise your eyebrow in that sexy way you do. I want to know what you're thinking all those times you drift away from me. I want to know about everything that matters to you. I love you.'

What?! I hadn't expected him to say it. Yes, I'd hoped, but I'd never actually believed it would happen. And certainly not then. But he'd said it – he'd really, really said it. I thought I might burst with happiness, or at the very least jump up and down on the bed like an overexcited kid. I took a deep breath to calm myself.

Everything was going to be OK.

Nat.

Loved.

Me.

His features were a little blurry in the darkness, but his eyes were wide. I think he was almost as surprised as I was. I leaned across and kissed him. Not much more than a peck, very chaste.

'I love you too.'

We sat in silence for a moment or two. I didn't know what to say or do. This was all new to me.

I was the first to speak. 'No one's ever said that to me before, you know.'

Nat kissed me the same way I'd just kissed him. 'I find that very hard to believe. You are *extremely* lovable.'

'It's true. Not the me being lovable bit . . . but, you know . . .' I gulped hard, trying to swallow the emotions that threatened to overwhelm me.

'Well then . . . every other guy you've been out with must have been an idiot.'

'You don't know how right you are.'

I lay back down and Nat followed suit. Side by side, hand in hand, staring at the ceiling.

'You never talk about other guys before me.'

This was dangerous territory. I had to be careful.

'And you don't tell me about your ex-girlfriends, do you? It's all in the past. None of it matters now.'

'Ex-girl*friend*. Singular. There's only one.'

'Really?' I tried (and failed miserably) to keep the surprise from my voice.

'Yes, really. Amy. I went out with her for three years. We broke up before I went to Nepal. And that's it – my entire relationship history.'

I was surprised by how it made me feel, hearing about this girl who must have known Nat so much better than I did. Three years is a very long time. Jealousy bubbled up inside me, turning everything sour.

'Did you . . . love her?' I *had* to ask.

'Yes.'

I said nothing. Nat raised himself up on one elbow. 'But it doesn't mean anything now. Like you said – it's all in the past.' He brushed my cheek with his hand. 'So . . . what about you? You can tell me – I can take it.' He smiled down at me, expectant but relaxed.

I'd hoped that we'd managed to bypass this awkward moment altogether. Surely we would have talked about it sooner if we were ever going to? But no . . . It had to raise its ugly, stupid head now, trying to ruin what should have been the best moment of my life so far. I wouldn't let it happen. I wasn't going to tell Nat about my past and see that happy look on his face replaced by hurt and disappointment and disgust. *No way.* Things were going too well. But I didn't want to lie to him by conjuring up some kind of semi-innocent, rose-tinted version of my past. He deserved better than that. So I did something despicable instead . . .

'Sal got pregnant.'

The ultimate diversionary tactic. Hardly a subtle, sleight-of-hand trick, but it did the job.

❧

Something's wrong with Ethan. I can't wake him. I shake him and shout at him but nothing happens. His breathing seems normal, but he won't wake up.

He lay down next to me last night. He didn't say anything after the mind-reading weirdness. I was freaked out and confused and aching with sadness. So many questions in my head. But I didn't ask any of them – something stopped me. And now it might be too late.

Got up this morning and left him lying on the bed. He looked peaceful.

But now he won't wake up.

What if he doesn't wake up?

I'm scared.

I won't leave him. Not now.

I have to finish this. I *have* to.

My despicable tactic with Nat certainly worked. A little *too* well. There was a moment or two of silence before Nat responded.

'*What?*' His voice was croaky.

I sighed. 'Sal got pregnant. That's why we fell out.'

Nat sat up and turned on the bedside light. I shielded my eyes and shuffled myself into a sitting position. Then I looked at Nat. His expression was hard to read.

'Wha— When did this happen?'

I felt sick that I was doing this to my best friend in the world. Betraying her trust, just to get myself out of a slightly sticky situation. But there was no going back now.

'I don't even know. She won't tell me what happened.'

'*Seriously?* You must know something. Why on earth wouldn't she tell you?'

'Nat, I *don't* know. She completely shut me out. All I know is it must have happened around Easter. She . . . um . . . she had an abortion a couple of months ago. I would have gone with her, but we fell out and . . .' I didn't know what else to say without sounding pathetic.

Now Nat looked like he was the one who felt nauseous. 'Jesus. I never thought it was anything like that. How . . . is she? Now, I mean. It must have been awful for her.'

I was touched at his concern. 'She's doing OK, I think. It'll take her some time to get over it, I suppose. But I think she's doing better.'

'And you really have no idea what happened? Who she . . . slept with?'

'No! I *told* you. Why won't you believe me?' I hated being asked the same thing twice. It drove me crazy.

'I'm just . . . surprised, I suppose. It seems like the kind of thing best friends might talk about, that's all.'

He was right and it made me angry. Angrier than it should have done. 'Look! Will you just stop talking about it? She didn't tell me anything. I haven't got a fucking clue what happened, and I probably never will, so just . . . leave it.' I turned away, not wanting Nat to see the tears that were beginning to blur the edges of my vision. I felt his hand on my shoulder, but I shook it off.

'Grace, I'm sorry. I just wish you'd told me about this sooner.'

I jumped up from the bed and whirled round to face him. 'WHY? What difference does it make? Why can't you stop going on about it? It's none of your business anyway!' I made no effort to hide the tears now. And I didn't bother to wipe them away as I stood over Nat, breathing heavily. He looked stunned. He'd never had to witness my temper before.

After a moment, he spoke quietly and deliberately. 'None of my business? Is that how you really feel?'

'Yes! I should never have even told you!'

'Why did you, then?'

He had me there. 'Look, Nat. Could you please . . . just go? I can't deal with this right now.' I was surprised at my own words, but part of me knew that if we continued this conversation it was going to end *really* badly.

'If that's what you want.' I'd more than half expected him to try to reason with me. Or at least be angry that I was kicking him out in the middle of the night. But he didn't even seem to care.

I nodded and watched as he pulled on his clothes. I wanted to say sorry, to tell him to stop, to stay with me. But the words wouldn't come.

Nat turned to face me when he reached the door. We looked at each other for the briefest of moments. Here was a last chance for one of us to say something, anything, but neither of us took it. His face was an emotionless mask; tears were still trickling down mine. And then he was gone.

I waited to hear the front door close before slumping on the bed and crying so hard I thought I might never stop. I was angry and sad and confused. I'd made a terrible mistake. I knew full well that I'd taken all my frustration and resentment at Sal for not trusting me and dumped it on Nat. All because he cared enough to ask about it. All because he loved me.

But what was with all the questions? Asking over and over again about what I knew and didn't know and why I hadn't told him. I didn't *have* the answers.

I didn't sleep for the rest of the night. Instead, I took the knife from my desk drawer and slowly and carefully re-opened the cuts I'd made on my legs that day. And then I made some more.

I examined the damage the next morning. It was not a pretty sight: like some kind of modern art gone badly wrong. There was so much blood on the sheets – more than I'd have thought possible. The blade of the knife looked rusty.

I couldn't face it. I pulled the duvet back over my head and fell into a dreamless sleep.

When I woke up, there were a few blissful seconds of not remembering, before it all came crashing back. I replayed things over and over in my head, and kept returning to the image of Nat's face just before he'd left. He'd looked at me the way you'd look at a stranger on the street. How could you go in a matter of minutes from telling someone you loved them to looking at them like that? How was that even possible?

I knew the whole thing was my fault. It would never have happened if I hadn't been trying to weasel out of telling him about my past. I could have just lied, or been vague, or told him he was my first. Or maybe not. Maybe I could have told him the truth and maybe he would have understood and maybe I would have felt as if a gigantic weight had been lifted and I could finally breathe again.

I checked my phone, hoping to see the little envelope in the corner of the screen. And there it was!

My heart hammered in my chest and I knew that everything was going to be fine. Until I saw that it was a SIM update from the bastard phone network. Bastardbastardbastard.

I threw the phone on the floor and gave it my best evil stare, considering what punishment to inflict on it next. Then I thought better of it and texted Sal: 'Come round? PLEASE? Nat's not here. x'. A few minutes later I got a message back saying she was on her way.

I had a quick shower, trying my best to ignore the pain of the hot water running down the cuts on my legs. I felt much more positive about things as I got dressed and put my damp hair in a ponytail. Sal would know how to fix things with Nat. I couldn't tell her exactly *what* we'd argued about, but I felt sure I could come up with something plausible. She'd kill me if she found out what I'd told him. And she'd have every right to. Best friends didn't do that to each other, not ever. I was the worst best friend in the world.

The doorbell rang much sooner than I'd expected. I hadn't had a chance to put the sheets in the wash. I grimaced as I looked at the state of them. It was OK though, Sal and I would just stay downstairs. Still, I quickly stowed the knife back in the desk drawer and chucked my dressing gown over the bed, somewhat haphazardly. It was the best I could do.

I bounded down the stairs and opened the door to let Sal in, and then accidentally burst into tears before she could sit down. That wasn't supposed to happen.

Sal manoeuvred me over to the sofa and let the tears run their course. She hugged me and told me everything was going to be OK, which was nice to hear even though I didn't believe it. When the crying died down to a mere sniffle, Sal offered to make a cup of tea. I waited on the sofa.

She emerged from the kitchen with two gigantic

mugs of tea. 'Get some of that down you.' I took a scalding gulp, relishing the pain.

'Now, what did he do?'

'What do you mean?' My brain wasn't functioning.

'Nat – what did he do? He must have done something for you to be in such a state. Tell me, and I'll go and punch him on the nose.' Just the thought of that made me smile.

'Nothing. *He* didn't do anything. It's all my fault.' I launched into the story of the weekend so far. Sal listened carefully, sipping her tea.

She interrupted only once. 'He told you he loved you?'

'Yeah, he did. And I was so happy. Then somehow it all went wrong. We got into a stupid argument and I got really angry and asked him to leave. He didn't even try to change my mind, even though it was like stupid o'clock and the buses wouldn't have been running. He just . . . left.'

'You got into an argument when he'd just told you he loved you? How on earth did you manage that?!'

My mind raced through the possible lies I'd concocted for Sal's benefit, before I made a decision.

'OK, here's the thing. Please don't be angry with me . . .'

'Why would I be angry with you? Don't be daft!' But I could see the first flickers of worry in her eyes.

'I'm really, really sorry, but I told him what happened with you.' I cringed, waiting for Sal's reaction. I must have looked pathetic – like a dog that had just peed on the carpet.

'You told him about . . . ?'

I nodded. 'He kept asking and asking about why we fell out, and I didn't know what else to say. I'm sorry.' I struggled to meet her eyes.

Sal shook her head slowly. 'You didn't know what else to say?! Come off it, Grace. You could have told him anything – you're the best liar I know. Jesus! I can't believe this!' She put her face in her hands.

'Hey, come on, it's not that bad. He's not going to *tell* anyone. But I still shouldn't have told him. I fucked up and I'm sorry. I'm really, really sorry.'

Sal didn't look angry or upset – more resigned than anything else. Resigned to the fact that her best friend couldn't be trusted.

'So . . . do you think you can forgive me for being a Class A idiot of the highest order? Honestly, I don't know why you put up with me!' My weak attempt at humour drew a scathing look from Sal.

'I don't know why I put up with you either.'

'Because me being such a loser makes you look good?' That managed to coax a small smile.

'Yeah, that must be it. Let's just forget about this, OK? Obviously I wish you hadn't told him, but it's done now. As long as you're sure he won't tell anyone? Especially Devon.'

Christ, I hadn't even *thought* about Devon. 'He won't tell anyone, I promise. And you have to know that you *can* trust me, even though it might not look that way right now.'

'But you still haven't told me why you argued. Why would you telling him about me . . . why would that start an argument? It doesn't make any sense.'

There was no point in lying now. The worst was surely over. 'He asked who you'd slept with and then wouldn't believe that I didn't know. And he kept asking, and I told him it was none of his business, and I suppose it just spiralled out of control from there.' I paused, wondering how far to go down this road. 'He thought you would have told me. And I think I got so angry with him because . . . well, I suppose I thought so too.'

'Oh, I get it. So somehow this is *my* fault now?'

'No no no, that's not what I meant at all. I was just trying to be honest with you. The only one to blame here is me.'

'But you're still pissed off about it, aren't you? About the fact that I didn't tell you.'

'No, not at all!' God, this telling-the-truth malarkey wasn't all it was cracked up to be. I continued, 'Well, maybe I'm a little bit hurt that you won't tell me. I just can't see what difference it makes.'

'Grace, you're just going to have to get over this. I can't keep having this conversation with you. I'm trying to forget about the whole thing, and do you know what would really, really help me do that?'

I looked at her expectantly. She laughed. 'Alcohol!' I laughed too, relieved that things were still fine between us – at least on the surface. Maybe there was something to be said for telling the truth after all.

I cracked open one of Mum's best bottles of wine, and over the next hour or so Sal listened to my Nat woes. She tried to reassure me that everything was going to be OK with him, that one little fight didn't necessarily mean that we were going to break up, that arguing was a perfectly normal thing for couples to do. Eventually I started to believe that maybe things weren't so bad after all. She persuaded me to text him an apology: 'I'm SO sorry about last night. I was an idiot – my fault completely. Ring me later? x'

I felt better as soon as I'd sent it, even though I didn't actually think it was my fault *completely*.

Ninety per cent maybe. The other ten per cent was down to Nat's general nosiness. But I was happy to take the blame if it meant he'd stay with me. He'd said he loved me, for Christ's sake. I wasn't just going to let him slip through my fingers.

He texted back about ten minutes later: 'OK. Am covering a shift at the pub tonight. Might not be able to call. Talk tomorrow. x'

It wasn't quite what I'd hoped for, but Sal seemed pretty positive about it when I showed her. She managed to convince me that he was probably distracted and busy at work, and that the only thing I needed to take any notice of was the kiss at the end of the message.

She poured me another glass of wine and stood up. 'How about some food to soak up the vino?'

The fridge revealed a few rashers of bacon, the sight of which was enough for Sal to convince me to create my legendary bacon, pasta and peas. It was her favourite.

Soon the pasta was boiling and the bacon was sizzling in the pan. Sal's phone rang in the living room. She must have got a new ringtone – some incredibly cheesy song from before we were even born. She picked up the phone and looked at the display to see if it was worth answering. She was almost as obsessive as I was about screening her calls. She didn't look particularly thrilled at what she saw. She turned and saw my quizzical look. 'Er . . . I've got to get this. OK if I take it upstairs?' I vaguely wondered who could be calling and why she didn't want me listening in, but I was distracted by the pasta, which was threatening to boil over.

Sal ran upstairs and I turned my attention back to the cooker. A minute or so later I was getting the plates out of the cupboard when I suddenly remembered. *My room*. I completely panicked: *Sal must not see the state of my room*. The plates clattered on to the work surface as I rushed out of the kitchen and scrambled up the stairs. *Please let her be in the bathroom or in Mum's room or in the hall or . . .*

She was standing just inside my room with her back to me. The phone was clasped to her ear. I heard her say in a quiet, weird voice, 'I'm going to have to call you later.' She snapped the phone shut.

'Sal, I . . .' I couldn't think of anything to say. I looked past her and saw that I hadn't done a very good job of covering the bed after all.

She turned slowly towards me, a look of horror on her face. Her voice was barely a whisper. 'What have you *done*?'

'OK, listen, it's not as bad as it looks. Just come

downstairs and we'll talk about it.' I reached out to try to take hold of her arm, but she shook me off.

'Jesus, Grace! Look at this!' She picked up my dressing gown and dropped it on the floor, revealing the worst of the bloodstains. It *did* look bad – even worse than I'd remembered.

'It's not as bad as it looks, honestly. I just . . . I was in a bit of a bad way last night.'

Sal shook her head slowly, surveying the scene.

'Sal? Say something. Please?'

Instead of speaking, she grabbed my sleeve and tried to pull it up my arm.

I pulled my arm away. 'What are you doing?! Stop it!'

'Show me.' Her voice was eerily calm.

I shook my head. 'Come on, let's just go downstairs.'

'I'm not going anywhere until you show me.'

'I'm not going to show you anything, so can we just leave it? Please.'

We stood in silence for a few moments, neither of us willing to budge.

'I want to see what you've done to yourself. Show me your arms. Now.' I'd never seen her like this before. It was scary.

I did as I was told and rolled up my sleeves. Sal

took each arm in turn and examined it for scars. There was nothing to see – nothing new at least. She looked confused.

I spoke quietly. 'My legs . . . I cut my legs.'

A look of pure disgust flickered across her face. 'What is *wrong* with you?'

'Look, it's no big deal. I can't help it – you know that.'

'But *this*? It looks like someone died here or something.'

I sat down on the edge of the bed. Sal stood there, unable to take her eyes off the scene before her. I was desperately trying to think of something to say – anything that would bring this conversation to an end.

'I couldn't stop myself. I just kept cutting.' Sal was still shaking her head; I was clearly going to have to do better than that. 'It made me feel better . . . I'm sorry.'

'*Sorry?!* Jesus, Grace, do you have any idea how wrong that sounds? How can cutting into your own flesh, making horrific scars all over your body . . . how can that possibly make you feel *better*?' Sal's voice got louder as she continued, 'Do you ever think about how *I* feel? I worry about you *all* the time.'

I was taken aback by her outburst. I thought we'd got over the whole cutting thing. It was just something

I did. As normal to me as brushing my teeth or filing my nails.

'There's no need to worry. I've got it under control.'

Sal snorted with derision. 'Yeah, course you have. Looks that way to me. This is the very picture of control.' She picked up a blood-spotted pillow and brought it so close to my face that I thought for a mad split second that she was going to try to smother me.

Now *I* was getting annoyed – my mood slowly but surely ratcheting up to meet hers. I grabbed the pillow out of her hands. 'Give it a rest, Sal. Sarcasm doesn't suit you.' She looked surprised. Clearly she hadn't expected me to talk back. She really should have known better.

She took a deep breath. 'Right, that's it. I have to go.'

'What? Why? Aw, come on! Don't be like that. I was only messing – sarcasm really suits you.' I attempted a smile.

'This isn't a joke, Grace. I'm going. I just don't know what to say to you right now.' She turned her back on me.

I jumped up from the bed and put myself between Sal and the door. 'Look, I'm sorry. Please don't go. Can't we talk about this?'

'I'm sorry too.' Sal shook her head as she neatly sidestepped me. 'But there's nothing else to talk about. You can't go on like this. You know that, don't you? If something happened to you, I'd never be able to forgive myself. Try to put yourself in my shoes . . . I've tried to understand . . . but this? This is too much for me to deal with right now.'

'Sal, I . . .'

'Just think about it. Promise me that,' she said, back to her usual, gentle self all of a sudden. I nodded. 'I'll call you tomorrow, OK?' She gently touched my shoulder, before leaving the room.

Another mute nod from me and then she was gone. The second time I'd been abandoned in the past twenty-four hours. I threw myself down on the bed and the tears came all too easily. After a minute or so the smoke alarm began to beep. *The bacon. Fuck.*

I lay in bed that night, under a fresh, over-starched duvet cover, mulling over the colossal pile of crap that my life had become. Trying to work out how (or if) I could make it all OK again.

Eventually I grabbed my phone from the bedside table and fired off two text messages in quick succession:

'I'm sorry. Things are going to change from now on – I promise. Love you.'

'I'm sorry (again!). I want to fix this. I love you.'

Subtly different, but basically the same message to the only two people I cared about.

I slept badly, my head a tangle of nightmares and dark thoughts. Every time I woke up, I checked my phone for messages, feeling more and more wretched. Finally, at about 3 a.m., I had to accept that neither of them was going to reply – at least not until morning. I tried not to think about what that might mean.

day 28

Ethan's skin feels cold and clammy. His skin looks paler too, with an almost blueish tinge. That can't be good. Last night I lay down beside him, pulling the duvet over us both. I lay my hand on his chest, so that I could feel it rise and fall, rise and fall, trying to reassure myself that everything would be OK as long as it kept doing just that.

This morning I woke up with my head resting where my hand had been the night before. His breathing hadn't changed. I got up and stretched. I feel . . . well, I feel good. Strong and vital. I haven't eaten for two days, but I'm not hungry. Not even a little bit. That can't be normal.

❧

I know what I have to do. I've never been so certain of anything.

I have to finish what I started.

I just hope there's time.

❧

Sal was as good as her word. She called at lunchtime and told me she hadn't got my message until that morning – something about turning her phone off cos she was so knackered. Our voices stumbled over one another's as we both tried to apologize. I promised not to cut again. I sat and watched myself in the mirror – watched myself lie to her. Sal was upset, even crying at one point. She kept on insisting that *she* was the one who should be apologizing. It was weird, but I figured she was just hormonal.

Nat didn't answer his phone the first couple of times I tried him. I didn't leave a message. I watched some crap on MTV, trying my best to concentrate on the trials and tribulations of some indistinguishable blonde chicks: Heidi/Lauren/Blah/Whoever.

After an hour, I took a deep breath and tried Nat again. One ring, two, three, four, five and then he answered. I couldn't tell much from his 'hello', apart from the fact that he seemed a bit out of breath.

'Hi, it's me.' Suddenly I had no idea what I wanted to say.

'Hi, you.'

I took heart from the fact that he hadn't hung up on me straight away. 'Can we meet up? I really need to talk to you.' Somehow I managed to refrain from begging.

'Grace, I . . . OK. Where do you want to meet?'

YES! There was still a chance, however slim it might be. We arranged to meet in a pub round the corner from the one where he worked. I chose to meet him there for three reasons: there was no danger of anyone we knew being there; it would be practically deserted at this time of day; and there would be alcohol.

I arrived early and ordered a vodka and Coke to settle my nerves. I tried to sip my drink in a nonchalant yeah-I'm-perfectly-happy-drinking-by-myself-in-the-middle-of-the-afternoon way. The barman looked over from time to time. It was sort of annoying. I crunched the ice cubes; the cold made my teeth tingle. I checked the time on my phone, again and again. Nat was late – nothing new there. It suddenly occurred to me that maybe he wouldn't show up. What if he'd changed his mind?

No. He wouldn't do that to me. He was different from all the others. And that's exactly why I loved him.

But there was something to be said for the simplicity of a meaningless relationship. You're far less likely to get hurt. You move on to the next one, memories already beginning to fade before you've even scrubbed away the smell of him in the shower. Apathy is the key. And so what if that apathy dooms the 'relationship' (if you can even call it that) to failure from the very start? Shrug your shoulders because you don't know any better – it's all you've ever known. It's all you're good for anyway.

I shook myself and checked the time AGAIN. God, I hoped Nat arrived soon. These thoughts were not helping. I downed the rest of my drink and quickly headed to the bar for another. I didn't want Nat to see that I was already on my second one. I settled myself back down and continued to watch the door.

It had started raining outside, and people were rushing past, shoulders hunched against the weather. A couple of guys in suits hurried by, trying in vain to shield their expensive haircuts with newspapers. The door opened and an old man in a tweed suit trundled in with a scruffy little dog at his feet. He left his huge rainbow-coloured golf umbrella by the door. The dog shook himself vigorously and water flew everywhere. It was cute, if you like that sort of thing.

I was so distracted by the dog that I didn't even notice Nat until he was halfway across the room. I gave him a little wave that made me feel stupid the moment I'd done it. He nodded, saw that I'd already got a drink, and detoured towards the bar. I watched him as he ordered his pint, smoothing back his damp hair, then nervously tapping his fingers on the bar. He'd ordered a Guinness, which took aaaaaaages. I just wanted to speak to him, to look in his eyes and get some kind of clue as to how this was going to go.

And then he was sitting in front of me, looking incredible.

'Hey.' A solid start from me, I thought.

'Hey.' Right back at me. Eye contact. *My heart hurts.*

'So . . .' I wasn't sure how to start. I really should have practised what I was going to say, but then maybe I'd have come across as being insincere. Nat said nothing and took a sip from his pint.

I tried again. 'I'm sorry. I'm so, so sorry.'

He nodded, but still said nothing.

'Nat, I hate myself for how I acted. There's no excuse. I get angry way too easily – always have. Just ask Sal.' I silently kicked myself for mentioning her. 'Do you think . . . maybe we could get past this?'

He looked at me for a few seconds. His eyes seemed more blue than ever, and that made me want to cry. 'Grace, I don't know—'

entangled

Something in his tone of voice scared me. It sounded detached, and somehow final. So I interrupted. 'I
can't lose you. Not now.' I could feel the tears getting
ready to flow, so I took a sip of vodka to try and distract them.

Nat shook his head. 'I don't know if this can work.'
He gazed into his Guinness as if it held all the answers.
A liquid Magic 8-Ball.

'It *can* work. It *is* working. Well, it was until the
other night. And I've said I'm sorry. I love you. You
know that, don't you?' The desperation in my voice
was painful.

He nodded, somewhat reluctantly. 'But maybe it'd
be better for both of us if we just . . .' He wouldn't
look at me.

'Just what?' Even though I knew full well what he
was trying to say.

'If we . . . ended things.' He looked up sheepishly
to gauge my reaction.

I took a deep breath and tried to concentrate extra
hard on the logo on Nat's T-shirt — anything to stop
the tears. Silence stretched out between us. A tear escaped and trickled down my face, tickling my cheek
in an especially irritating way, but I did nothing to halt
its progress. It dripped onto the table in front of me.
Stupid, disobedient tear.

'Grace, please don't cry.'

'I'm not crying!' *Yeah, right.* 'I don't understand why you're saying this. I love you, and I thought . . . well, you said you loved me. Did you even mean it?'

'It's not that simple.' Again with the sheepish look.

'I think it is. I don't want to lose you over this. Things were good. I mean, they were, weren't they?' He nodded, which gave me the tiny bit of encouragement I needed to carry on. 'Please give me another chance? Give *us* another chance.'

He was shaking his head again, so I let the full extent of my desperation show. 'I need you. I don't know how I'd cope . . .' It was true, but it felt wrong saying it – like it was cheating somehow.

Nat reached out for my hand. 'Shh, don't say that. You'd be better off without me.' His voice was soft and he looked troubled.

'How can I possibly be better off without you? I don't just go around telling random boys that I love them, you know. I've never felt this way about anyone, and it scares me. But I thought . . . I *think* we could have a future together. Don't you?'

'I don't want to hurt you.' He looked so unhappy, but I definitely detected the first hint of doubt in his voice. *Maybe this isn't a lost cause after all.*

'You think *this* isn't hurting me? I know this can work. Just give it a chance – that's all I'm asking for.' I reached out to hold his other hand. I wasn't going to let go. If I could hold on tight enough then maybe I wouldn't drown.

He sighed and looked deep into my eyes. I blinked away another round of tears and willed him to say the right thing. I hoped and wished and willed with every fibre of my being, praying that the positive vibes would flow through my fingertips from my body to his.

This was it. *Everything* rested on his next few words.

⌒

Ethan's getting colder, I think. I lay down next to him and tried to warm his body with mine. It didn't work. I fell asleep.

I dreamed we were back in the park, sitting on the swings. There was an empty gin bottle on the ground next to me. Ethan was swinging back and forth, back and forth. He looked all blurry and I couldn't work out why. Was I drunk? Or was he moving so fast I couldn't focus on him?

I heard his voice inside my head, but it sounded like my voice too. 'Keep going, Grace. You're so close.'

I woke up feeling sort of good. Sort of right.

❧

Nat said yes. He was willing to give it a go.

'Really?' I asked in a small voice. I didn't want to make any sudden movements or loud noises. Slow and quiet.

'Yes, let's do this.' He didn't look *entirely* convinced, but I was sure that was only temporary. I was going to prove to him that he'd made the right decision. *I will be the best girlfriend ever.*

'I do care about you, Grace. Never forget that.'

I brought his hand to my mouth and kissed it gently. 'I know you do.' I paused, considering my words carefully. 'Do you want to . . . do you want to come back to mine? Mum's not back till tomorrow.' All of a sudden I felt shy.

Nat shook his head. 'I can't – I have to get back to work. I'm only on my break.' He lifted our entwined hands from the table so he could look at his watch. 'In fact . . . I'm late as it is. I'm really sorry.'

'Don't worry about it – it's fine.' *Liar.*

He let go of my hands and downed the rest of his

drink. I did the same, just to mask my disappointment.
'Right, let's go. I'll walk with you.'

We left the pub in silence. It was still raining outside, so we ran round the corner to the pub where Nat
worked. We stood in the doorway, both of us slightly
damp. I tried not to think about how bad my hair must
look.

'I'll call you tomorrow. Got some lame family thing tonight.' He leaned down to kiss me, all too
swiftly. I wanted more. I put my hand to the back of
his neck and pulled him closer, but I still couldn't get
close enough. I wanted to take him home with me and
make things all better in the only way I knew how. But
it looked like I was going to have to wait.

Before I knew it I was standing alone in the doorway, feeling relieved and unsure and happy all at once.

The next day, I couldn't face waiting at home for Nat
to call, so I went round to Sal's for lunch. The added
bonus was that I wouldn't be home when Mum got
back from London. She always made a show of wanting
to spend quality time with me when she got back from
one of her trips. It never lasted. After about half an
hour in my company, she'd suddenly remember that
she needed to call Alison or Suzy or the hairdresser

or *anyone*. I swear to God she'd rather dial a random number and talk to a complete stranger than have to spend time with me.

Everything was nice and normal at Sal's house. Her mum folding the washing, Cam wandering around playing on his DS, getting in everyone's way and shouting, 'Die! Die!' every few minutes. But Sal was being weird. She was acting super-polite and kept making sure I had a drink and did I want any more salad? Anything for pudding, perhaps? It was disconcerting. It had always been a case of 'get it yourself' when we went to each other's houses, but she was acting as if I'd never so much as set foot there before.

I put it down to the fact that she felt awkward about the way she'd acted the other night. I thought we'd dealt with all that nonsense on the phone yesterday. I was half tempted to say something to put her at ease, but I was reluctant to bring up the subject again. Instead I did my best to act completely normal, hoping to reassure her that everything was OK between us.

After lunch, we headed up to her room. I lounged on the bed, while Sal connected her iPod to her stereo. We listened to music and talked about nothing important. It was nice just hanging out with her, and after a while she seemed to relax — as if she'd suddenly remembered that we were best friends and perhaps she could feel comfortable in my presence after all.

My phone rang and it made me jump. How had I managed to forget that I was expecting Nat to call? I'd hardly slept the night before, trying to work out how best to play things. I just wanted everything to get back to normal as quickly as possible. I wanted this 'hiccup' (I'd decided that's all it was) to be a distant memory, something Nat and I would maybe remember in years to come and laugh about how silly we'd been. I wanted that more than anything. But it couldn't even begin to happen until I was able to at least spend some time with him. I was so desperate to see him that I nearly pressed the disconnect button on my phone in my eagerness just to hear his voice.

But I was sorely disappointed. It was Mum, dammit. Why the fuck was she calling me? Maybe she'd discovered that I'd wrecked one of her best pans. Maybe she'd decided to cook some big meal to celebrate her homecoming? *Unlikely.* Then I realized that she was calling on her mobile.

'Grace, darling, it's me.'

'Hi.'

'Listen, I'm afraid I'm going to be staying down here a few more days. You'll never guess who I bumped into yesterday! Uncle Mick . . .you remember him, don't you? Of course you do! Your father's friend? Well, he's got a flat here – a penthouse, no less – and he said he'd love to have me stay for a few days. That way we can have a proper catch-up. I hope that's OK? It's so long since I've seen him – we have so much to talk about! Anyway, there's plenty of food in the freezer, and if you need anything else, there's money in the penguin jar.'

I could hardly get a word in. My mother was babbling like never before. It was painful. My end of the conversation consisted of words like 'yeah' and 'fine'. I did, however, manage to squeeze in a question about Uncle Mick's wife. Strangely enough, Mum didn't seem entirely comfortable with that particular subject. Messy divorce apparently, all very recent.

And then she couldn't get off the phone fast enough, which suited me just fine. I was pleased that I'd have the house to myself for a bit longer, especially as it coincided nicely with Operation: Making Things Normal with Nat.

Sal had pretty much got the gist of the conversation by listening to my half, but I filled her in on the rest.

She rolled her eyes. 'Your mum is ridiculous! I don't mean to be rude or anything, but I don't know how you put up with her sometimes.'

'What do you mean?'

'Well, doesn't it bother you that she's away *all* the time?'

'Are you kidding? I *love* it when she's away. It's the only time I get a bit of peace and quiet.'

'If you say so . . .' She didn't seem to be buying it, but she really should have known better. I'd never exactly hidden my feelings towards the woman who gave birth to me.

'Trust me – you'd feel exactly the same if you had a mother like mine. Your parents are so cool, you have no idea. You're so lucky.'

'I wouldn't go that far. But I suppose I'm glad they're around – well, most of the time anyway. Don't you get lonely, being in the house on your own?'

I gave this some thought. 'Not lonely, exactly. And certainly not lonely for her . . . if that makes any sense. It's not like I'm sitting there pining away, wishing we could make popcorn and watch *Beaches* or some such crap, or have a heart-to-heart and talk about boys. Ha! Just the thought of it . . .' I stared into space, struggling to picture the scene. It was no good. Even my overactive imagination couldn't pull that off.

'What about this "Uncle Mick" then? Do you think . . . ?'

I shrugged. 'I don't know what to think. I haven't seen him in years. Not since . . . not since the funeral.'

'Oh.' The mention of the funeral was Sal's signal to back off. Usually whenever the conversation strayed into 'Dad' territory, the subject would be changed as quickly as possible. But today was different . . .

'He was Dad's best friend at uni. Dad said the two of them were like peas in a pod – they did everything together. A bit like us two, I suppose. Mick and his wife used to come and stay with us for a week every summer. Can't think of her name. She was pretty and blonde and didn't smile much, that's all I remember. Mick was cool. He could always make me laugh, even when I was in the middle of a tantrum. Him and Dad were like some sort of comedy double act.'

'And you haven't seen him since . . . ? That's such a shame.'

'Yeah, it's weird. I'd completely forgotten about him until just then. I swear my memory's faulty. It's strange how someone can be such a big part of your life and then just . . . disappear.'

My phone rang and interrupted my thoughts. This time it was Nat. I picked up and gestured to Sal that I'd take the call out in the hall. Nat and I chatted about nothing for a bit, then arranged for him to come over at eight.

I lowered my voice. 'I've missed you . . .'

'But you only just saw me yesterday.'

'That's not quite what I meant . . . I want you,' I said as quietly as possible.

'Oh, riiiiight. I'm so dense – sorry. I've . . . er . . . missed you too.'

'Really?' I could have kicked myself. Why did I have to sound like a needy little girl?

'Yes, really. I'll see you later.'

'See you.' I disconnected the call, wondering if I should have added an 'I love you' at the end, but perhaps that would have been too much, too soon. I leaned against the wall for a moment and closed my eyes.

A little voice piped up, 'Who was that?'

I opened my eyes to find a pair of eyes peering up at me from the stairs below, hands grasping the banisters as if he was a prisoner down there.

'None of your business!'

'Was it your *boy*friend? Do you luuuuuurve him? Have you kissed him yet? With tongues?' He stuck his tongue out at me and wiggled it around.

I laughed. 'That's none of your business either! What do you know about kissing anyway? Have you got a girlfriend?'

'Urgh, no. Gross! I'm NEVER having a girlfriend! Never, ever, ever in a million years! Girls are worse than cabbage.' And with that made perfectly clear, he clattered back down the stairs.

I returned to Sal's room. 'Your brother is hilarious! And possibly gay.'

She was sending a text message at lightning speed. She pressed send and then looked up at me. 'I'll have to take your word for that. So . . . things are definitely back on with Nat then?'

I hadn't told her the whole story yet – I'd been sidetracked by Sal acting weird and then Mum calling. I quickly filled her in, recounting my conversation with Nat *almost* word for word. I made sure that I sounded slightly less pathetic than I'd actually been. There was no reason for Sal to know about all the tears.

'So . . . that's good then, isn't it?' She didn't sound sure.

'Er, *yeah* it's good! I really thought it was over.'

'Sounds like you did a pretty good job convincing him otherwise.'

Her words made me feel odd somehow. 'Well, I didn't force him or anything! I just reminded him what we had.'

'You really do love him, don't you?'

'Of course I do. Why? Didn't you believe me before?'

'I don't know what I believed. I suppose . . . well, it's all quite new, isn't it? You were always so scathing about love and relationships.'

I shrugged. 'What can I say? I was an idiot. I had no idea what I was talking about. People do change, you know. Why are you being weird about this? Aren't you happy for me?'

That seemed to shake her up a bit. 'Sorry, of *course* I'm happy for you. I just don't want you to get hurt, that's all.'

I softened somewhat. 'I'd be hurting a whole lot more if he'd dumped me.'

Sal merely nodded, still chewing at her fingertips. I noticed she'd drawn blood.

'Hey! Since when do you bite your nails? That's disgusting!'

She took her hand away from her mouth and looked at me all shifty. 'I don't bite my nails . . .'

'Yeah, right.' I looked at my watch. 'I'm going to have to head off, if that's OK? I need to sort the house out a bit before Nat comes round. And sort myself out – I look like shit.'

Sal sighed. 'You *never* look like shit, Grace.'

'Aw, thanks, honey, but you have to say that –

you're my best friend.' As I leaned over to give her a quick hug, her phone beeped with an incoming text message. She ignored it.

'Right, I'll call you tomorrow and give you all the gory details.' I winked at her.

Sal grimaced. 'You can keep the gory details to yourself. I'll take the PG-rated version.'

I laughed and skipped out of the room, feeling buoyed and positive about everything.

When I saw the state of the house, my positivity levelled out somewhat. I changed into my trackie bottoms and an old T-shirt and got to work, washing dishes, vacuuming, plumping cushions. Well, I plumped two cushions before I realized what I was doing. *Mum* plumps cushions; *I* do not. I took my bedding out of the tumble dryer and checked it carefully. It was as good as new, thank God, so I decided to change the sheets on my bed for the second time in two days. My spare set (tartan, if you can believe it) didn't exactly conjure up the mood I was aiming for.

By the time I was finished, the house was looking pretty damn good – as good as it ever could, anyway. I was exhausted, so I slumped down on the sofa and flicked on the TV. It was just before six, so there was plenty of time to get myself looking halfway decent – I just needed a little break first. I surfed the channels and eventually found *Friends*. I'd only seen that particular episode twice, so I settled down to chill out for the next twenty minutes or so. I told myself (and quite strictly too) that I was only allowed to watch this *one* episode, and that was it.

Next thing I knew, the doorbell was ringing. Shit. Shitshitshitshitshitshitshit. One look at the clock on the mantelpiece confirmed my worst fear: eight o'clock on the dot. He wasn't even late. *Why isn't he late? He's* always *late, dammit!* I sprang from the sofa and presented myself in front of the mirror. *Eeeeesh. Not good* at *all*. I wiped at the corner of my mouth to get rid of a tiny bit of drool. I let my hair down and flung my head forwards and backwards a few times. The result wasn't quite just-stepped-out-of-a-salon, more just-escaped-from-an-asylum. But it was going to have to do. It was too late to do anything about the clothes, but at least my trackie bottoms weren't harbouring any nasty stains. The T-shirt was way too small and my big toe stuck out of one of my mismatched socks. Oh well. I quickly sniffed my armpits, which didn't send me reeling in disgust. I smelled like nothing – no deodorant, no body lotion, no perfume, no nothing.

I opened the door to find Nat standing there, looking (and smelling) like it was our first date. He took one look at me and laughed.

'Wow! You look –' I cringed, not wanting to hear how he was going to finish that sentence – 'different!'

'I fell asleep after doing the housework and didn't have time to have a shower and get changed, and then you had to pick this *one* time to be on time. Tell you what – you help yourself to a drink while I run upstairs. I won't be a minute . . . just *stop* looking at me like that!'

He was still laughing. 'Grace, shut up and kiss me.' I had no choice but to obey. God, he was good at the kissing.

After a few minutes, he led me over to the sofa. He sat down and pulled me down next to him. 'Can I get you a drink, or something to eat?' He shook his head and moved his hand to tuck a bit of my unruly mane behind my ear. He stroked my cheek ever so gently with the back of his hand. He was looking at me strangely and it made my heart feel funny and jumpy. 'Well, can I at least put on some decent clothes? I feel all . . . icky. And you look all . . . not icky.' He shook his head, still saying nothing. 'Nat! Say something! You're being weird.'

Instead, he kissed me again. I melted. Finally, when

I'd practically forgotten my own name and decided that I wanted nothing more than to go on kissing him forever, he pulled away. 'You look amazing.' His sarcasm earned him a punch. 'Ouch . . . that hurt!'

'Liar!'

'Well, it *could* have hurt.' He pouted. 'It hurt my feelings anyway.'

'Yeah, yeah, whatever. If you keep taking the piss out of me, I'll punch you harder next time . . .'

He kissed me again before I could say anything more: a mightily effective shutting-up-Grace technique.

'I'm not taking the piss – trust me. I've never seen you look so beautiful. I mean it.'

'You're mental. Or is there something wrong with your eyes?' I waved my hand in front of him, inches from his face. 'Can you see this? How many fingers am I holding up?'

He grabbed my hand and held it in both of his. 'You look fresh . . . and young . . . and cute . . . and really . . . *really* . . . hot.' Each pause was punctuated by a kiss. I melted more. He actually seemed to mean it. And who was I to argue?

'Young? Not too young, I hope?'

Another kiss. 'Nah, don't worry . . . I think you're still legal.'

I sank back into the sofa. Nat followed, his lips never leaving mine. I could barely form a coherent thought, such was my blissed-out state. I was vaguely aware that this was going a *lot* better than I could have ever hoped. This was better than normal – better than *anything*, in fact.

And somewhere in my mind – my pink and fuzzy soft-focus mind – something clicked: the cuts. The fresh cuts. He could hardly miss them, could he? There were so many, and they looked so bad. Much, much worse than before. He wouldn't even want to *look* at me, let alone touch me. I silently cursed my stupidity: this reunion was going to be over before it began.

I don't know how, but Nat realized that something was up. He pulled away and looked at me intently. 'Are you OK?'

I paused – I knew that my answer was crucial.

The choice, as I saw it, was a simple one:

Carry on as if nothing was wrong, and hope that he wouldn't freak out when he saw what I'd done to myself.

OR . . .

Tell the truth, and probably scare him off for good.

Why do I keep doing this to myself? Will I never learn?

I manoeuvred my way out from underneath Nat and straightened out my T-shirt.

'What's the matter, Grace?' The concern in his eyes almost made me change my mind. Almost.

I covered my face with my hands, before whispering, 'There's something I have to tell you.'

'What is it? You can tell me anything. I don't want any more secrets between us.' He leaned forward and put his arm around my shoulders. It felt heavy and comforting, but I didn't want to be comforted — not yet.

I stood and turned to face him. I watched his face as I started to pull down my tracksuit bottoms. He raised his eyebrows and smiled at first, having obviously misunderstood my actions. And then his smile slipped away, and was replaced with . . . with what? I couldn't really tell. It certainly wasn't the full-on disgust I'd expected. I resisted the urge to pull up my trousers straight away, and tried not to think about the fact that I was wearing an old, greying pair of pants.

'Say something, Nat. Please say something.'

Nat's expression was unreadable as he knelt on the carpet in front of me and gently pulled my trackies back up. He reached for my hand, and looked up into my eyes. 'It's going to be OK.'

I blinked back tears and crumpled down to

meet him on the floor. He put his arms around me once again, and held me as I cried and cried and cried.

Eventually I sniffed and took a deep breath. 'Not looking so fresh and cute now, am I?'

He laughed and wiped away my tears. 'Hmm, perhaps not . . . I still *would* though.'

'Liar. But thanks anyway.' I leaned my head back against his chest.

'I'm not lying! Do you want me to prove it?' His hand crept towards the drawstring of my trackie bottoms.

I caught his wrist and held it fast against my stomach. 'Don't. How can you even *think* about having sex with a freak like me? I'm repulsive.'

'Don't say that.'

'Why not? It's true.'

'It's not, and I don't want you thinking like that. So you cut yourself sometimes? Big deal. I don't care.'

'*What?*'

'Look, we all have our ways of dealing with stuff when it gets too much for us. Your way just happens to be more . . . extreme than most. I hate that you feel you have to do this to yourself, and it makes me sad that you're going to have these scars long after you've realized that there are better ways of dealing with your feelings, but I *am not* repulsed by you. I thought you knew that.'

I had no idea how to respond. I didn't know what to think.

'Grace, look at me. If I thought I could do or say anything to make you stop, then I would. But that's not how it works.' He paused, and said more quietly, 'You did this after our fight on Saturday, didn't you?'

'I'm sorry. I didn't mean to. I was just so upset and I thought I'd lost you and I didn't know what to do.'

'Hey, hey . . . It's OK. I was upset too.'

'Yeah, but you didn't go home and start slicing yourself up, did you?'

He shook his head. 'Maybe not, but I did kick a wall really, really hard . . . I think I might even have broken a toe.'

I smiled. 'Really? That wasn't very clever, was it?!'

'I know. I felt like a right twat, hobbling home in the middle of the night. Anyway, what I'm trying to say is that we're going to have more arguments – I guarantee it.' I frowned at him. 'Come on, you know it's true. People argue, all the time, about the stupidest things. And we will too. But let's not leave things like that again. OK?' He acknowledged my nod, before continuing. 'Let's talk things through properly. And then maybe you won't . . . feel the need to hurt your-self.'

'You're right. I don't want that happening again. I can't promise anything though . . . about the cutting.'

'I'm not asking you to. I'm just saying let's both do our best to minimize the situations where you feel you have to do it. You have to *talk* to me when you're feeling like that. You can promise me that, can't you?'

He looked so earnest and sensible and utterly ador-able, I had no option other than to agree. 'I promise.' We kissed. 'You're pretty amazing, you know? I can't believe how cool you're being about this. I didn't ex-pect you to be so . . . calm.'

'Well, maybe I'll make a half-decent doctor after all, eh?' he said.

'I think you're going to be the best doctor in the whole world.' I kissed him again, harder, deeper. 'Doc-tor Scott has a nice ring to it, don't you think?'

'Why, thank you, Miss Carlyle. Hmm, I think you're running a bit of a temperature. I'm afraid I'm going to have to prescribe immediate bed rest,' he said in a stupid posh voice, accompanied by a wicked glint in his eye.

I burst out laughing and cuffed him round the head. '*That* was the cheesiest thing I have *ever* heard!'

'Hey! I thought that was some of my finest work!'

He clambered up off the floor and headed to the stairs, pulling off his T-shirt and chucking it back towards me. 'Well, *I'm* going to follow doctor's orders, even if you're not. You can do what you want: watch TV, file your nails, whatever.' His nonchalance was pretty convincing. Well, it would have been if he hadn't ruined the effect by giving me *that* look. The look that left me completely powerless and just . . . aching.

I followed.

He undressed me.

The cuts melted away with his touch.

I was a priceless china doll in his hands.

That was it. The return to normality I'd been hoping for. Except it was a new, better kind of normal. I vowed never to come that close to losing him again. I wouldn't allow it to happen.

And if I came to rely on him and need him a little bit *too* much, then where was the harm in that? The cuts on my legs started to heal. Every time I looked at them, I was reminded how lucky I was to still have Nat. I never got complacent, not even for one second. Nat meant everything to me.

❧

Mum came back from London. I'd kind of hoped she might stay there and just send me some money every month for food and stuff. But my fantasy came crashing down when I heard the click of the key in the door, and then, 'Grace, be a dear and help me with my bags.' It was always the same routine.

The bags were even more excessive than usual. The damage to her credit card must have been serious. *There goes my inheritance.*

'Now, put the kettle on and we can sit down and have a chat.' Jesus, this was worse than ever. But I did as I was told. It didn't pay to argue with a woman who was *that* good at shopping: she clearly always got what she wanted.

I hugged my mug to my chest, vaguely hoping that it would provide some kind of protection against the onslaught of chat.

'So, what have you been up to these past couple of days?'

'It's been over a week,' I muttered.

'Well, what have you been up to for the past week?' Her pretend patience scratched at my nerves.

I shrugged, getting into the role of moody little cow. 'Nothing.'

'Really, Grace?! You must have done something!'

Yeah, you're right. My boyfriend told me that he loved me and then we got into a massive fight. I cut myself so badly I thought the bleeding was never going to stop, and then I fell out with Sal cos she was so upset about it. Then I made up with my boyfriend and we had quite a lot of sex. Er . . . that's the edited version anyway.

God, it so was tempting – just to see the look on her face. This woman had no idea about my life. She didn't even care.

I sighed. 'I watched a bit of telly, went into town a couple of times. Sal came round.'

Mum nodded, already distracted, and clearly dying to tell me about her trip. I obliged grudgingly. 'How was London?' I knew she wouldn't even notice my entirely disinterested tone.

'Wonderful! I bought a fabulous pair of heels – you can borrow them some time if you like.' I said nothing. 'Anyway, Selfridges was *amazing*, as usual. I saw lots of things that would be perfect for you, but I didn't buy anything in case it didn't fit. Wouldn't it be lovely if they opened a branch near here and then we could go shopping together? Or . . . maybe . . . you could come with me next time I go to London. That would be fun, wouldn't it?' I couldn't think of anything worse, and I almost felt bad because she looked like she really believed that it *would* be fun. 'You know that dress I saw on the Internet? Well, it fitted me perfectly and it was on sale . . . and I couldn't say no. Aren't I naughty?!'

Dear God, what is she on about? I had to stop this before I threw my tea in her face.

'How was Mick?'

'You're so impatient, Grace! I was just getting to that.'

Things my mother told me about meeting up with Mick even though I wasn't in the slightest bit interested (but it was my fault for asking)

1. She bumped into him on Oxford Street of all places. (Her words, not mine.)
2. It was so lovely seeing him again after all these years. (Again, her words.)
3. He hadn't changed a bit.
4. He was doing very well for himself.
5. His penthouse had three bedrooms, each with an en-suite bathroom. (Big fucking deal.)
6. He took her to the Ivy. He's a regular there, apparently. Blah blah blah.
7. They stayed up late and *talked* for hours.

Way too much information.

'Why did you stay in his flat? Isn't that a bit . . . weird?'

'What an odd thing to say! Why would it be weird?'

'Well . . . you know . . . he's just got divorced, and you're . . .'

'I don't know what you're trying to imply, Grace Carlyle, but I can assure you, it was all completely above board. Mick is one of my oldest friends.' She pushed back her chair, went over to the sink and rinsed out her mug. She'd barely even touched her tea. It looked like our special mother–daughter time was coming to an end.

I got up to leave the kitchen, taking my tea with me. I was *so* close to making a clean getaway.

'Mick was asking after you. He said he'd really like to see you some time . . . if that's OK with you?' She sounded nervous.

I turned round, reluctant to continue the conversation. When it finally came, my answer surprised me almost as much as it surprised her. 'No.'

'What do you mean, "no"?'

'I don't want to see him.'

'Why ever not? Grace, you are acting *very* strangely. Are you all right?'

'I'm fine.'

'Then why don't you want to see Uncle Mick?'

'He's not my uncle. Don't call him that. I haven't seen him in years. Why the hell would I want to see him now? I can barely even remember him anyway,' I lied.

'But he was your dad's best friend! Surely that means something to you.'

'Then why haven't we seen him since the funeral? It's pretty obvious that he just wants to get in your pants now that he's divorced from what's-her-name!' I didn't know why I was acting like this. Maybe I just wanted to hurt her. I didn't need a particular reason for that.

'Grace! How dare you say that to me?!' She was shocked, but she didn't deny it, did she?

'Oh, whatever, Mum. You know it's true.'

'You apologize right now.' Her tone was threatening.

'I've got nothing to apologize for,' I said snottily. And I left her sitting there, surrounded by her shopping.

Back in my room, I wondered whether I might have overreacted ever so slightly. It was hard to tell. I was unsettled by the Mick thing. Why did he have to turn up now? Did they really just meet on the street, by accident? I couldn't escape from the awful, nagging feeling that Mum might have slept with him already. That was just too gross to think about, but I couldn't help myself. It would certainly help explain her overt niceness to me when she got back – talk about over-compensating. But why *him*? There were thousands of blokes out there that she could have gone for, so why did it have to be Dad's best friend? And why did it bother me so much? *Doesn't she deserve to be happy too?*

I spent the next few days avoiding Mum. I stayed at Sal's for a couple of nights. I didn't tell her what was up – there was no need. I was able to push Mum and Mick right to the back of my mind with all the cob-webs and other extraneous matter.

Everything else was good, and that was all that mattered. I concentrated on what was important: Nat. He was going back to university in three weeks' time. And I was going back to school next week. I fully intended to spend every possible minute with him before he left. I'd tried talking to him about how things would work between us when he was back at uni, but he'd just told me not to worry. Everything was going to be fine, apparently.

I was running out of time to put my Nat and Sal

plan into action. I was determined that they were going to be friends.

Nat had bought a couple of tickets for a gig near his university, and I thought it would be the perfect opportunity to throw Sal into the mix. We were hanging out in Nat's room a couple of days before the gig when I made my move.

'Why don't we invite Sal to the gig?'

Nat looked up sharply. 'Why?'

'She's my best friend, that's why! I thought it would be fun for us three to hang out, that's all. But if you don't want to . . .' I left the sentence hanging in the air.

'I thought it was going to be the two of us.'

'Aw, come on! It's just one night.' I scooted down onto the floor to lie next to him and started to massage the back of his neck. 'And I think Sal would really enjoy it. It'd be good for her to get out . . . She hasn't exactly had the easiest time of it this summer, has she?' I knew that would do the trick.

'Fine. Bring her along.'

'Are you sure? I don't *have* to.' *Disingenuous or what?*

He rolled his eyes. 'Are you always this good at getting what you want?'

I laughed and shrugged. 'Pretty much. I got you, didn't I?'

He thought for a second before answering. 'Yeah, I suppose you did.'

❦

One down, one to go.

'Sal . . . ?' In between bites of my Big Mac.

'Yeeeeeees?' She stretched out the word as far as it would go.

'What are you up to on Monday?'

'Hmm, let me think . . . Monday, you say? I'm going to have to check my *very* busy schedule, but I *think* I might be free. Well, as long as I get all my pencils sharpened for school on Tuesday.' She took a big slurp of her milkshake and looked at me expectantly.

'Good, cos you're coming out with me and Nat.'

Another slurp of milkshake. 'Now I'm pretty sure I'd remember if I'd arranged to do something like that.'

Sal was a slightly tougher nut to crack. It was obvious that she wasn't up for it, but I wore her down, countering every reason she gave for not coming with us. It was over in a matter of minutes.

Eventually she sighed. 'You're impossible when

you get like this! You're not going to take no for an answer, are you?'

I laughed. 'Ah, you know me so well! So that's settled then. You can come round to mine to get ready beforehand, and then we can meet Nat at the station. Maybe we should get a couple of cans to drink on the way? Shit . . . what am I gonna wear? What are you gonna wear? We'll have to make sure we look completely awesome. I bet there will be lots of fit boys there. Maybe you'll—'

'Grace . . .' The warning in her voice was clear.

'But—'

'But nothing! You'd better promise right now, or I'm not going.'

I sighed in melodramatic fashion. 'I promise. But I can't say the same for Nat – he might have a lonely, unbelievably gorgeous friend in mind for you.'

'He won't,' she said quietly.

'Nah, course he won't! All the friends *I've* heard him talk about are girls anyway, so the odds aren't in your favour.' I laughed. Sal did not.

When Sal arrived on Monday, my bed was buried underneath a mountain of clothes and I was standing there in my jeans and bra, hands on hips.

'What's up?'

'I have NOTHING to wear. Nothing! Not one thing! This is hopeless.'

'Calm down. You've got loads of clothes.'

'Yeah, but nothing's right!'

Sal started sorting through the pile I'd discarded, carefully folding things and putting them back in the wardrobe as she went. Before long she'd pulled out a black top and held it up against me. 'Yup, that's the one.'

'That? But it's so old! And so boring. Don't you think it's a bit too casual?'

'Nope. We're going to a proper studenty club, re-member? Dressing down is the only way to go.' She rummaged in the drawer of my dressing table and pulled out the purple necklace she'd given me a few months ago. 'Here. Try it with this.'

Of course she was right – as usual.

'Thank God you're here. You're a lifesaver!' I said, as I struggled to fasten the necklace in the mirror.

'Here, let me.'

I checked her out in the mirror as she concen-trated on the fastening. She was wearing a *lot* less make-up than I was, and her hair was in a simple ponytail, which made her look young and sort of innocent. I was slightly worried she might get ID'd, but knew better than to say anything now. She was wearing jeans and a black top too, but we could not have looked more different.

Nat was leaning against the railings at the station when we arrived. This 'being on time' thing was becoming a habit. He watched our approach and made a big show of checking his watch.

'What time do you call this?!'

'Yeah, yeah, you can blame Sal. She's almost as incapable of being on time as you are . . . well, were.' I kissed him.

Nat said hello to Sal and they shared an awkward hug. I was pleased they didn't shake hands or anything lame like that. The train was just pulling into the station, so we legged it over the footbridge and made it onto the train just in time. Sal sat opposite me and Nat, and we cracked open the beers Nat had brought. We chatted about this and that and the conversation flowed easily without too much effort from me. I was pleased that despite their initial lack of enthusiasm for the evening, they seemed to be enjoying each other's company.

'I like your necklace, Grace. Is it new?'

I beamed at Nat, and then at Sal. 'Nah, I've had it for a while. Sal bought it for me – she has impeccable taste, doesn't she?'

Nat nodded vaguely and was about to say something when Sal piped up with a change of subject. 'Grace told me that one of your friends works behind the bar at this place we're going. Will she be there tonight?'

Nat nodded and swigged his beer. 'Yeah, Anna will probably be working. We might get a couple of free drinks from her, if we're lucky.'

'So, what's Anna like? Is she on your course' I wanted to know what I was up against.

Nat shrugged. 'Yeah, she is. Unbelievably clever – she helped me out a lot with anatomy last year.'

'Anatomy?' I couldn't help but giggle.

'Grace . . . how old are you?' he chided.

'Sorry. So . . . does she have a boyfriend?'

Nat shook his head. 'Nah, she was seeing someone for a bit just before the holidays, but I think she dumped him. Anna isn't really into relationships – she thinks they're a waste of time.' *Hmm, don't like the sound of this one at all.* In fact, she sounded suspiciously like the Old Me.

'Is she pretty?' I just couldn't help myself. I glanced over to catch Sal's eye, but she was staring out of the window.

'Yeah, I suppose she is. My mates seem to think so

anyway.' Nat clearly hadn't been reading his How To Be
A Perfect Boyfriend handbook. Of course, the answer
I was looking for was something along the lines of: 'I
have no idea. Everyone pales into insignificance now
that I'm with you.'

'I'm looking forward to meeting her.'

'She'll probably be too busy to talk to us much, so
don't take it personally.'

The rest of the journey passed uneventfully. Nat
told us a bit about the bands that were playing. Sal
feigned interest even though they didn't sound like her
cup of tea at all. I reminded myself that the quality
of the music was irrelevant; tonight was about much
more than that.

On the walk from the station to the club I noticed
that Nat didn't hold my hand like he usually did when
we were out and about. I thought it was sweet that he
obviously didn't want Sal to feel left out. I resolved to
remember not to act too coupley. I was pretty sure I
could manage that for a few hours at least.

We had no problems getting into the club, and Nat
bought Sal's ticket, ignoring her protests. He insisted
that this was *his* treat. I patted his bum to show my
approval in the most subtle way possible, a gesture
he seemed not to notice. The club was a sweaty little
dive. The ceiling was low and every visible surface was

painted black. Old posters and flyers peeled from the walls. I liked it immediately. The tiny stage was empty for the time being, but the bar was heaving. Sal and I stood behind Nat as he gradually edged his way to the front of the queue. I took the opportunity to check that Sal was fine and dandy. She said that she'd feel a lot better when she'd got a drink in her hand, so it sounded like she was up for getting wasted. I approved wholeheartedly.

Nat waved at a girl behind the bar. As soon as she saw him, she squealed excitedly (I hated her already) and leaned right over the bar to hug him. *OK, you can let go now*. But she held on for a good few seconds too long. She called to another girl behind the bar to say she was taking her break. The other girl looked pissed off and gestured to the hordes of thirsty customers. Anna (at least I *assumed* that's who it was) skipped around the side of the bar without a backwards glance. And then she hugged Nat again, which I thought was entirely unnecessary.

Sal slipped into Nat's place in the queue and I heard her order three pints from pissed-off bar girl. So I was left standing awkwardly sort of behind Nat while Anna fired questions at him.

'Dude! Where have you been all summer? Why didn't you call to let me know you were coming? I could have got you in free. Is Si here too?' *Dude? Do real people actually talk like that? And who on earth is Si?* I was certain Nat hadn't mentioned him. I wasn't liking this one little bit. I took the opportunity to look Anna up and down. She *was* pretty, and obviously too cool for school. She wore a ring through her nose and another through her lip. Her features were even, and might have been unremarkable had it not been for her eyes, which were piercingly blue and twinkling at my boyfriend in a way I didn't feel completely comfortable with. Her hair was sort of short and streaky, and messy in that just-got-out-of-bed-but-not-really-this-has-taken-ages way. She wore a black T-shirt with the club's name on it and she'd cut off the sleeves and knotted it just under her breasts (which were bigger than mine). Her stomach was toned and flat, and her baggy jeans hung carelessly off her hips. A swirly bit of tattoo peeped above her waistband, and I didn't even want to think about where it might end.

'Anna! Shut up for a minute! This is Grace . . .' I abruptly halted my appraisal and returned my gaze to those laser eyes.

'Hi, Grace, I'm Anna. Nice to meet you.' she said, friendly enough.

'Hi, nice to meet you too.' We shook hands, and Anna looked at Nat with a question in her eyes.

'Grace and I have been going out for a couple of months.'

'*Really?* You mean this is your *girl*friend? Well, well, well! Then it's *doubly* nice to meet you.' Anna winked at me conspiratorially. 'Just between you and me, I thought he was never going to get a girlfriend. Well, there was that one chick he wouldn't shut up about, but that was a good few months ago now. God, I thought he was never going to get over her . . .'

'Sal! Over here.' I'd spotted her trying to elbow her way through the growing crowd, doing her best not to spill a drop of beer.

Anna started to say something, but Nat talked right over her to ask her whether she'd done the set reading for the summer. He was sort of a geek, but by the sound of her answer, Anna was too. He took one of the pints from Sal and thanked her, before turning away from us to continue his highly fascinating conversation with Anna. I appreciated not being bored to death with medical terms I didn't understand. And it gave me the chance to give Sal the lowdown on the situation, along with my thoughts on Anna. After a couple of minutes I noticed Anna looking over Nat's shoulder, scoping out me and Sal. I guessed their topic of conversation must have taken a turn towards more interesting things — like me.

Sal turned my attention towards the stage, where the first band was just about to start. A lot of people migrated towards the front, but we agreed to stay put. When they started playing, Sal and I looked at each other and burst out laughing. They were beyond terrible, but pretty entertaining to watch, if only because the lead singer was a shirtless boy with a very nice body.

A little while later, Anna and Nat drifted back towards us.

'Hi, you must be Sal.' Anna smiled broadly, and stuck out her hand for Sal to take.

Sal looked confused, but shook the proffered hand anyway. 'Yeah, er . . . hi.'

'Nat was just telling me about you. You're Grace's best friend?'

Sal nodded.

Anna sighed wistfully. 'I've never had a best friend – someone to share *everything* with. You two are so lucky.' *Man, this girl is a proper weirdo.*

Nat pushed his wrist in front of Anna's face and tapped his watch. 'Hadn't you better be getting back to work?'

I was surprised at his rudeness, but glad that he wanted to get rid of her just as much as I did.

Anna stuck her tongue out at him, then looked

back at me and Sal. 'Well, it was lovely to meet both of you ladies. I can see Nat's got his hands full with you two! Laters!' She lavished us with one final impish grin before disappearing into the crowd.

Sal shoved her drink into my hands, saying she was desperate for the toilet. I was bursting too, but before I could ask Nat to hold our drinks, Sal had bolted. I followed a couple of minutes later, after quizzing Nat about his weird friend. He'd merely shrugged and said, 'That's just Anna,' as if that explained everything.

Sal was washing her hands when I found her, staring vacantly into the mirror. 'Feeling better?' She flinched as if I'd crept up on her.

'What do you mean?'

'Just that you were desperate for the loo, remember?'

'Oh yeah. Much better.'

'Wait for me, will you?'

My chosen cubicle was disgusting, but the graffiti did a good job of distracting me. I was surprised people could be so creative in such adverse conditions. When I came out, I asked Sal what she thought of Anna, while I washed my hands with extra thoroughness.

'She's pretty.'

'Pretty weird, you mean?' I paused. 'Do you think she fancies Nat?'

Sal shrugged. 'How would *I* know?'

'I dunno. I bet she does though – I saw the way she looked at him.'

'Why do you even care? *You're* the one he's going out with.'

'I know, I know. It's just . . . she's all cool and pierced and . . . *older* than us.'

Sal looked at me like I was crazy. 'What's *that* got to do with anything?'

'I don't know! She just makes me feel like a stupid little schoolgirl. Like there's some big joke I'm not quite in on . . . you know?'

Sal shook her head. 'I think you're reading too much into it. Don't worry about it. Now let's get your paranoid head back out there. I don't know about you, but I fancy getting some shots in.'

I smiled. 'Now *that* is the best idea I've heard in ages.'

We linked arms and headed back into the fray. The number of people there seemed to have doubled in the short time we'd been gone. It took us a couple of minutes to find Nat, who'd managed to get a table in a reasonably quiet corner. We downed the rest of our drinks, and Nat headed off to the bar to get the shots. Sal and I had barely settled into our old routine of making up bizarre life stories for the people we were watching when Nat emerged from the thronging crowd. He brandished a tray laden with enough shots for a small army (well, a football team at least), and was looking mighty pleased with himself.

He sat down and carefully placed the tray in front of us. 'Check it out!'

'I take it you didn't pay for them?'

'A tenner for the lot.'

'Won't Anna get in trouble?' *I hope so.*

'Nah, she was pretty sly about it. She wouldn't care if she got fired anyway.' And then he sort of muttered, 'Plus, she owes me.'

'For what?'

He shrugged. 'I'm always buying her drinks when we're out.' *So he goes out with her a lot? We'll have to see about that.*

I doled out the shots. 'Right, let's drink.'

And so we did. I began to think that maybe Anna wasn't so bad after all. Anyone who supplied free drinks was OK with me . . . as long as she kept her hands off my boyfriend.

A few shots down the line, a new band started up. They were loud and brash, and actually tuneful.

I jumped up, somewhat unsteadily. 'I'm going to the front. Who's with me?'

Sal and Nat exchanged glances. Nat said, 'Maybe later,' at exactly the same time as Sal said, 'Not right now.'

'Man, how boring are you two? Fine, I'll see you in a bit.' I turned and weaved my way towards the stage. I wasn't in the least bit bothered about being on my own. The alcohol was flowing through my veins and I just wanted to jump up and down until I could jump no more. And it'd be good for Sal and Nat to have a chance to chat without me watching them like a hawk, willing them to like each other.

I managed to wheedle my way into the pack of people dancing and jostling in front of the stage. Calling it 'dancing' was stretching it a little bit: people were bouncing off each other, elbows flying everywhere. I threw myself into it with complete abandon, jumping around and sweating *a lot*. These guys were awesome. It felt as if the bass burrowed into the very core of me until I became part of the music itself. God, I was *properly* wasted.

After half an hour or so, I stopped jumping and dragged my fingers through my sweaty hair. I was dizzy and thirsty and elated. Time to head back to the others, after a quick trip to the toilets to check myself in the mirror. Amazingly, the eye make-up was still in place. Somehow it looked better than it had before – nicely smudged, like I wasn't trying so hard. My reflection stared back at me, slightly bedraggled, but alive and sparkly in a way I'd never noticed before. I smiled at the girl in the mirror; a real smile just for me and me alone. *Is this what happiness feels like?* I laughed and threw a scrunched-up paper towel, which hit my reflection on the nose.

As I approached our table, I saw Sal and Nat, their heads close together. He was saying something in her ear, and she was shaking her head vigorously. Her face had a stubborn set to it. Whatever they were talking about looked way too serious. I hoped he hadn't said anything to upset her.

'Hey, guys,' I had to almost shout.

Nat looked up guiltily, which made me sure he'd said something stupid to Sal. 'Hi.'

I sat down and picked a shot glass from the tray. They hadn't drunk many in my absence. Sal took one too and we downed them simultaneously.

'So . . . what were you two talking about?' I asked casually.

'Nothing much,' said Nat.

'Didn't look like nothing much to me! Tonight's

supposed to be fun, remember? No more serious debates, OK?' Nothing – not even burning curiosity about what they'd been talking about – was going to ruin my mood.

We drank another shot each, and I told them all about my 'spiritual' dancing experience. They laughed at me. We sat and drank more. Nat didn't seem the slightest bit interested in watching the bands, which seemed a little strange, considering he'd bought the tickets in the first place.

When Sal headed off to the toilets, I took the op-portunity to snuggle up to Nat. He smelled really good, and I didn't even feel self-conscious about the fact that I might not, after all the dancing. I kissed him, but he seemed a bit distracted.

'Are you OK?' I asked.

'Yeah, I'm fine. Are you having a good time?'

'I am . . . Are you?'

He nodded.

'What were you and Sal talking about before? She looked kind of upset.'

'Oh . . . nothing. Really.' My facial expression told him he was going to have to do better than that. 'All right, all right. I was teasing her about Devon.'

I smacked him on the arm, semi-playfully. 'You idiot! You *know* she's a bit funny about him. Just watch what you say – I really want her to have a good time tonight.'

'Sorry. Won't happen again. Promise.'

I laughed. 'Now, hurry up and kiss me before she gets back.'

The kiss was rudely interrupted by Sal stumbling into the table as she sat back down. I took one look at her and knew that something was wrong. She was pale and there was a sheen of sweat on her face.

'Sal? Are you OK?' I reached out and put my arm around her shoulder.

She shook her head slowly. I thought she might cry. 'I feel . . . sick. Grace, would you mind getting me a glass of water?' Her voice was weak and unsteady. I half stood, unsure whether I should do as she asked, or if it would be best to stay with her. I looked at Nat helplessly.

'Go. I'll look after her.' He scooted his stool round so he was sitting close to her. Reassured, I squeezed Sal's shoulder, before rushing in the direction of the bar. The timing was bad; seemingly everyone in the place had decided to get a drink while the next band set up their gear. It must have been a good five minutes before I got near enough the front to be able to catch Anna's attention.

She greeted my request for water with a questioning eyebrow. I explained that Sal wasn't feeling well.

'She obviously didn't appreciate Si's chat-up line.'

I asked her what she was on about.

'Simon? He's a mate of ours. Hmm . . . I take it you haven't had the pleasure yet? Hardly surprising, I guess – he's a bit of a sleaze. Nat would want to keep you as far away from him as possible! I saw him talking to your friend a couple of minutes ago, and she wasn't looking too happy about it.'

I tried not to let my confusion show. I hated being in the dark like this. 'Simon? Yeah, I think Nat's mentioned him. Which one's he? Can you point him out?'

She craned her neck to scan the crowd. 'I can't see him anywhere. He must have gone off to find another victim.'

I thanked Anna for the water and left the bar, trying my best to digest this new piece of information. How had this Si bloke managed to freak Sal out so badly? It didn't make any sense.

When I got back to the table, Nat was talking quietly to Sal, his hand resting on her back. As soon as I sat down, he got up and walked away. 'Back in a couple of minutes,' he said in a hard, tense voice. I nodded distractedly and turned my attention to Sal.

She gulped down some water before thanking me.

'Thanks, Grace. I feel much better now – not quite sure what came over me. Too much to drink, I guess.' A weak shadow of a smile.

'Who's Simon?' I asked.

Her eyes went wide and panicky. I continued, not wanting to upset her, but determined to get to the bottom of this. 'Anna said she saw you talking to some boy called Simon. A friend of Nat's?'

Sal said nothing.

'Sal? What's the matter? Did he hit on you? Is that why you're upset?' I tried my best not to sound like I thought that was kind of a ridiculous reason.

She nodded.

'What did he say that was so bad?'

'Nothing really.' She paused and looked around, like she was worried we might be overheard. 'I came out of the toilets feeling a bit dizzy and sick anyway, and then he was suddenly all over me – he wouldn't leave me alone, and I felt all claustrophobic . . . like I was about to have a panic attack or something. I swear I'm never drinking shots again.'

'Did you know he's a friend of Nat's?' She shook her head. 'I'm surprised Nat's friends with someone like that . . . Are you sure you're feeling OK now?'

'I still feel a bit dizzy. I think it might be best if I go home.'

'We'll go as soon as Nat gets back.'

'No, no, there's no need for you guys to come. I'll be fine.'

There was no way I was letting her go off by herself with Sleazy Simon on the loose. 'Don't be daft. We're coming.' I checked my watch. 'We wouldn't be able to stay much longer anyway – the last train's at midnight.'

Nat returned just as we were gathering our bags together. 'We're leaving – now.' He looked angry.

'I was just going to say the same thing! But what's up with you? What's happened?' I touched his arm.

'Nothing. Let's just go, OK?'

I wasn't going to argue. He was scaring me.

The three of us left the club with Nat in the middle, his arms guiding me and Sal in the right direction. No one said a word on the walk to the station.

On the train, Sal promptly closed her eyes and fell asleep. She must have been drunk after all – she *never* fell asleep on public transport.

I whispered to Nat, 'Now can you tell me what happened?'

He was calmer now, but he looked really, really

tired. He sighed deeply. 'Sal told me that Simon had been harassing her, so I went to have a word with him, that's all.'

'And this is a friend of yours?'

'Was. He *was* a friend of mine. Until I realized what kind of person he is.'

'What kind of person is he? Lots of guys come on to girls like that, don't they?'

'Not like Si does.' He glanced over at Sal and added quietly, 'He's not the sort of person you want Sal to be talking to.'

'There's more, isn't there? Why did we have to leave in such a hurry?'

He nodded. 'I . . . I hit him.'

'What?! Why the hell would you do something like that?' Nat had *never* struck me as the violent type. I could not have been more shocked.

He sort of mumbled, 'I don't know what came over me. I was just so . . . angry. And Sal was so upset . . .'

'God, Nat. I can't believe you did that!' I wasn't sure how I felt. Part of me was disgusted and shocked, definitely. But I have to admit that a little part of me was also sort of thrilled: he'd been a knight in shining armour, protecting Sal's honour. 'Did he try and hit you back?'

'No . . . he was sort of . . . sprawled on the floor. Which was why I thought we'd better make a quick exit.' He looked embarrassed.

I shook my head in wonder. 'I would never have imagined you doing something like that – ever.'

Nat stared out the window into the blackness.

'Me neither,' he said softly.

❧

We put Sal in a taxi at the station, and then Nat flagged one down for me. I kissed him goodbye and thanked him.

'Thanks? What are you thanking me for?'

I shrugged and kissed him again. 'I dunno. For being more than I deserve? For being all brave and strong and coming to Sal's rescue?'

He shook his head and stared at the ground, muttering something that sounded like, 'Stop taking the piss.'

'I'm not! Come here, you.' I hugged him and held on tight. I whispered to him as the taxi driver shouted about not hanging around all night. I remember the words all the more clearly because they make me feel so stupid now. They seem extra loud when I hear them in my head:

'I love you for always doing what's right.'

The next day was hard. As it turned out, the combination of being back at school and having a killer hangover was not a good one. I barely managed to make it through English without throwing up. The three-page reading list we were supposed to get through by the end of the year certainly didn't help. At least taking the train to see Nat would give me some much-needed reading time.

At lunchtime, Sal and I secured our usual table at the cafe round the corner from school. I ordered a bacon sandwich, and Sal ordered a salad – which made me snort with derision.

'A salad? Are you feeling OK?'

She shrugged. 'I just fancied something different, that's all.'

'If you say so . . . weirdo.'

Sal chucked a bit of lettuce at me. It hit my cheek and landed in my lap.

'Urgh. Keep that filthy green stuff away from me!' I threw it back in Sal's direction. I missed though – I always did throw like a girl. 'I need fat, fat and more fat today. This hangover is a bastard. Anyway, how come you're looking all bright-eyed and bushy-tailed? You drank just as much as I did . . . Oh my God, you'll never guess what Nat told me on the way home last night! He HIT that Simon fella! Properly punched him. Can you even believe it?'

Sal paused with a forkful of salad halfway between her plate and her mouth.

'*What?*'

'I *know*! It's weird, isn't it?'

'Why did he do that?' She returned the fork to the plate without taking a bite.

'I dunno! I suppose he was defending your honour or something. It's kind of sweet in a way, don't you think?'

Sal was shaking her head. 'I can't believe he did that.'

'Yeah, I thought it was maybe a bit extreme, but apparently that Si is a proper sleazebag. Bet he's had it coming for ages.'

'God. I never would have thought . . .'

'I *know*! He just doesn't seem like a "punching" type of guy, does he? It makes me think of him in a whole new light.'

Sal returned her attention to her salad as I continued to ramble on about how perfect Nat was, and how I'd been so sure that he was a nice boy who'd never harm a flea, and now, well, he was a bit more *dangerous*. And definitely a bit sexier too.

✦

The common room was too frantic, considering the fragile state of my head, so I ventured into the library after lunch. It was cool and calm and quiet and everything you'd want a library to be. Completely deserted too – just the librarian and me. She was reading *Glamour*, somewhat furtively. Not exactly the reading matter I would have expected from a librarian. I wondered if she was worried that the Library Inspector might come to call and make her hand back her Licence to Library. I settled at a table round the corner, leaving her in peace to discover this season's must-have trenchcoat or whatever.

I was halfway through the first chapter of *Emma* and beginning to remember just how much I despised Jane Austen when I suddenly felt that I was being watched. You know how you just *know*? Maybe the librarian had clocked me as Not a Regular Library Visitor and had decided to check I wasn't defacing the books or sticking chewing gum under the table. I turned around in my chair, but all I could see was books, books, books. I got up and peeked around the corner of a shelf. The librarian was still engrossed in her magazine, absently scratching her head. Huh. I sat back down and tried to get on with my reading. But that nagging feeling wouldn't go away.

A mammoth sneeze broke the silence and confirmed that I wasn't going crazy after all. I jumped up from my seat and headed in the phantom sneezer's direction, ready to tell off whichever snivelling little first year had been spying on me. And bumped smack bang into someone a lot taller than I'd been expecting. Devon.

He dropped his handkerchief and the book he'd been holding. *A handkerchief? In this day and age?* Maybe *he'd* been reading a little too much Jane Austen lately. He scrabbled on the floor to gather his stuff together before standing to face my somewhat puzzled expression.

'Grace . . . hi. How's it going?' He sneezed again, a little more stifled this time.

'Hi . . . and bless you! What are you doing hiding back here?'

His face flushed to match his ruby red nose. 'I wasn't. Hiding, I mean. I was looking for a book. Um . . . this one, in fact.' He held up a battered old copy of *To Kill a Mockingbird*, as if that proved he hadn't been acting shiftily.

I nodded. 'That's one of my favourites. I used to wish I was Scout. Even tried calling my dad "Atticus" for a while, before . . .' I abruptly shut my mouth. I was pretty sure I hadn't told anyone this before. Not that it was particularly interesting or shocking. But still, it was personal.

'Really? I didn't think it would be your kind of thing. I mean, not that there's any reason it shouldn't be. It's a great book, after all. It's just that I thought you were more . . .'

'More what? Mills and Boon? Jackie Collins?' I teased him.

'No, no, nothing like that. Er . . . I'm going to stop talking now.'

'You don't have to! Do you want to come and sit with me?' I'd gone and surprised myself again.

He seemed slightly taken aback at the invitation and I sensed he was about to say no, so I grabbed his arm and pulled him towards my table. 'Pleeeease? I'm bored. And surely it beats lurking around back there all by yourself?'

Devon muttered something as he reluctantly slumped into the chair opposite mine. It sounded like 'I wasn't lurking'.

And so there we were: me and my boyfriend's little brother. Hanging out. Sitting in the library, chatting. Well, semi-whispering actually. The initial awkward weirdness disappeared sooner than I would have expected. Slowly but surely Devon came out of his shell of shyness. He had a lot to say, which shouldn't have surprised me, but did. He agreed with me about Jane Austen, and hated both Brontës too. Our conversation was pretty much confined to books at first, but little by little we moved onto other subjects.

It turned out we felt the same about a lot of things. We talked about music and compared the worst songs on our iPods. He told me about a song he thought I'd like and we listened to it, our heads huddled together, one headphone each. Being so close, I couldn't help but notice that he smelled really, really good. The song was beautiful.

My hangover was forgotten. And if I wasn't mistaken, a slight flirtatiousness had crept into my voice, without me even noticing. He had a cute smile – a little bit crooked. I liked it.

The bell went, and I decided to skip history. Devon looked at his watch briefly but carried on talking. I wondered if he was missing a lesson too. He'd probably never missed one in his life.

We talked all afternoon and it felt like the most normal thing in the world. It had gone four o'clock by the time the librarian kicked us out. I packed my neglected copy of *Emma* into my bag. 'Well, I suppose I'd better get going. I said I'd meet Sal in town after school.' This was the first mention of either Sal or Nat. And the mere mention of her name seemed to break whatever spell we were under.

'Right, yeah, I'd better get home . . . things to do, you know . . . It was fun though – talking to you, I mean. You're different . . .' Every ounce of awkwardness was back – and then some.

I nodded, not altogether sure what to say to that. 'Yeah, well, thanks for this afternoon. You saved me from Death by Boredom.'

'Any time.' Devon smiled, but it was a slight, tight sort of smile. He looked me in the eyes for the longest time. I couldn't look away; I didn't want to look away. He was the first to break eye contact. He looked down and fiddled with the straps on his bag. If I hadn't seen his lips move, I'd have hardly believed what I heard next.

'What do you see in him?'

❧

I don't know what to think about Ethan.

He's fading.

I'm starting to give up hope.

Hope. I'm not even sure what I'm hoping for any more.

~

What do you see in him? The words were tinged with bitterness.

'What did you say?' I'd heard all too clearly, but I really didn't know how else to respond.

Devon looked at me, his expression unreadable. 'You heard me.'

'Yeah, I heard you. But what kind of question is *that*?'

'I'm curious.'

'Curious?'

He nodded, a little less sure of himself now. 'Yeah . . . I just wanted to know . . . Never mind. Forget I said anything.' He turned his attention to the noticeboard we were standing next to and started picking at one of the drawing pins with his fingernail. Back to Devon, Master of Awkwardness. But I hadn't imagined the bitterness in his voice, had I?

'Devon, I don't know what to tell you . . .'

'You don't have to tell me anything. Just forget it. Please.' He still wouldn't look at me.

'I don't mind, honestly.' I paused, not knowing what he wanted from me. 'Nat's not like anyone else I've been with.' *Cringe. I sound like a right slag.* 'He makes me feel good about myself. And I trust him.'

Devon looked up. 'Do you?' He asked the question ever so quietly.

I nodded.

'You . . . love him?' His eyes burned into mine. There was something beyond weird happening between us, and whatever it was made me hesitate before answering his question.

'Yes.'

He closed his eyes for just a second, but it was long enough for me to notice his long eyelashes, just like Nat's. 'He doesn't deserve you.' The words were barely more than a whisper.

And then he turned and bolted away down the corridor before I was able to process what he'd said.

~

What the fuck? What the hell is he on about? Why would he say that to me? I thought it was Sal he had a crush on, not me. I couldn't wait to see what she made of it all. I briefly wondered if Devon was just jealous that Nat had a girlfriend and he didn't. And then I felt mean for thinking that.

I hopped on a bus into town and texted Sal to say I was on my way. My phone buzzed straight away, and I was sure it was going to be Sal, making some sarky comment about me being the late one this time. But it was from a number I didn't recognize:

'Sorry about that. Pls don't tell anyone – I was out of order. Sorry. D'

I had no idea how he'd got my number. Maybe he'd nabbed it off Nat's phone? I wondered whether I should text him back, but since I couldn't think of anything to say I decided against it.

I mulled things over for the rest of the bus journey. The idea that Nat didn't deserve me was absurd. *I* was the one who didn't deserve *him*. Any idiot could see that. Well, any idiot who knew the truth, anyway. Clearly Devon had no idea what I was like. I was sort of pleased.

I'd really enjoyed hanging out with him that afternoon – even more than I was willing to admit to myself. But why did he have to go all weird and spoil things? It was annoying.

I was so immersed in my mulling that I very nearly missed my stop. I jumped out of my seat and semi-sprinted down the aisle, accidentally clouting some guy round the back of the head with my bag. He swore at me just as I was about to say sorry, so I kept my apology to myself. Served him right anyway – he had an unusually large head.

I ran from the bus stop to the shop where I was

meeting Sal. We always met in the same place when we were in town. It wasn't as if there was much choice – there were only about three half-decent shops. Sal wasn't waiting outside, so I headed inside. I was twenty minutes late, but that was pretty standard for Sal, so I knew she wouldn't have been waiting too long – if she was even there yet.

The shop was busy and it took me a while to find her. She was in the lingerie section, holding two bras and staring vacantly into space. She didn't notice me until I was right in front of her, waving my hand in front of her face.

'Oh, hi.'

'Hi, space cadet. What planet are you on right now? Hmm . . . Planet Va-va-voom, by the looks of those!' I gestured at the bras. They were lacy and black and nothing like the underwear Sal owned. Well, none that I'd seen.

'These? Er . . . yeah . . . I wasn't . . .' She started to put them back on the rail.

'But you totally *should*. At least get this one. Ooh . . . and get the knickers too . . . Here you go.' I held out the matching set and raised my eyebrows suggestively. The knickers were tiny.

Sal shook her head. 'I don't think so . . .'

I tutted. 'Well why were you even looking at them

then? That's *proper* pulling underwear. Hey, you weren't planning on going on the pull without me, were you? Cos that is just not on!'

'Don't be ridiculous. It's just . . . I'd already looked at everything else in the shop about four times, cos you're so bloody late. I'm not buying them . . . I mean, they're not really *me*, are they?' She looked so embarrassed I wanted to hug her.

'OK, fair enough. Sorry I'm late, but I've got a really good reason. You won't *believe* it! But first things first, you should *absolutely* buy this underwear. Even if you don't want to wear it now, you'll be thanking me when Mr Fabulous comes knocking on your door. Trust me on this one.'

Sal shook her head again, but I could tell her resistance was flagging.

'You know I'm right. Every girl should have some kick-ass underwear at the back of her knicker drawer – just for special occasions . . . And you never know when that special occasion might be. Do it. By the power vested in me as bestest friend ever, I ORDER you to buy these.'

Sal rolled her eyes, grabbed the hangers from me and headed off to the cash desk. *Result.*

We left the shop, after a lot of muttering from Sal about not really being able to afford her purchases.

'Soooo . . . aren't you going to ask me why I was late?'

Sal obliged. 'Why were you late then?'

'Ah, all in good time, my dear. I reckon this kind of gossip definitely calls for a drink. What do you say? Might help the hangover – hair of the dog?'

Sal wasn't sure. She looked at her watch and ummed and ahhed a bit.

'Come on . . . you know you want to. We can celebrate your first foray into ooh-la-la lingerie.' That comment got the withering look it deserved, so I tried one last avenue of attack. 'I'm buying?' That clinched it.

&

A few minutes later we were settled on a sofa in a bar I'd never been to before. I slipped off my shoes and tucked my feet underneath me, took a sip from my stupidly big glass of red wine and relished the moment. There was nothing quite like having a sweet morsel of gossip to impart. I could tell Sal's patience was wearing thin, but that just made it more fun for me.

When I couldn't bear it any longer, I launched

into the story. 'Guess who's got a secret admirer?'
A sufficiently intriguing start.

Sal listened quietly as I told my tale, occasionally
interrupting with the odd comment or two, such as,
'But you've always thought Devon was a loser, haven't
you?' *Fair point.*

I was nearly one hundred per cent honest about
everything that had gone on. And if I happened to omit
the fact that I'd been kind of flirting with him, then who
could blame me? I hadn't quite come to terms with the
idea that I was finding Nat's little brother more attractive the more I got to know him. *Eurgh.* It was just plain
wrong. Anyway, I was pretty sure the feelings would go
away if I ignored them for long enough . . .

When I eventually got to the good bit, Sal's reaction didn't disappoint.

'He said *what?*'

'I know! Hysterical, isn't it? It was like something
out of a cheesy soap. *"He doesn't deserve you!"* I almost
laughed in his face!' Not strictly true.

'Why would he say something like that? What's it
got to do with him?' Sal's annoyance was clear.

'I dunno. I guess—'

'It's none of his business! Why can't he keep his
nose out of it? It's pathetic.'

'All right, calm down.' I laughed. I hadn't expected

Sal to get quite so cross about it. Well, I hadn't expected her to get cross *at all*, actually. 'No need to get your knickers in a twist. Oooh . . . speaking of knickers . . . let's have a look at what you bought. I desperately need some new underwear. Now that Nat's off back to uni I've got to make sure I keep things . . . interesting, y'know? Don't want him getting distracted by any skanky student girls – like that weird Anna girl.'

It was a lame attempt to change the subject, and Sal was having none of it. 'What else did he say?'

I shrugged. 'Nothing really. He pretty much scarpered before I could say anything back to him. He did text and apologize though.'

'What is he playing at?' She leaned back into the sofa and sighed.

'Er . . . it's pretty obvious, isn't it?'

Sal looked confused.

'Duh. He fancies me, doesn't he? Little Devon's got a crush!' I shushed the little voice inside my head – the one that was calling me a bitch.

'A crush? On *you*?'

'Of course! It's so obvious. Why else would he be all weird and jealous of Nat? Asking me if I loved him and all that!'

Sal nodded slowly. 'Maybe you're right.'

'Well, I can't think of any other reason he'd be so weird. Can you?'

She was biting her nails again. Suddenly I felt bad.

'Hey, are you OK about this?'

'About what?'

'Well . . . I know Devon's always worshipped the ground you walk on. I'm sure he'll be over me and back to following you around in no time. It's just cos I'm with Nat – that's the only reason, I'm sure of it.'

'Whoa there, Grace. Are you . . . ? You think I'm jealous, don't you? You actually think I'm *jealous*!'

I shrugged. 'Not jealous exactly . . . I mean, I know you're not interested in him. It's just that it's nice to be wanted, isn't it? Even if you don't want that person back – it's sort of flattering.' I couldn't seem to think of the right words – the words that would make Sal not be annoyed with me.

'You are unbelievable! You know that, don't you?'

'What?! What did I say? I'm sorry, OK? It's not my fault that two boys like me and . . .' I stopped myself short. Just in time – I hoped.

'And what? And no one's interested in me? That's what you think, isn't it?'

'No, not at all. I never said that! Look, let's talk about something else. I'm sorry. I didn't mean to upset you.' But I wasn't sorry. Not really. I had no clue why this harmless bit of gossip had suddenly turned into something sinister.

She sighed and closed her eyes for a moment. 'It's OK, Grace. I'm sorry I overreacted. I think I'm just tired after last night.'

I put my arm around her and pulled her towards me. 'Hey, that's OK. Let's forget about boys for a bit, eh? Sometimes I feel that all I ever talk about or think about is Nat, or something vaguely Nat-related. And that can't be healthy, can it? What's happened to me, eh?'

Sal leaned her head towards mine. 'Maybe that's what happens when you love someone. You really love him, don't you?' she asked quietly.

'I do. It scares me, Sal. It really scares me. What if I lose him? Sooner or later he's bound to realize what I'm like. He could do so much better. Why can't he see it?'

'Don't say that. You're a good person. He's . . . lucky to have you.'

'Do you really mean that?' I felt small and pathetic, needing reassurance, needing someone to tell me that I was OK after all. Not a freak. Not a bitch. Not a slag.

Sal turned to face me. She looked as if she was ready to cry, but her voice was steady. 'Of course I mean it. You *deserve* Nat. And he deserves you . . .

You two are right for each other. Anyone can see that.'

I felt a rush of affection and hugged her. 'Thank you. That means a lot. You always know the right thing to say. Sometimes I wish I was more like you, you know.' I'd never voiced this thought before. Possibly because it was ultra lame.

Sal snored with derision. 'Yeah, right, course you do.'

'It's true. I don't know – it's like you're my moral compass or something . . . You always do the right thing. And I *try* to do the right thing, I really do. But it always seems to get fucked up somehow, and there's no one to blame for that but me.'

Sal's eyes searched mine. 'Don't say things like that. It's not true. I like you just the way you are.' She squeezed my hand.

'Thanks, honey. You are the awesomest best friend I could ever have wished for.'

Sal shook her head dismissively. She never was comfortable with getting a compliment. It was one of the things I admired about her. I was all too ready to gobble up any praise anyone deigned to throw my way.

We stayed in the bar till closing time. Sal hadn't really wanted to, but I'd managed to convince her it was the right thing to do. It was fun. Fun like the old days fun. We talked about things that we used to talk about — before all the drama.

Later, I waited with Sal at the bus stop. When the bus eventually arrived, she stumbled onto it, but not before slurring a question in my direction. 'Why do I let you talk me into these things?'

'Because you LOVE me, and I know what's best for you!' I half shouted, half sang back at her. People on the bus looked at me weirdly, so I treated them to a little bow as the bus pulled away.

I looked at my watch and pondered for a second. Nat was working the late shift. He'd be locking up right about now. I smiled to myself, and reached out to hail a taxi.

It started raining almost as soon as I got in the cab. The motion of the windscreen wipers and the sultry tones of late-night love songs on the radio lulled me into a semi-doze.

'Oi! Sweetheart!' The cabbie's tone made it clear this wasn't his first attempt at waking me up. 'We're here! If here's where you want to be. Looks like you've missed last orders. Sure you don't want me to take you home? A pretty little thing like you shouldn't be wandering around on her own this time of night.'

I tried to remember where I was and why. 'Eh? No, that's OK. I'm meeting my boyfriend.' I still got a kick out of calling Nat my boyfriend. *Saddo.*

'Well, if you're sure . . .' He seemed strangely concerned about my well-being. It was disconcerting. I paid the fare, told him to keep the change and got out of the taxi as quickly as possible.

'You take care, y'hear?' He leaned out of the open window and gave me a meaningful look.

'Er . . . yeah . . . will do.' *Weirdo.* He drove off and I stood in the rain. It was serious, proper rain – no messing. I looked up to the sky and let the water hit my face. It felt good. I didn't think of the havoc it must be playing with my hair and make-up; I was totally focused on the fact that I'd never really noticed how brilliant rain was. Why were we always trying to shelter from it when it could make you feel so good? OK, I admit it, I was not entirely sober.

After a minute or two getting soaked to the skin, I turned my attention to the task at hand – Operation: Get Naked with Nat. The 'closed' sign was hanging on the back of the door, and the pub was mostly in darkness. I was worried I might be too late, but as I stepped closer to the window, I saw movement inside. I cupped my hands around my eyes so I could see better. And there he was, the object of my late-night lust. He was wiping down the pumps, ever the conscientious employee. But he was speaking to someone on his mobile at the same time – so maybe not *that* conscientious. I watched as he smiled that beautiful smile. God, he was hot.

He put the cloth down and leaned against the bar, clearly engrossed in his conversation. I was going to knock on the window, but something made me stop. I didn't want to interrupt him. It didn't seem right; I could wait. Plus, it was nice just watching him – seeing him *be* Nat. Maybe a slightly different Nat to the one I knew. It struck me that there would always be a part of him that didn't (and shouldn't) belong to me. It's all too easy to think that the people you care about go into some kind of suspended animation when you're not around. That they only truly come to life when they're with you, and don't really exist without you. I mean, you *know* that's not true (you're not stupid, after all), but that *other* part of their life is kind of irrelevant – to you at least. But watching Nat, I felt differently. He was a one hundred per cent real person, even without me. And that made me happy.

It was maybe five minutes later that he hung up. He looked at the phone for a moment or two, tossed it in the air and then slipped it into his back pocket. Still he stayed leaning against the bar, staring into space.

I knocked on the window.

He jumped, which made me laugh. Maybe he thought I was some drunk, ready to batter down the door to get a pint after last orders. Or maybe he was a bit of a wimp, scared to be alone in the pub on a dark and stormy night. Or maybe he was just daydreaming about me.

I squished my nose up against the glass as he came over to unlock the door.

'Grace, what are you doing here?'

Huh. Not quite Grace-what-an-awesome-surprise-come-here-and-let-me-ravish-you-right-this-second.

'I wanted to see you.' I banged my elbow against the door frame as I passed it. *Ouch*.

'You could have called to let me know you were coming.' He kissed me. A fleeting, cursory sort of kiss.

'What? Can't a girl surprise her very brave and slightly dangerous boyfriend any more? What *is* the world coming to?' I was more drunk than I'd thought.

'You're wasted, aren't you?' He turned away from me and started putting chairs up on the tables.

'Maybe a leeeetle bit,' I held my thumb and fore-finger together to indicate just how little. 'Sal and I needed to ease our way through our hangovers. How are you feeling anyway, after all the drama last night?' I went to him and put my arms around his waist.

He shrugged. 'It was nothing.'

'I'd hardly call decking someone "nothing" . . . you know, it's actually kind of sexy.' I tried to look all se-ductive, but judging by the expression on Nat's face I'd got it a bit wrong.

'What are you on about? There's nothing "sexy" about it. I shouldn't have done it.' He wouldn't look at me.

'Why did you, then? All that guy did was hit on Sal . . . not exactly the crime of the century, is it?' Saying the words made me actually appreciate how strange a thing it had been for Nat to do.

'She was upset.' His voice was quiet and dark.

'She overreacted, is what I think.' Another realiza-tion. Something wasn't quite right.

'You don't know what you're . . .' He stopped himself, then started again. 'Look, Si's a wanker of the highest order and I wouldn't put anything past him. Can we just forget about the whole thing? Please?'

He put his arms around me and I nodded into his shoulder, but something really wasn't right. We were two mismatched pieces of a jigsaw puzzle. He smelled of work and sweat. Sort of sour, actually.

I pulled away from him. 'I should get going. I feel a bit sick.'

'But you've only just got here . . .' He leaned down and nuzzled at my neck. His breath was too hot.

'It's really late, and I've got school tomorrow.' Again I pulled away.

Nat smirked. 'Okaaaay, if you say so . . . but we've got the place to ourselves . . .' He patted the bar. 'What do you say? Ever done it on a bar before?' He laughed and it sounded wrongwrongwrong in my ears.

'No.' And his smile disappeared. *What's wrong with me? Why don't I want to?*

'What's up with you? That's why you came here, isn't it? I *know* you, Grace. Come on . . . it'll be fun.' He pinned me up against the bar and kissed me hard. I relaxed into it, knowing that this was the one way to silence the voice that was whispering to me, telling me something was wrong. I did my best to ignore the voice: how could I trust it when I didn't know who it belonged to? I was with Nat, and that was all that mattered. Wasn't it?

Nat's breathing was loud and urgent and his mouth tasted different to me. I was kissing a stranger. And the stranger was unbuttoning my jeans.

I pushed him off me. 'No!' The word came out louder than I'd intended. Nat was shocked, and I couldn't blame him. This had never happened before.

I softened my voice and tried to pretend that I was still me and Nat was still Nat, and I was just tired and drunk and everything would be OK in the morning. 'I'm sorry. I really have to go. I'm way too drunk for this.'

He said nothing for a moment, ego clearly bruised. Then he seemed to shrug it off in a heartbeat. 'Fair enough. The bar's still pretty skanky anyway . . . wouldn't want you sticking to it, would we?' He smiled and he wasn't a stranger any more. 'Let me call you a cab. My treat.'

We waited for the cab and he carried on clearing up as if nothing had happened. And we chatted as if nothing had happened. After all, nothing *had* happened. Had it?

I texted Nat when I got home: 'Sorry about tonight. Love you. x'

Got a message straight back: 'No worries. x'

I was in a pretty foul mood for the next couple of days. People at school seemed to sense it and mostly kept out of my way. Sal tried to find out what was up, but *I* wasn't even sure, and I couldn't even summon up the energy to talk about it.

In the evenings I stayed holed up in my room, not doing much of anything. I talked to Nat a couple of times and everything seemed fine. I wanted to see him so badly, but he had some random aunt visiting and he was expected to show her round town and keep her entertained. I wasn't quite sure why his mum couldn't do that, or Devon for that matter. But apparently he was her favourite nephew – no surprise there. Everyone loved Nat. He was golden.

By the time Friday came along, it felt like I hadn't seen him for ages. It had been three days. Random auntie had a lot to answer for. Nat and I were planning to hang out on Sunday, so I just had to somehow survive one more day at school and one day at home. Not sure which was worse. Sal and I went out for lunch. Fish and chips on a Friday was the best way to start the weekend.

'Urgh, I'm so glad this week is over. I can't WAIT for the weekend.'

Sal nodded. 'Me neither.'

'What are you up to anyway? Fancy doing something tomorrow? I could really do with getting out of the house. I can't handle being around Mum at the moment – she's driving me loopy.'

'Sorry, can't tomorrow, I'm afraid. Family day.'

'*Family* day? Since when do you have family days? I thought every day was a family day chez Stewart?'

'Yeah, I know it's lame. But Dad's decided we're going on some kind of day trip.'

'Christ. Nightmare.' But I was actually thinking it sounded sort of nice. That's the kind of thing dads are good at, I guess. Planning stuff. Looking at maps and brochures for stately homes or something. 'What is it with families at the moment? They're everywhere, ruining my plans. Nat's got his aunt monopolizing every minute of his time, and your dad's scuppered my Saturday! How inconsiderate!'

Sal smiled. 'Sorry, I'd get out of it if I could. You know how annoying Cam gets on car journeys – not exactly my idea of a fun day out. Tell you what – why don't we do something on Sunday?'

'No can do, sorry. I'm seeing Nat for the first time in forever. Well, first time since Tuesday anyway.'

'No worries.' Sal shrugged, but I could tell she was a bit pissed off. We usually spent at least one weekend day together, if not both.

'But maybe the three of us could do something?'

I offered – pretty generously, I thought. *Please say no please say no please say no. I want him all to myself.*

She must have read my mind. 'Nah, you're all right, thanks.'

I was relieved, and I immediately felt ashamed for feeling *quite* so relieved. But Nat and I needed some alone time. Hopefully this time both of us would stick to the script. I certainly planned to, anyway.

I decided to go for a wander after lunch to walk off some of the fish and chips. Free periods were the only thing that made school tolerable. Sal had a free period too, but said she had to get a book back from Devon. I meandered down the side of the playing field, trailing behind some shiny new first years embarking on their first ever cross-country run. I never did understand exactly why we were expected to parade around outside the school grounds in nothing more than a T-shirt and some tiny gym knickers. Ritual humiliation, I suppose. It was enough to put you off sport for life, but somehow I'd managed to get through it and now I loved running more than anything. Not that you'd have guessed it though – I hadn't been running in ages. Maybe that explained my mood.

I was half-tempted to run after the first years but a) I wasn't exactly dressed for it (biker boots and teeny-tiny skirt), and b) it would be a weird thing to do, even for me. So I watched them run and stumble and meander into the woods ahead of me.

And then the herd of runners was out of earshot and I was utterly alone. It was peaceful. I found a comfy-looking tree stump and perched on it like a gnome. I got out my notebook and chewed on the end of a pencil. For the first time in months I felt like writing something – I just wasn't sure what.

Writing and running. Two of my very favourite things. It struck me that I hadn't done much of either since I'd met Nat, and that made me feel sad. Like I'd lost a little part of myself. Or given it away. These were the things that defined me, or at least I used to think they did. But how important could they be if I was willing to drop them as soon as I got a boyfriend? What else would I be willing to give up for him?

Before I could think of something to write, my phone rang, scaring the life out of me and making me drop my pencil. The cheery ringtone sounded all wrong in the silence of the woods. I didn't recognize the number and nearly didn't answer it, but curiosity got the better of me.

'Grace? Er . . . hi, it's me. Er . . . Devon, that is.' He sounded unprepared, as if I was the one who'd called him, instead of the other way round.

'Hi, how's it going?'

'Yeah, fine. I mean, not exactly fine. Um . . . look, where are you?'

'In the woods behind school. Why? Is Sal with you?'

'No, er . . . no. She's not here.'

'I thought she was meeting you in the library after lunch.'

'Can I come and meet you? I really need to talk to you.' He sounded like he was on some sort of covert mission, scared of being discovered by the enemy at any moment. He really *was* an odd one.

'Look, if this is about Nat and that crap about him not being good enough for me, then I don't want to hear it. And how did you get my number anyway? I was wondering after you texted the other day.'

'I . . . got it off Nat's phone.'

'I don't reckon he'd be too happy about that – do you?'

'Who fucking cares what he thinks?!' I'd never heard him swear before and it sounded wrong. 'Grace, you *have* to listen to me. He's—'

'No, I really don't.' I talked over him, but I definitely heard the words 'messing you around'. Now I was cross. 'I could do without you putting ideas in my head. It's really none of your business, but if you must know, everything's just fine between me and

Nat. And it'd be even more fine if you'd keep out of it. I won't have anyone ruining this for me, OK? I'm going to talk to Nat as soon as your aunt's gone. I think he has a right to know what his little brother's up to behind his back.' I left it at that, feeling better for venting my feelings. Sure that I was in the right. Until . . .

'*Aunt?* What aunt? What are you talking about?'

I went to the bathroom to splash my face. When I was drying my hands I noticed something was different. Something impossible.

My scars have gone. Every single one of them. This cannot be real. I checked out my thighs, just to be sure. Not one scar, just milky smooth skin. It is real.

And somehow I knew what had happened. I didn't know how I knew, but I *knew*.

I went to Ethan and lifted the covers I'd wrapped around him.

His arms are criss-crossed with silvery lines. My scars.

Two of the scars are different from the rest. Thick rusty red scabs running up the inside of each wrist. They have yet to heal.

The other scars are as familiar to me as my own

reflection. But these two . . . they're different. They're new.

~

Ethan's breathing is slowing, I think.

I wish there was something I could do.

~

'*Aunt*? What aunt? What are you talking about?'

I disconnected the call. He called straight back, so I turned off my phone. I retrieved my pencil from the forest floor and wrote a single word in my notebook:

LIES

I underlined it three times, pressing harder and harder on the paper. *Lies.* Unless Devon was spectacularly unobservant and simply hadn't noticed a middle-aged woman roaming round his house over the past few days. Unless Devon was staying at his dad's house at the moment. *Unless . . . unless . . . unless nothing.*

Nat had lied to me. It was so fucking obvious. I was surprised I hadn't realized sooner – it's not like me to be so trusting. Clearly he was still pissed off about the other night. That's why he was avoiding me. The knock-back must have hurt him more than I'd thought. *God, boys are so fragile. One night they're punching some-one's lights out, and the next they're all put out cos their girlfriend won't put out (for once).*

I sat on my toadstool in the woods and thought about how best to handle this. *What to do what to do what to do?* Nat had lied. This was not good. But he had lied for a reason – he was upset. And we'd arranged to see each other on Sunday. So was it really so bad if he wanted some time out?

Yes. Yes, it was. He shouldn't have lied. If he'd just told me he wanted to lay low for a couple of days, I'd have understood. *Now who's lying?*

I wanted to call him and confront him about the lie, just to see what he'd say. But it would be much bet-ter to do it in person. That way I'd be able to see the truth in his eyes (I was sure of it).

Sunday. I'd wait till Sunday. That'd be the best way to play it. I could be patient . . . if I tried really, really, really hard (and hid my phone somewhere to avoid temptation). Sunday. It would all be sorted then. I felt better as soon as the decision had been made.

~

It was harder than I'd thought – not calling him. I skived off the last couple of lessons of the afternoon and wandered around town, trying my best to think about anything but him.

Mum made me sit down for a 'proper dinner'. It was pure torture. She tried to talk about Mick, but I refused to talk back, which took the wind out of her sails somewhat. I shovelled food into my mouth at record speed, desperate to escape to my room.

The rest of the evening was spent battling indigestion, which at least gave me something else to focus on other than Nat. When I turned on my phone there were eleven missed calls from Devon and five messages, all of which I deleted immediately. I didn't want to hear it. I wouldn't couldn't shouldn't let myself hear it.

I went to bed early so I didn't have to think. But I dreamed about him.

Got up late on Saturday and went for a long run. This was the first step to getting back to being me. A wheezing, sweaty, beetroot-red me. I was so out of shape it wasn't even funny. I wouldn't let this weakness happen again.

Mum was out shopping, so I had the house to myself – the silence was a relief. More missed calls from Devon. Got my laptop out and read the last thing I'd written: a couple of chapters about a girl spookily similar to me. *Lame*. I'd even given her my middle name. *Lame squared*.

I deleted it and started writing a story about a psychotic gnome who hung around in the woods, waiting for unsuspecting schoolgirls to kill and eat. Also lame. But fun.

I forgot about Nat for a whole afternoon. It felt good to be lost in fiction, where everything was so much more straightforward. The characters (mostly) did exactly what I wanted them to. I pulled the strings and they jumped. I felt powerful and good and happy.

At about nine o'clock my phone buzzed with a message. Devon was really starting to fuck me off now. Why wouldn't he leave things alone?

But it wasn't Devon this time. It was Nat:

'Can you come over now? I need to see you.'

That was unexpected, but a huge relief. I replied to say I'd be there in half an hour and then changed my clothes. I looked in the mirror and took a deep breath: better to get things sorted out tonight. First, he'd have to beg my forgiveness for lying, then he'd have to beg me to sleep with him. And I wouldn't turn him down this time.

～

Devon was waiting at the front door like some kind of geeky gatekeeper. He started to speak, but I held up my hand to silence him.

'No. I've got nothing to say to you. I'm here to see your brother.'

Devon shook his head and spoke quietly. 'I was just going to say that he's upstairs.'

'Right. Well, thanks for the info.' I shuffled past him. He smelled good.

As I trudged up the stairs I could feel him still watching me, but I turned around just to be sure. He was leaning against the door, staring up at me. His expression was pained.

I paused outside Nat's room. Music was blaring. A song we both loved. I smiled to myself.

My hand was on the door handle. I wondered if I should knock. *Not that he'll be able to hear me. And he IS expecting me . . .*

I opened the door.

I saw lots of things.

The crack on the ceiling, longer and wider than ever before.

A textbook splayed on the floor, spine broken.

A glass of water on the desk, half empty.

Nat on the bed.

With Sal. Not me.

My eyes were broken and my brain was too.

He was sitting with his back against the wall. She was lying down. Her head was on his lap. My head was not. He was wearing jeans and nothing else. She was wearing jeans and a bra. Bare feet. I wore trainers.

He was touching her arm. Not mine.

He was looking at her and she was looking at him and I was looking at them.

My heart was spilling out of my mouth onto the carpet.

I was looking at them and they were looking at me. We were all looking, and no one was speaking.

Music was blaring.

A door was slamming and feet were running. And running. And running. And running.

My eyes were broken and my brain was too.

My heart had been left for dead on the carpet.

My feet were running faster *faster* FASTER.

I ended up at the park. The den at the top of the climbing frame was waiting for me. I hugged my knees to my chest, desperately trying to hold myself together so I didn't splinter into a thousand pieces. If I let go, no one would ever be able to put the pieces together again.

I was sweating and cold and nothing.

My phone rang. Sal. My phone rang. Nat. My

phone rang. Sal. Sal. Sal. Sal. Sal. Sal. A text message. Mum: 'Where are you? 'I want you home by midnight.'

Me: 'Staying at Sal's. See you tomorrow.'

All I could see was the two of them. The *wrong* two.

$1 + 1 = 2$

$1 + 1 + 1 = $ broken shards of me

A text from Sal:

'Grace, PLEASE answer your phone. I need to talk to you. I'M SORRY. This wasn't meant to happen. It's all fucked up. PLEASE call me. Where are you? I'm sorry. Call me. x'

I threw the phone out of the window. I wouldn't be needing it.

I kept thinking about the bra she had on. That bra she bought the other day. Brand-new underwear for a special occasion. The special occasion of fucking my boyfriend.

I kept thinking about him touching her arm. The easy intimacy that doesn't just come from nowhere.

I kept thinking about them looking at each other. Gazing.

entangled

I kept thinking about
    slicing flesh
        welling blood
            dizzy high
                relief.

❧

Later. A too-bright all-night cafe. Still thinking, drinking cup after cup after cup of coffee until I threw up on the table. Got chucked out. *No tears, not yet.*

The night went on and on and I dreaded the dawn. I didn't want tomorrow to come. But it did.

Sunday morning and joggers and dogs and people with cappuccinos and newspapers. Up early, making the most of the day. Ignoring the ghost girl wandering among them.

Dazed. *Gazed, gazing, touching, wanting.*

Public toilets. Ghost girl staring back at me in the mirror.

Who are you?

Nobody.

❧

My house. Waiting outside, keys in hand. Another door to open.

Mother waiting on the sofa.

'Where have you been?' Softly softly, but I could hear the steel.

'I told you – I slept over at Sal's.'

'Hmm . . . did you have a nice time?'

'Yeah. We went to a late showing at the cinema. I thought Mr Stewart would be able to drive me home, but he's away at some conference or something, and I didn't have enough money for a taxi. Sorry.'

'Really?'

'Yeah.' I headed for the stairs.

'Sit down.' All steel now.

'I'm really knackered. I just need to get some sleep.'

'SIT down. Now.'

Nothing to do but obey.

'When did you become such a good liar, Grace Carlyle?' Lips pursed, anger barely contained.

I didn't even try to argue. Past caring.

'Sal called last night, asking where you were. She was worried. I've been up all night waiting for you, worrying. I nearly called the police.'

A derisive snort from me.

'Would you like to explain exactly what it is you find so funny? Just look at yourself! YOU'RE A MESS!' Shouting, spitting anger at me. She grabbed hold of me and hauled me in front of the mirror above the mantelpiece.

'Look at the state of you. You look half dead.'

I looked. Greasy hair and pale face and dark circles and eyes. Green eyes that looked more like grey. Broken eyes.

Half dead? More than half, nearly all the way.

'Are you on drugs?'

A giggle from me, high pitched and manic.

'Well? *Are* you? Look at me, Grace.' More man-handling, shaking me. My head clinging on to my shoulders for dear life. 'Answer me, for Christ's sake!'

'No, Mother. I am not on drugs, but thanks for asking. It's nice to know you care.'

'What's that supposed to mean?'

'What do you think it means?' No anger. A voice detached from my body.

'Of course I care, you stupid little girl. But you don't make it easy sometimes.'

'It's not my job to make it easy. You're supposed to be the parent, remember?'

She was furious now. Even more so because I wasn't.

'Grow up, Grace.'

'Oh, I grew up a long time ago. Shame you weren't

around to notice. Shame you never thought to ask where I was all those *other* nights.'

That stumped her, if only for a moment.

'What other nights?' Defeated, deflated, tired.

A smirk from me. 'The nights when I was with *boys*, Mother. A lot of boys. Having quite a lot of sex, if you must know.'

'Grace!'

'What did you *think* I was doing? Playing with dolls? Having a teddy bears' picnic?'

'Be quiet!'

'You can't honestly tell me you're *surprised*? You know what they say . . . like mother, like daughter.'

'Stop it! Stop talking NOW!' Time for tears. But not from me, not yet. 'Your father would never have stood for this sort of behaviour . . . he'd be ashamed of you.'

'Whatever. He shouldn't have *fucking* killed himself then, should he? If he cared so *fucking* much.' I felt something then – a flicker of feeling, of caring. I stomped on it, hard.

'Go to your room. Right now.'

'Whatever you say, *Mother*.'

She hated me, and I was glad.

Questions. Lots of questions, all fighting for my attention. I hid from them under the duvet, but they seeped in somehow. Drip-drip-dripping poison into my head.

Drip. When was the first time? *Shh, don't listen.*

Drip. Who made the first move? *It doesn't matter. Hush.*

Drip. How could they do this to me? *That's what people do. Hurt.*

I slept. A confused, restless sleep.

Dreamsandthoughtandquestions all mixed up and upside down and the wrong way round.

Cut. Cut them out. Deeper. It's the only way.

The poison was stronger than me. I was powerless to resist. *Cut.*

I woke up to a new question: Why did he ask me to come over? He can't have *wanted* me to see that . . . can he? Unless that was his own unique way of dumping me? *No. Think harder.*

And then I knew: It hadn't been *Nat* who'd wanted me to see.

⁓

Later. Mum crept in. I pretended to be asleep. She stroked my cheek and her touch made my skin creep and crawl and itch. She stayed a few minutes, and before she left she whispered, 'I love you.' *Liar.*

⁓

Monday morning. Happy sunlight streaming through the window. *Today's the day.* I smiled at the ghost girl in the mirror. She looked different today. I showered and dressed and put some make-up on and went downstairs.

Now for the tricky bit . . .

'Morning, Mum.'

She was sitting in the kitchen with her back to me. She said nothing.

I stood behind her chair and hugged her, like I used to. I whispered, 'I'm really, really sorry about yesterday. I didn't mean any of it. I was just tired and upset – Sal and I . . . fell out on Saturday night.' I kissed her perfectly powdered cheek. 'I know it's no excuse, but I'm sorry.' *There. Done.*

She patted my arm and I knew I'd succeeded. 'I'm sorry too, Grace. I didn't mean that . . . about your father. It was just . . . some of the things you said . . .'

I slid into the chair next to her and took her hand in mine. 'I made it up. I just said the first thing that came into my head – I was being a total cow. Sorry.'

She looked into my eyes and didn't see me. She never did. She believed what I wanted her to believe. Always. 'Really, Grace. You're a funny one, aren't you? Let's just move on. I tell you what – why don't we have a girls' night in tomorrow? Just the two of us. It would be good to . . . talk. I know I haven't been around much recently, and things haven't exactly been easy for us since your father . . . but I think we should start spending some more time together. What do you say?' Her face was hopeful. It made her look younger.

'Mum, it's OK. I'm a big girl – I can look after myself. And you deserve to live your own life. Things are just fine – don't you worry about me.' It was easier than I thought. The words all came out in the right order and my voice was light and soft and . . . daughterly. 'But tomorrow sounds good.' *Yeah. Tomorrow.*

'Lovely! Oh, I nearly forgot. Sal phoned yester-day – quite a few times actually. But I thought it was best to let you sleep. Sounds like she wants to make up though, doesn't it?'

I plastered on a plastic smile. 'Yeah. Great. Well, I'll talk to her at school. It'll be fine.' We smiled at each other and I worried that my face would crack open.

᠈

After break, double English. Sal was there, of course. The look on her face when I sat down next to her was pretty special.

'Grace, hi. I didn't know if you'd be here. I . . . don't know what to say.' *How come I've never noticed how mousey she sounds?*

'Have you got your *Canterbury Tales* with you? I left mine at home.'

'*What?* Are you serious?'

'What?'

'Grace, we need to talk . . .'

The teacher arrived and started droning on and on and on and I took notes. I wrote extra neatly and used a ruler to underline all my headings. Sal was scribbling furiously next to me. She tore out a page from her notebook and slid it across the desk to me:

'I'm sorry. Please can we talk? We NEED to talk about this. I'm so so so sorry about Saturday, but it's complicated. There are some things you need to know.

(*Yes, like when you started fucking my boyfriend.*) This was never supposed to happen, just let me explain. I need you to know that you're my best friend and the last thing I wanted to do was hurt you.'

I wrote back: 'Have you got your *Canterbury Tales*?'

She sighed, frustrated now. Grabbed the paper back from me: 'Please. Just hear me out. Then if you want nothing more to do with me, that's fine. I need to explain – about Nat, about Easter, about everything. Lunchtime?'

Me: Can't today. Sorry.

Sal: Tonight then?

Me: Got plans. Sorry. Free tomorrow night though. (*Yeah, tomorrow's perfect.*)

Sal: I really think we should talk today.

I was bored now: Tomorrow or nothing.

I looked at her, stared her into submission. She nodded a meek little nod.

I shot out of the classroom as soon as the bell went. I didn't want her following me. I wanted to get to the woods, but I only made it halfway down the corridor. I couldn't allow anyone to see me – the library was the only option. I ducked in among the reference shelves. Only just made it in time before the tear ducts let loose: a total onslaught. Sobbing in silence.

Explain about Easter? What about Easter?

Think about it.

No no no no no no no. It can't be true. It's not possible. No. Yes.

Don't think about it.

Stop it. Stop it now. This isn't part of the plan. It doesn't change anything. Think about something else, anything else. Look at the books.

I pulled an encyclopedia of British birds from the nearest shelf and sat on the floor. *Look how many different types of seagull there are . . . count them, memorize them. Read the Latin names . . . again and again and again.*

Gazing, touching, wanting, fucking.

Footsteps. 'Grace? Grace, is that you?'

I wanted the book to swallow me up. But it didn't.

Sophie knelt down in front of me. 'Grace! What's the matter?'

'Nothing. I'm fine.' Choking sobs betrayed me.

She sat down next to me and put her arm around my shoulders, whispering, 'Shhh, it'll be OK,' over and over again. I leaned into her.

More footsteps approaching. I didn't dare look up.

Sophie hissed at whoever it was. 'Go on, piss off!' The footsteps fled. I laughed, still crying.

'That's better. More laughing, less crying. Do you want to tell me what's wrong?'

I shook my head.

'You know you can trust me, don't you?' *You can't trust anyone, ever.*

But I nodded anyway.

'Do you want me to go and find Sal?'

I shook my head again, harder.

'Is there anything I can do to help?'

'No,' I whispered. 'Thank you.' *Right. Pull yourself together now.* I took a deep, juddery breath. 'I think I'm OK now.' *Liar.*

Sophie wasn't buying it. 'Well, let's just sit here for a bit longer. We don't have to talk.'

I was pathetically grateful. I wasn't quite ready to face the world yet – I needed to put my armour on more carefully this time. Make sure there were no chinks. I leaned my head against hers and we sat in silence.

☙

I nearly told her. So nearly. But I had to stick to the plan.

The bell went and I dragged myself to my feet. A

358

rush of dizziness so that I had to steady myself against the shelf.

Sophie got up too. Her knees made a cracking sound, which made us both smile. She pushed her glasses up the bridge of her nose. 'I . . . I hope you're feeling better. If you ever . . .'

I nodded. 'Thanks for being so great. I feel loads better now.'

It suddenly hit me: this would be the last time I ever saw her. Breathing was difficult. I hugged her fiercely. 'You're a real friend, you know that?' She looked puzzled, but I ploughed ahead. 'What you did today – it . . . really helped. Don't ever forget that. I'm sorry for being such a bitch. I wish things could have been different.' *Shhh. She'll guess. Stop talking.*

'Hey, it's OK. We *can* be friends, Grace. I'd like that a lot.'

I felt all hollowed out. 'Me too.'

I walked away. Hating myself even more than I hated *them*.

Don't look back. Stay strong . . . Not long now.

The afternoon was fine. My armour protected me from everything and everyone and, most of all, from me. Listened carefully in lessons, took notes about battles

entangled

and kings and things. Memorized the dates and names.

And then it was over. School was over. Everyone streamed out of the school gates, just happy that another Monday was done and dusted.

I saw Devon waiting at the bus stop. He saw me too. I walked towards him and he looked worried, guilty, trapped. The bus arrived and he barged to the front of the queue, desperate to escape.

I let him go. He didn't matter, not really.

~

Home. An envelope for me, from Nat.

Terrible handwriting, just like mine.

No stamp or postmark – delivered by hand. I peeked out the window in case he was watching. He wasn't.

Why hadn't he waited to see me?

You don't want to see him. It won't make any difference. It's better this way.

~

I sat on the sofa, the envelope sitting next to me.

Read it. Don't read it. Read it. Don't read it. Don't read it. Don't read it. Don't read it. Don't read it. It will just be lies. Lies and excuses and more lies.

You can't trust anyone, ever.

I ripped it into tiny pieces – pieces so small no one could ever put them together again. I scattered them into the recycling bin.

§

Dinner with Mum in front of the telly. *Pass the salt, please.*

Washing the dishes. Putting everything back in its place.

Studying the knives in the knife block. Choosing.

§

Time to go to the park one last time.

Time to go, Grace.

§

And that was that. Mission accomplished. Monday was over.

I was over.

Or so I thought.

§

Ethan's gone. I woke up and he was gone.

He left me. Just like Dad. No. Not like Dad.

I'm not scared any more. I don't need Dad. Or Ethan. Or Nat. Or Sal. Not really.

I'm alive and strong and shiny and new and I think I'm going to be OK.

All I have to do is get out of here. Soon.

The door isn't locked. I KNOW the door isn't locked. Ethan wouldn't lie to me.

One more sleep and I'll be ready.

One more sleep.

Dreamy, drowsy, drugged. Wake up, sleepyhead.

I can't open my eyes. Why can't I open my eyes? Try harder. No good. My eyes are broken. Listen then. Silence. No, not quite silence. Beeping sounds, far far away.

Whooshing too. Like the tide: in, out, in, out. On and on and on. Shhh. Go back to sleep. Sleep is good. You can sleep forever.

Wake up, sleepyhead.

Aw, please let me sleep. I'm so very tired.

No. Get up. Open your eyes. Move your arm at least.

I try. Arm disobeys. At least I think it does, but I'm not sure where it is. Try harder. Find it, feel it. It should be connected to your shoulder. There it is, with a hand on the end, and fingers too. Try moving a finger. Nope, can't. I can feel something though. What is it? Feels familiar, nice. A hand in mine: warm and comforting. A boy's hand, I think. Mmm, you smell good.

Are you Ethan?

Who's Ethan?

I don't remember.

❧

Voices. People with voices, saying things I don't understand. Long words. Ask them where you are. Ask them why you can't open your eyes. Ask them ask them ask them what's wrong with you. Speak. Now. I CAN'T I CAN'T I CAN'T. Screaming inside my head. My eyes are broken and my brain is too.

Hush. Don't worry. Maybe you've fallen asleep watching ER again.

❧

A new hand. Smaller, colder. And a voice.

'Wake up, sleepyhead. It's time to wake up now. Come on, open your eyes, just for me. I know you can do it if you try. No? . . . Well, squeeze my hand . . . Even just a little bit. Please?' My hand is floating, higher. Still at the end of my arm, I think. Shhh. I'm trying to sleep.

'Well, we'll try again tomorrow. You rest up and we'll try again. Yes, tomorrow you'll be stronger, I just know it.'

Silence. And then, 'Don't you dare leave me. Don't even

*think about it. I won't let this happen again. I WON'T.
You hear me? You try harder tomorrow, OK? Just. Try.
Harder.' The same voice, tight and choked. It's choking
me.*

~

*Beeping beeping BEEPING louder and longer and it won't
stop.*

No whooshing. The sound of the sea has stopped.

*The hand is ripped away from me and I'm mov-
ing fast, I think. Things are whirling around me. Voices
loud and louder. Hands touching me. Not his though. Not
his.*

*What's happening to me? Shhh, just sleep. Don't worry
your pretty little head about it. Night, night, sleep tight.*

*OK. If you say so. Tell everyone to be quiet though. How
can anyone sleep with that racket going on?*

Pounding, pounding, pounding. My chest hurts.

*Breathe. In and out. In and out. The whooshing is back
and so is his hand.*

*I smile. On the inside though, so no one can see. A
secret smile just for me.*

~

*Another voice. I have no choice but to listen. A girl-voice.
Sounds upset. I try to work out if there's a hand in mine, but I*

can't tell. Just a dull throbbing sensation in my wrists, which is weird.

'I hope you don't mind me coming. I couldn't not come. This is all my fault.' This could be interesting.

The voice goes on. 'I still can't believe you did it.' Did what? Why so cryptic?

'I don't know if you can hear me . . . Of course you can't hear me! This is so stupid, but . . . I need you to know that I'm sorry. I'm so, so sorry. This whole situation is a mess. And I can't help thinking that if I'd just told you the truth from the start then none of this would have happened. I'm sorry.' Enough with the sorry! Just get on with it.

'I met him first, you know. I'm not just saying that to be a bitch. It's true. I was at Devon's, and he was there. And I liked him straight away, and he . . . liked me. I've never been able to tell with boys before, but with him I just knew. He had some mates over for a party – it was all a bit crazy. Devon got fed up and went to stay at his dad's. I should have left too. But I didn't. I liked him so much. We had loads in common. We talked for ages. Sorry if you don't want to hear this, but I need you to know the truth.

'I drank too much. I didn't mean to, but I was nervous and . . . I was having a good time. I felt like a different person. I knew something was going to happen with him. I really, really wanted something to happen. But he got wasted too – playing stupid drinking games. He fell asleep on the sofa

while I was in the kitchen. Idiot. And then I . . .' And then you what?

'One of his friends had been eyeing me up all night. Simon. He saw that I was about to leave and begged me to stay. It was easier to say yes than no. He dragged me up to dance with him, and it was sort of fun. I remember thinking that this must be what it's like to be you — just doing what you want and not caring. I've always wondered how you do that.

'Simon kept on topping up my glass and I just didn't care. We danced for ages, and then he kissed me. And I kissed him back. I wasn't thinking. And then we must have gone up to Devon's room. And I . . . don't really remember much. I don't remember how it happened. I don't think I said no, but I can't believe I didn't. Does that make sense?' *I have no idea.*

'I just know that I woke up feeling sick and sore and I knew what must have happened, but it was almost like I couldn't believe I'd actually done it. Simon was asleep next to me and I just got dressed and ran. I felt disgusting. I don't know why I didn't tell you. I should have told you, I wanted to, but . . . I don't think I'll ever forgive myself for . . .'

There's a sound like a door opening.

'Oh, sorry. I didn't realize anyone was in here.' *A boy-voice.*

'That's OK. I have to go anyway.'

'*Don't go. Please. I think we should talk.*'

'*Not here. Not now. You should stay — talk to her.*' Her? *I think 'her' must be me. But who are they, and who is Simon for that matter?*

Don't think about it don't think about it don't think . . .

'*I don't know what to say.*' *He sounds petulant.*

'*How about sorry? That might be a good place to start.*' *Ouch. A door slamming shut hurts my ears. I listen hard for the boy-voice, but my ears are full of nothing. Just the beeping and whooshing. Comforting. I'm just starting to drift away when he speaks.*

'*This is so weird.*' *I hear a loud exhalation, and I think I feel it on my arm.* '*Just for the record, I* don't *think you can hear me. Nothing I've read about this sort of thing has convinced me.*' *Ha. That's what you think, buddy.*

A deep sigh. '*But I* am *sorry, you know. This should never have happened. I did care about you, but it was messed up from the start. You want to hear something funny?*' *I can tell it's going to be anything but funny. His voice is sour.*

'*Remember the night we met? I'd just got back from uni, and the first thing I did was go round to her house. I'd been thinking about her ever since we met. I'd emailed and called and texted, but she just ignored me, and I couldn't work out why. I was pretty gutted. God, why am I even bothering to explain? You can't hear a word I'm saying.*' *YES, I CAN!*

'Anyway, she refused to see me that night too. And then I met you at the bus stop. I thought I'd try to forget about her. And it was working, till I found out you two were friends. It was so fucked up. I know it's no excuse, but I was confused. I . . . I thought I was falling in love with you, but I couldn't get her out of my head. She knew how I felt, but she said she wouldn't do anything to hurt you. She made me promise not to say anything – even made me pretend I'd never met her before.'

His voice goes quiet. 'When you told me about her getting pregnant . . . I blamed myself. I knew it must have been Simon – he's such a sleazy fucker and he'd acted so damn smug after that party, but I never knew why. I begged Sal to see me. I kissed her that night, but she said if I broke up with you she'd never forgive me. She really loves you, you know that?

'And then that night. You shouldn't have had to see that. But nothing actually happened. We never . . .'

It hits me. Like a physical blow to my heart. That night. I remember That Night.

I don't hear another word he says.

~

Nat. Sal.

Don't think about it. Don't. Think.

But I have to. I want to. I need to.

entangled

Just go to sleep.

No!

You don't want to remember. Just drift away. It's better this way. Trust me.

No!

You'll be sorry.

We'll see about that. We'll see.

~

I remember. All of it. And it hurts. More than I'd have ever thought possible.

I know where I am and what I've done and why I can't move or speak or open my eyes. And I'm scared.

It was all a terrible mistake.

I'd like to not be here. I'd like to go home now.

Please.

Please.

~

The hand is back, nestled in mine. The right hand. Or the left. But it feels right at least.

Music is playing. The same song over and over again. I've heard it somewhere before, I think. It's beautiful.

The music stops. And then he speaks. 'I hope you don't mind listening to that. I thought . . . you might wake up. Stupid of me, probably. I didn't tell you before, but it reminded me of you the moment I heard it. I don't know why.'

A pause and then his voice is closer — right next to my ear. 'I'm here for you, if you need a friend. I know I might not be your first choice, but I reckon we've got more in common than you think. Don't laugh.' I'm not.

'I'm sorry for what I did. You shouldn't have had to find out that way. If I'd thought for even a second that something like this would happen, I would never have . . . But you wouldn't listen, and I couldn't think of any other way. You're so stubborn! You're even being stubborn now, aren't you? Pretending you can't hear me. Ignoring me. It's really kind of rude, you know.'

But I CAN hear you, I shout inside. I won't ignore you, ever again. I promise. I could do with a friend right now. A friend like you.

'It's OK, you don't need to say anything today. But I'll be back. Tomorrow, and the next day, and the next day, until you're so sick of me you get right up out of that bed and walk out of here. It's going to happen. Trust me.' I think I do.

I feel the gentlest of kisses on the back of my hand. And then he's gone.

❧

The small hand is back again, but this time it's warmer.

'I'm sorry, Gracie-bear. I'm sorry.' Gracie-bear? I've heard *that before, I think. But what does it mean? 'I know I should have said it years ago, but I was too wrapped up in myself. I wasn't there when you needed me . . . I was hurting so much. And I knew you were too, but somehow I just couldn't bring myself to do anything about it. I couldn't be who you needed me to be. I missed him so much. He was everything to me. I'll never understand why he did it. Why he left us.' Her voice is small and sort of heartbreaking. The hand squeezes mine and I would really like to squeeze it back. I try my hardest, but it's no good.*

'I didn't know how to be without him. He was all I'd ever known. I know that's no excuse, but I want you to understand . . . things are different now. I'm here for you. And I always will be, even when you don't want me to be. That's the way it's supposed to be. I won't let you down, I promise. You just have to wake up and let me prove it to you.'

I believe this voice. And I know who it belongs to.

I try and try and try to move my hand, just to let her know that I can hear her. My brain is sweating with the effort. I concentrate on my little finger and think think think about it moving. And I try and I try and . . .

Nothing.

But I'll try again. Tomorrow, and the next day, and the next.

I won't give up.

I won't ever give up.

acknowledgements

Entangled took its sweet time making its way from my head to the page, and a relatively short time making its way from the page to the book you hold in your hands. Lots of lovely people helped me along the way. Extra-special big thanks to . . .

Jan Sherwood, my favourite English teacher, for not laughing at my early writing attempts.

BWC. Our meetings got me through the whole 'actually-having-to-write-the-book' thing. Non and Kate K., I owe you big time. Nonster, you know I couldn't have done this without you. Thank you thank you thank you for encouraging/nagging me every step of the way. You are a star. Go fish!

The All-American Rejects, Fall Out Boy, Cute Is What We Aim For, Elliot Minor and Jack's Mannequin for writing the soundtrack.

Chris (Kissyfur), Ed, fabulous cousin Sarah, Liz

(Frodders), Dan, Laura, Smoo, JNT, Stephanie K. and Megan L. Each one of you has been supportive, enthusiastic and/or excited just when I needed it the most.

Awesome Sar, for recognizing that elusive first line lurking in the middle of my manuscript, and for being, y'know, awesome.

My agent, the marvellous Victoria Birkett, and the equally wonderful Nancy Miles, of the Miles Stott Children's Literary Agency. Meeting you both on that sunny day in Marylebone was truly one of the highlights of this whole journey. You took a chance on Grace, and for that I will ALWAYS be grateful.

Roisin Heycock (editor extraordinaire), Parul Bavishi (publicity guru), Talya Baker (copy-editing genius) and all at Quercus. I couldn't have wished for a better home for *Entangled*.

My new blogging and Twitter buddies, for sharing in the excitement and for understanding that getting what you've always dreamed of can be kind of scary too!

Lastly, and firstly, and always, my parents, Elspeth and Rob for well . . . *everything*. And for being (sort of!) patient when I wouldn't let you read my writing.

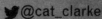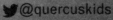

for news, blogs and more information
visit us online:

www.catclarke.blogspot.com

www.catclarke.com

Twitter @cat_clarke

www.quercusbooks.co.uk

Twitter @quercusbooks @quercuskids